THE POETIC EDDA
PART I : THE GODS

THE POETIC EDDA
PART I : THE GODS

Rendered into English
by
ANNIE GISVOLD and KNUT HARRIS

KDP Publishing
Amazon, UK

Copyright © 2023 by Annie Gisvold and Knut Harris
All rights reserved
Printed in the UK; Print on demand

First edition, 2023

Cover design by Annie Gisvold: Water colour depicting Freya from Tissø, Denmark

This book is sold subject to the condition that it shall not, by way of trade or otherwise, be lent, resold, hired out, or otherwise circulated without the publishers' prior consent in any form of binding or cover other than that in which it is published and without a similar condition including this condition being imposed on the subsequent purchaser.

Requests for permission to reproduce material from this work should be sent to:
annie.annieamg@gmail.com
or
knutharris@gmail.com

KDP ISBN   9798371586520

ACKNOWLEDGMENTS

We would like to thank Marit Jerstad, reader em. at Oslo Metropolitan University, for reviewing our translation and for giving honest and helpful feedback; and Elizabeth Ashman Rowe, reader PhD at Clare Hall Cambridge, for encouraging comments. We are grateful to Gro Steinsland, prof. PhD em. at the University of Oslo, for her extensive authorship on the religion of the North and for giving useful feedback; and to Torgrim Titlestad, prof. PhD at the University of Stavanger, for imparting his knowledge of the political history of Norway in the Middle Ages.

Scholars and translators, whose works we have often consulted, are Ludvig Holm-Olsen, *his translation of the Elder Edda into Norwegian: 'Edda-dikt'*; Ursula Dronke: *'The Poetic Edda, Mythological poems'*; Carolyn Larrington: *'The Poetic Edda'*; Andy Orchard: *'The Elder Edda. A Book of Viking Lore'*; Jackson Crawford *'The Poetic Edda, Stories of the Norse Gods and Heroes'*; and Knut Ødegård, *his translation into New Norwegian reflecting recent scholarship, 'Edda I & II'*.

We wish to express our thanks to Leiv Olsen for making available to us his treatise on the age of the Eddic poems in Codex Regius, and for several helpful comments on our manuscript.
Two pillars of Old Norse scholarship in the 19th and early 20th centuries need to be mentioned: Sophus Bugge, for his work on ON texts and interpretation; and Fredrik Paasche, for his literary expositions of the same material.

ABOUT THE AUTHORS

Annie Gisvold, b. in Trondheim, 1949; studied art and ceramics at Oslo National Academy of the Arts, has a degree in art education and spec.ed.; she worked many years as a studio potter; was for many years member of a puppet theatre; has edited articles on Nordic as well as Classical mythology in the encyclopedia CAPLEX, for J.W. Cappelens Forlag, Oslo 1990 – 2004; translated into English "Water-colour on Porcelain", by Arne Åse, Oslo University Press 1987; a large part of her childhood was spent in Canada and she is therefore bilingual.

Knut Harris, b. in Drammen, 1956; studied Nordic Language and Literature and other subjects at the University of Oslo; has continued working with ON texts; together with Marit Jerstad he has written "Voluspå – gudinnene og verdens fremtid" (which translates to: "The Sibyl's Prophecy – the Goddesses and the Future of the World"), Saga Bok, Stavanger 2013; he has also been engaged in metalwork, carpentry and story-telling; and was a member of a puppet theatre for many years.

Contents

ACKNOWLEDGMENTS 5
ABOUT THE AUTHORS 6
ABBREVIATIONS 9
INTRODUCTION 11
BIBLIOGRAPHY 42
The Sibyl's Prophecy 52
The Tale of the High One 74
The Tale of Vavthrudnir 117
The Tale of Grimnir 133
The Tale of Skirnir 149
The Song of Harbard 161
The Poem of Hymir 175
Loki's Quarrel 187
The Poem of Thrym 205
The Tale of Alviss 215
Baldr's Dreams 225
The Story of Rig 230
The Song of Hyndla 245
The Song of Grotti 261
The Spells of Groa 270
The Tale of Fiolsvinn 275
The Song of the Spear 289
APPENDIX I 293
APPENDIX II 295

APPENDIX III 296
APPENDIX IV 301
INDEX of MYTHOLOGICAL NAMES 303

ABBREVIATIONS

Alv	Alvíssmál	Alviss' Speech
AM		Arnamagnean Collection
appr.		approximately
AS		Anglo-Saxon
Bdr	Baldrs Draumar	Baldr's Dreams
cfr		confer
cp		compare
CR		Codex Regius
Dar	Darraðarlióð	The Song of the Spear
etc		etcetera
f, m and n		feminine, masculine and neuter
Fjǫls	Fjǫlsvinnsmál	The Tale of Fiolsvinn
GKS	Gammel Kongelig Samling	Catalogue system of the Danish Royal Library in Copenhagen
Grím	Grímnismál	The Tale of Grimnir
Gró	Grógaldr	The Spells of Groa
Grott	Grottasǫngr	The Song of Grotti
Hár	Hárbarðsljóð	The Song of Harbard
Háv	Hávamál	The Tale of the High One
Hym	Hymiskviða	The Poem of Hymir
Hynd	Hyndluljóð	The Song of Hyndla
Icel.		Icelandic
Lok	Lokasenna	Loki's Quarrel

OHG		Old High German
ON		Old Norse
pl		plural
Ríg	Rígsþula	The Tale of Rig
sg		singular
Skír	Skírnismál	The Tale of Skirnir
Þrym	Þrymskviða	The Poem of Thrym
Vaf	Vafþruðnismál	The Tale of Vafthrudnir
Vsp	Voluspá	The Sibyl's Prophecy
*	asterix	denotes reconstructed words and names

INTRODUCTION

Baldr had bad dreams; they told him that he was going to die. Then his mother, Frigg, went and asked all things in nature to swear an oath that they would promise her not to harm Baldr. One small plant, however, the mistletoe, seemed to her too young and meek to swear an oath. The aesir thought it was great fun to throw stones, daggers and arrows at Baldr, because nothing could harm him. Then the sly Loki intervened by furnishing Baldr's brother, the blind Hod, with a twig of mistletoe. He helped Hod to sling the twig at Baldr, the twig turned into an arrow and killed him. Then Frigg and all of nature wept over the dead Baldr, something which we can witness every day when rocks and boulders are wet with the morning dew.

The religion of the North

According to pagan belief, the world was a dynamic universe where everything was treated as being alive. Life began when heat from the South melted the ice from the North, and when drops of ether formed into the celestial cow Audhumbla and the primeval androgynous giant Ymir. Nourished by Audhumbla's milk, Ymir grew to an enormous size, and since he was both sexes, he-she bred the race of giants. At the same time the celestial cow brought forth the primeval god Bur by licking him out of a salt-stone. From Ymir's body the gods shaped the material world and everything in it, from the clouds in the sky to the mountains of the earth, from the soil of the lands to the waters and salt seas. The elements were basically alive, and mythological beings populated all levels of existence and all areas of life. The interaction between these beings, these forces, created a dynamism in which people needed to find their place. An everflowing exchange of information, possessions and power characterized their world. It was essential for them to find solutions to their problems through negotiations, deliberations and co-operation.

There were oppositions between the individual gods of the pagans, and in *The Song of Harbard*, even between Thor and Odin. The poem *The Story of Rig* differentiates between three layers of society: thralls, farmers and nobles. This division into three is seen also in the mythology of the North by the differentiation of divinities into giants, vanir (the fertility gods) and aesir (the war gods). In Old Norse the giants are called *iotuns*, and in the present translation the terms giants and iotuns are used interchangeably.[1] The mythological geography shows the same partition into three: the iotuns living in Utgard, the gods living in Asgard, and mankind placed between these two, with their home in Midgard. Odin and Loki also personify the blending of opposites. Odin was half god and half iotun, his father Bur being a god, while his mother Bestla was of the iotun clan; Loki was half iotun, his father being the iotun Farbauti, and his mother Laufey/Nal who was perhaps an elf. Other examples of this unity between opposites are for instance the alliances beween the vani god Freyr and the beautiful iotun woman Gerd, and between the vani god Niord and the powerful iotun woman Skadi.

Loki has a special place in the mythology, as he is the one who instigates calamities and the one who is forced by the gods to mend them. He is Odin's blood-brother, and like him Loki is capable of taking on various shapes. In the form of a beautiful mare he gave birth to Sleipnir, Odin's eight-legged horse, which could travel through all worlds. With the giantess Angrboda, he had three formidable children: Hel (the Ruler of the Dead), the Fenris Wolf who eventually swallows Odin, and the World Serpent whose venom kills Thor at Ragnarok.

It is interesting to observe that in this vast universe of mythological beings who strive and struggle, conquer and are defeated, man's psychology is described in an impersonal way. What we in our present-day culture perceive as something we ourselves think, feel or do, was expressed in Old Norse without a grammatical subject: *mér thikkir* = 'methinks', *mér synisk* = 'seems to me'. In the same

---

[1]*Iotuns*: On the question of the role of the iotuns, see Gro Steinsland: 'Giants as Recipients of Cult in the Viking Age?', cfr. our Bibliography.

way they would say: *snióvar* = 'it's snowing'; *rignir* = 'it's raining'. In other words, what goes on in our psyche was perceived as natural events.

The three clans of divine beings were, as already mentioned, *the iotnar* (giants, often personifying events or elements in nature), *the vanir,* and *the aesir*. All according to family tradition, one's occupation in life, and so on, a person would choose the deity one specifically and generally would invoke and trust, one's *fulltrúi*. A farmer would for instance revere Freyr and Thor, and a warrior would invoke the help of Odin. On the farms the women would be responsible for the worship of ancestral and guardian spirits. Many people felt that they had a particular guardian spirit, while at the same time they professed their faith in one of the major gods. The world was also populated by elves, dwarfs, trolls and hags. People believed that one's deceased ancestors could appear as elves, and that psychic properties even could be perceived in the shape of animals, which they called *fylgior*, 'followers'.

In this dynamic universe everything was given a name, bringing order and meaning. Names were not only given to geographical places, but even to one's sword, one's tools, and so on. Often these names would express an action or a quality, making them personal. A few examples close to Odin are: his ring *Draupnir*, 'he who drips'; his ravens: *Huginn*, 'he who knows', and *Muninn',* 'he who remembers'; or Odin himself disguised as *Grimnir* 'he who puts on a mask'. In several of the Eddic poems beautiful and poignant names of this kind are given.

Butter, beer, blood, fat and so on, were given to the gods. In their cult communal meals would probably have played a great part. According to law, farmers were obliged to brew beer since drinking bouts were an intrinsic part of the social order. As well as putting them in contact with the gods,[2] these gatherings also gave an opportunity to discuss and prepare issues for the

---

[2] «...*contact with the gods*»:   Beer was brewed from barley. 'Barley', ON *Byggvir,* was one of the servants of the fertility god Freyr.

next General Assembly, which they called the *Thing*.³ For communal meals meat was cooked or fried over open fire. It is known that there could be a cooking pit in the middle of the horg (ON *hǫrgr*), the old type of an outdoor altar. A striking example of a pagan sanctuary was unearthed in 2010 at Ranheim in Trondheim, Norway. This sanctuary was complete with a processional road leading to the central area where the horg and also a *hof* lay, an upright wooden temple. The processional road led from an area that in earlier times was most likely marsh land, indicating the ancient belief that such areas were sacred. The sanctuary at Ranheim showed no less than three consecutive stages of religious practice. It was discovered that the horg was erected directly on top of a grave site dating from appr. 400 BC. The second element of the pagan shrine was consequently the horg. It consisted of a circular platform, fifteen metres across and one metre in height, with a spiral pathway of white stones leading in toward the cooking pit in the centre of the horg.⁴ The third element was the hof, a wooden construction with cornerposts and intermediate posts carrying the roof, and between the posts a wall was erected of staves or upright planks. This manner of constructing a wooden building lived on in an adapted form in the Christian stave churches. Inside the hof there was a platform carried by smaller posts, probably supporting statues of gods. Some sagas tell of statues of Thor, Odin and Freyr. Hakon, Earl at Lade near Ranheim, is supposed to have had statues of Thorgerd Holgabrud and her sister Irpa placed inside his hof at Lade. These were tutelary deities, perhaps worshipped as the ancestral mothers of his family. The statues were decorated with

---

³ «...*called the Thing.*»:   The word *Thing* originally meant 'gathering' or 'the appointed time for the Gathering'.
⁴ "...*in the centre of the horg*":   See: «**Horg, hov and ve – a pre-Christian cult place at Ranheim in Trøndelag, Norway, in the 4rth – 10th centuries AD", by Preben Rønne**: Copy to google browser: http://www.rockartscandinavia.com/images/articles/preben_roenne_a11.pdf. (Preben Rønne, NTNU: "Horg, hov og ve – et førkristent kultanlegg på Ranheim i Sør-Trøndelag»: http://www.transpersonlig.no/ranheim.pdf)

jewelry, gold and silver, and perhaps also fitted with weapons, emblems, etc.

The concept of a living universe was clearly reflected in the art and architecture of the North. Animal ornamentation often decorated their artifacts. This may be seen on jewelry, weapons, details of clothing, furniture, pillars and portals, ships' bows, sacramental wagons, steles, etc. The force of the images were often enhanced by brass rivets. The chair posts of the high seat could be decorated with mythical figures, and one may imagine the grand effect when light from the open fire was reflected in the rivets. Immigrants to Iceland are reported to have brought their chair posts with them, and they also brought soil taken from where the temple posts had been standing. In this way they believed that their preferred gods and guardian spirits would continue to protect them.

In all likelihood the iotuns/giants were a class of very ancient deities in the cult of the Nordic peoples. Aegir, for instance, personifies the ocean, his name containing the same root as the Latin word *aqua*. His brothers were Logi, meaning 'flame' or 'fire', and Kari, meaning 'stormy winds'. The iotuns were huge creatures, big as hills and even mountains. An earlier worship of iotuns is for instance suggested in *Loki's Quarrel* where the giantess Skadi speaks of her shrines and sacred fields (ON: *vé oc vangar*).

The vanir were fertility gods. In the Bronze Age belief in fertility gods was widespread all over Europe and the Middle East. According to Snorri Sturluson[5], three vanir remained important in the the later pagan times and were worshipped along with the aesir. These three were Niord and his children Freyia and Freyr. Niord was associated with the sea, and his dwelling was called Noatun, meaning shipyard. His wife, the powerful iotun woman Skadi, preferred living in the high mountains where she had her dwelling Thrymheim. While Niord could not stand the sound of the howling wolves in the mountains, Skadi hated the shrieking of seagulls. Niord's son Freyr, who lived in Alvheim, is associated with horses

---

[5] *Snorri Sturluson:* 1178/79 – 1241; Icelandic author of *The Prose Edda* and *Heimskringla, etc.*

and racing. The goddess Freyia, Niord's daughter, is associated with love, fertility, magic and death in Norse mythology. She taught the aesir the art of *seiðr*, a specific technique of divination and of casting spells, both good and bad. Freyia also ruled one of the realms of the dead, and those who died in battle were divided between Odin's Valhall and Freyia's Folkvang.

The youngest class of deities was presumably the aesir, the war gods. In *The Sibyl's Prophecy* we are told of a war between the vanir and the aesir. Many have interpreted this as being a memory of the arrival of the cult of the aesir in the North. The history of the war gods reflects a cyclic concept of world events, from a happy and carefree Golden Age, through increasing difficulties, into an Iron Age of wars and strife, through their defeat and death at Ragnarok, until the cycle starts again with a new Golden Age. Ragnarok (the 'End of the Powers'), applies only to the male aesir. Some of the aesir's children are said to survive, and together with Baldr and Hod, who are released from Hel, they enjoy the dawning of the new Golden Age, thus starting a new cycle of life. It is interesting to observe that none of the goddesses die at Ragnarok. This might mean that people believed that the typological descendants of the Mother Goddess were immortal. Disir was a collective name for female deities, branching off into asynior, valkyries, norns, fylgior, elves, etc.[6] Observing the cult of the disir was mainly a task for women. Sacrifice to the disir (ON: *dísablót*) was an institution in pagan society. In *The Sibyl's Prophecy* the World Tree is showered with white loam. On the farms women gave ale in offering at sacred sites.

The number of burial mounds that exist shows that the custom of burying one's dead within the earth must have been common practice at one time in the pagan culture. Among the most famous burial mounds is the Sutton Hoo from the 6th and 7th centuries AD, in Suffolk, England. In some burial mounds jewelry, weapons, armor and all sorts of tools have been found deposited with the dead person. At Sutton Hoo, as well as at Oseberg in Vestfold, Norway, the dead were buried in a ship, and the deposited articles indicate

---

[6] See: Index of Mythological Names

that the dead in these burials were people of high status. Although burials still continued into late pagan times, cremation became more common, and in Iceland *brennuold*, the 'era of cremations', is a name for pagan times. In the Eddic tradition both types of burial rites are mentioned. Baldr and Nanna are burned with a ship gliding out to sea, whereas a dead and buried volva is called up from her grave by Odin in *Baldr's Dreams*. Cremation stopped with the advent of Christianity. After the conversion to Christianity in the 11th century, beliefs and customs of the pagan religion still had many followers for years to come. Ale offerings went on in Norway even until the present time.

Family, clan and society

The culture of the Viking Era[7] was developed by a surprisingly limited number of people. Around the year 1000 AD, for instance, Norway had a population of less than 200 000.[8]
Along the Norwegian coast there have been discovered quite a few circular yards, sites of enclosures, the purpose of which is unknown. It is surmised that these enclosures are the remnants of either thingsteads or military camps close to chieftains' seats. In either case these are traces of a common culture spread along the coast from the southernmost point of Norway and well into the polar regions, to Bjarkøy in the county of Troms. The merchant Ottar of Helgoland, in his report to king Alfred the Great of Wessex, told that this sea lane, *Norvegr,* was used for trade with Bjarmaland, OE: *Beormaland*, today's North-Western Russia. It is very likely that this is the origin of the name *Norway*, 'the way northward'.

---

[7] *Viking Era*: The Viking Era is commonly placed between 793 and 1066 AD. The origin of the term 'viking' has been widely discussed. Its early occurrance in OHG and AS may perhaps stem from a visit paid by King Rodulf to Theodoric in Ravenna, accompanied by warriors from tribes in the Oslofjord area (the so-called *Vika*).
[8] «... *less than 200 000.*»: Ref.: Bergljot Solberg, «Jernalderen i Norge», p. 240-41; Oslo 2019.

The origin of the term 'viking' has been widely discussed. Its early occurrence in Old High German and Anglo-Saxon could be connected to a visit by king Rodulf to Theodoric the Great in Ravenna. Rodulf was accompanied by warriors from different tribes, among others, warriors from *Vika*, the wide Oslofjord area in Norway. An early occurrence of a 'viking raid' is indicated in Denmark at Lejre, the historic royal seat. A great number of broken weapons, skeletons, etc, dating from the 4th Century AD, are taken to be the remains of unsuccessful Norwegian raiders, who must have reached the Danish shore by boat. For a long time onwards dominion over *Vika* was a matter of dispute between Danish and Norwegian rulers. Another assumption is that *vikings* meant warriors who could land in any *vík,* or bay, due to their advanced warships. A third guess links the seasonal viking raids to the verb *víkja,* 'to leave'. Their expeditions abroad, growing in size and regularity, meant a recurring drop in man-power back home, so *viking* may have designated 'one who regularly took his leave'.

People lived mainly on farms and crofts, and along the coast their livelihood was largely based on fishing where seamanship was a necessary condition. In the forests and high mountains they would hunt, and iron was extracted from marshes. Scandinavia had plentiful woodland, supplying oak for ship-building, as well as ash, aspen, pine and other kinds of trees which were used for building houses, furniture, tools, and so on. The wide range of wild animals included, among other species, bears, wolves, harts, boars, vipers, and squirrels, which all appear in the Eddic poetry. Plants like the mistletoe, crucial in the myth of Baldr's death, is also indigenous to the Scandinavian flora.

In those days there were no police, no schools, nor hospitals, no road maintenance, etc. Neither was there any bureaucracy since people lived in an oral culture. What they did have was a well-established judicial system, the Thing meetings. Also, we know that there were certain religious specialists, and among these the *thulr*, whose task would probably be to give recitals in ritual settings, and the *goði/gyðia,*⁹ who may perhaps be compared to a priest. We know from Icelandic society that a chieftain could also have the function of goði. The offices of both the thulr and the goði/gyðia, were attached to their temples. One who was not attached to a specific place was the volva, a soothsayer or prophetess. She performed her profession ambulating between the farms. A few stories that tell of the shamanist nature of her tasks and techniques exist. She could be asked to foretell aspects of the future concerning health, wealth and other important issues.¹⁰

One's family and relations were of great importance, providing assistance and security.
Life in general depended on the families themselves, and cooperation was absolutely necessary for society to function. The cooperative or community spirit (*dugnad*)¹¹ was a vital force, and there were few specialists. Most people were skilled in a variety of crafts. Tool-making, work in textiles, furs and leather, carpentry, and so on – everything was produced on the farms. Bigger projects meant that people had to gather for concerted efforts in order to get jobs done. Seasonal tasks like reaping, gathering sheep and cattle, etc, and larger tasks like erecting buildings would call for teamwork.

In a clan society it was important to keep track of one's relatives. Marriage meant more than linking two families, as it was not merely a romantic engagement between two individuals. Certainly it would be necessary that the two who were getting married should get along. The final decision, however, would rest with the heads of the families, whose main interest was to build alliances that could strengthen the power and position of the family. Divorce was however allowed both parts in the Nordic culture. If a woman demanded divorce, she kept her dowry and wedding gift. While married, it was the wife who directed household activities, carrying

---

⁹ *goði/gyðia:* The *goði* was the title for a man, while *gyðia* was the title for a woman.
¹⁰ *Concerning the volva:* See 'The saga of Eirik the Red' in 'The Complete Saga of the Icelanders' (see our Bibliography).
¹¹ *Dugnad:* «Working together on an enterprise».

the keys to the farm houses hanging from her belt. There were mutual obligations within the family, and blood vengeance would be one of them. Marriage could sometimes end in tragedy like the heroic poems of the Edda demonstrate, causing bloodshed due to conflicting interests. Honour was of utmost importance, and the duty of executing blood vengeance would fall on a person whose relative had been murdered, in order to retain his honour and that of his family.

In the pagan Nordic society, when a woman was giving birth, the ancient custom was for her to kneel, hugging a tree during labour. A reminiscence of this seems to be the word 'child log' (ON: *barnstokkr*) in the Saga of Volsung. After a child was born, the mother would hold it up before its father, who, by placing the child on his knee (*knésetja* : 'setting on the knee'), acknowledged it as his own. The child would then be offered salt allegedly on the edge of a sword, and sprinkled with water. At the same time the child was given its name and was received into the family with full rights to inherit. Another feature was that when a child was born, they believed that the female deities of fate, the norns, would gather to determine the child's future. To accept one's fate was an essential ideal in the Nordic religion. Yet if a child was born gravely handicapped physically or mentally, the custom was to put it out in the forrest, something which could also happen with children in cases of famine.

On the farms children began learning everything that was customary in their culture. They acquired the skills necessary for working a farm, for hunting, fishing and for transport especially at sea. They had to become self-sufficient in everything, and to learn all the skills that would enable them to produce what they needed. Besides learning how to prepare food, the girls, especially, would learn all that it took to make textiles and to prepare hides and furs. The boys would learn carpentry, they would learn how to forge tools and eventually weapons and so on. Other skills were how to erect fences and build houses. Children would be trained in sports, also in martial arts, and the training was intensive. Both boys and girls took care of the animals. As they grew up, the girls took part in dairy work and the children would learn horsemanship.

Eloquence was highly valued, since exchange of ideas and information was verbal only. People had a taste for pertinent remarks and poignant expressions, as witnessed in the Eddic poem *The Tale of the High One*. A statement made in an everyday situation could be expressed in the form of a proverb. They also developed a capacity for memory and techniques for memorizing. Today we have severe difficulties in comprehending how much they actually were capable of retaining in memory.

Along with the development of international trade and commerce, certain chieftains established their power over important trading posts and sea lanes. These chieftains needed men who were loyal, willing and able to fight for them. By and by, as some chieftains had gathered a great number of followers, the need arose for them and their retinue to be on the move from place to place. After having used up the resources on one farm, they would move to the next. *The Tale of Rig* shows that wealth was counted in farms, for this very reason. Local chieftains, earls and kings were constantly dependent on access to merchandise, especially of the luxury kind, in order to be able to deal out presents, thus keeping up their superior position. The raids of the Viking Era increased the possiblity for chieftains to give away valuables in exchange for loyalty and power. The Roman historian Tacitus (ca. 56 – 120 AD) observed that in his time Germanic kings did not have absolute power, and their position was not hereditary as they were chosen by their people. In principle they would be chosen for specific ends, for instance warfare, and according to Tacitus, they would rule more by their example than by giving strict orders.[12] Due to this type of government, the social organisation of Germanic tribes tended to remain fairly egalitarian.

As trade, travel and communications steadily increased, young men saw new possibilities for themselves, and a new kind of fellowship became established. A fellow (ON: *felagi*) was a person with whom one shared one's baggage when journeying, especially onboard ship. A fellow was a person you could trust, and establishing

---

[12] *About Germanic kings:* Tacitus: Germania, chapter 7.

fellowship in this way marked stepping outside of one's family. New bonds of fealty could even cause family members to kill each other if they had sworn allegiance to opposite parties. Competition between chieftains and between local kings gradually increased, and the idea of a national kingdom was budding.

The system of the Thing

The legislative and judicial assembly, the Thing, was basic to the culture of the North. The Thing system was organized according to geographical conditions. In Norway there were four levels of this system: one regional level, two county levels, four quarter Things (municipal level), and each of the quarter Things was divided in two, the so-called *hustings*. This is reflected in the English language today, cfr the Court of Hustings in the City of London. The regional Things themselves became established in the centre of the area of their jurisdiction, the *thingsteads*. In Norway *Frostathing* (in Trøndelag), *Gulathing* (in Sogn), *Eidsivathing* (in Oppland), the *Thing in Hologaland* (in Nordland) and *Borgarthing* (in Østfold) were regional Things. One may consider this form of social organization to be the first enduring democracy in the world.[13] By comparison, in the city-state Athens democracy lasted some 160 years and affected only the town itself. The Roman republic (509 – 27 BC) was an oligarchic representative system that bore little resemblance to that of Scandinavian democracy.

People who met at the Thing were free men, namely those who were in possession of a farm or a freehold, and each family was regarded as a unity. This meant that a widow who owned land would also be entitled to meet at the Thing. The alodial system of freeholds, to take a farm by alodial right, secured property for the families. In main it was the oldest son who inherited the farm. As already mentioned, women owned their dowries and bridal gifts and if they divorced their husbands, they kept this property, and both women and men had the right to declare themselves divorced before

---

[13] See: *T. Titlestad:* 'Norge i Vikingtid' (Norway in the Viking Era), p. 23-25.

witnesses. Basic to democracy was the function of the Thing to pronounce laws and to uphold them. At the Thing people would meet to discuss their conflicts, differences and to make political decisions; verdicts would be pronounced and fines would be meted out. The Thing system in Scandinavia had, however, two major deficiencies. One problem was the lack of national unity in that there was no common code of law. The other problem was that no law-enforcement existed. If the court at the Thing had decided in your favour, it would be up to you to collect your compensations and exert your rights. The Thing was usually held out of doors at *thingsteads*, defined meeting places. Wherever the Vikings sailed they would practise the Thing system, and if the need arose, they would even congregate aboard ship out at sea, 'Thing-at-the-mast'. Naturally they brought this system with them when they emigrated and also when they stayed abroad for longer periods at a time. The Scandinavian tradition of Thing meetings was continued by the immigrants to Iceland, and also by those who went to the British Isles, as witnessed by a great many place names.[14]

National jurisdiction came to be an Icelandic invention, and the people of Iceland may rightly claim to have established the first *national* democracy in the world. Ulfliot was chosen as the very first lawspeaker at the *Allthing*.[15] He had previously been sent to Norway to study the law system there in order to develop a general law system for all of Iceland. «Ùlfljótur's law», which was adopted in 930, was mainly based on the law at the Norwegian Gulathing. One famous Icelander who was elected lawspeaker twice was Snorri Sturluson, author of *The Prose Edda*, his ars poetica, a major source of Norse mythology.

---

[14] "...*place names*": Shetland has *Thingwall*; the Orkneys the same; Lewis, *Thiongal*; Isle of Skye *Tinwhil*;
Cromarthy Firth, *Dingwall*; Dumfriesshire, *Tinwald*; Northumberland, *Dingbell Hill*; Isle of Man has *Tynwald Hill*; Whitby, *Thingwala*; Liverpool, *Thingwall Hall*; Wirral, *Thingwall*; and in Ireland: *Thingmote* in Dublin.
[15] "...*lawspeaker at the* Allthing: lawspeaker was uniquely a Scandinavian legal position, based on common Germanic oral tradition. This office demonstrates the significance of the spoken word, that nothing was considered valid until it was pronounced.

When people assembled at the Thing, a special judicial-poetic formula was announced to invoke peace and order, the *Trygdarmál*, 'the Granting of Security'. Other rituals were performed to consecrate the courts at the Thing. A significant feature is that one third of the law had to be recited at each yearly meeting, so that over a period of three meetings at the regional Things the entire law would have been recited by the law-speaker. This shows the great importance attached to the spoken word in judicial matters: the law was regarded as valid only when it had been announced. Everybody was involved and everybody was given the possibility of knowing the law. Culture was integrated to such a degree that poetry and religion were not separate from judicial procedure. A radical example of the importance that was laid on law and order may be found in the Old Law at Frostathing, which stated that one was obliged to kill the king if he broke the law, or else one would forfeit all one's possessions. Obviously people realized that their society would crumble if law and order was not kept.

The Norsemen – warriors at sea

An absolute condition for the Viking Era were the viking ships. Reconstructions have shown that these ships could reach the speed of 17 knots. The vessels were slender, light weight and shallow. One could halt them in the wink of an eye by simply letting the crossbeam drop, and the ships could quickly be pulled across land on logs. They could also be rowed, since the gunwale was fairly low. It was the vikings themselves who rowed the warships. They attached their shields to the gunwale for protection against arrows and spears. All this made viking ships superior to other warships for several centuries.[16] Other types of vessels were also in use, both broader and deeper, which were suited for trade and commerce. Shipbuilding was a profitable business in Scandinavia, but especially in Norway, given her rich supply of slow-growing timber, and the builders were both Norsemen and Sami people. An important condition for the ships were their sails and riggings. The

---

[16] *"... several centuries"*:   'The Viking Ship Museum' in Roskilde, Denmark: https://www.vikingeskibsmuseet.dk/en/

ships were square rigged, and the sails were woollen, tightly woven by women, who made them water-tight, probably by use of wool grease (lanolin). This task of making the sail was just as time-consuming as building the ship's hull. The woven lengths of woollen material were dyed and sewn together to produce the huge broad-sails that were necessary for sailing the ships. The riggings needed ropes of unusual strength, and for this purpose the best material was the hide of walrus, hunted in the far North. The rugged Norwegian landscape, where one of the greatest resources was the fisheries and where hardly any inland roads existed, caused its inhabitants to become accustomed to travelling by boat and to learn the diverse techniques of fishing. This was a maritime culture, and Norsemen depended on the sea which was rough. However it was free of ice during the whole winter, so sea travel was possible, being the easiest means of transportation. This made it natural for them to experiment and develop good vessels, an enterprise which culminated in the famous war ships of the Viking Era.

The vikings were renowned for being exceptionally tough warriors. They believed that if you died in battle, you would gain a better after-life than if you died from old age or illness. A feature of their culture was to not show fear and by all means not to complain about one's wounds, aches and pains. To die with a manly proverb on one's lips was considered to be a worthy exit from this life. Since no other people had developed a nautical technology as sophisticated as the people of the North, their warriors, the vikings, 'ruled the waves'.

The Norsemens' relation to Central Europe

It is reasonable to suppose that the viking culture had its roots far back in history. The Gothic historian Jordanes[17] tells that Rodulf, who must have been the leader of several North Germanic tribes, joined the Gothic king Theoderic the Great (455-526 AD) in Ravenna. In his work *De origine actibusque getarum,* 'On the Origin and Deeds of the Goths', Jordanes mentions several clans

---

[17] *"...Jordanes"*:   East Roman historian from the 6th century AD.

from the Scandinavian peninsula, proving that there must have been a good deal of contact between the ancestors of the vikings and Central Europe.

On the Continent Charles the Great was building his empire. He had an advantage, being backed by the Pope, and Charles' ambitions culminated when the pope crowned him 'Emperor of the Romans' in the year 800 AD in Rome. One of Charles the Great's associates was the English scholar Alcuin of York. Through him and through his network in the monasteries, Charles exerted pressure against the pagan civilization. He waged perfidious war against the Saxons, who were still pagan,[18] and challenged the Danes. Realizing the threat, the vikings attacked the monasteries, an effective reaction against Charles' attempt of expanding his empire. This has caused a great bias in descriptions of the Nordic culture. The concept of 'vikings' has generally been coloured by the view of chroniclers and Christian historians portraying them as berserks and pirates engaging in rape, murder and pillage.

The relationship to Ireland was different. To begin with, the Irish form of Christianity varied greatly from the one Charles had adopted. After the missionary work of St. Patrick, the Irish converted around 500 AD to an old form of Christianity dating from the Roman period in England. Legend has it that St. James, one of Jesus' apostles, had visited Ireland and preached there. Secondly, there was extensive commerce between the Norsemen and the Irish. The Irish Sea was a seething, international market place, where slave trade also occurred. Dublin was founded by vikings in 840 AD as a fortified trading post. The Norsemen quickly became engaged in internal power struggles between Irish local kings, contracting alliances and marriages. Many became naturalized and got Irish names along with their Nordic ones. The *Ostmen*, 'men from the East', a special stratum of the population, were people who had their roots in Norway, and the same term was used in Iceland for Norwegians who visited there. In Scotland the Norsemen also had relations with the Picts, a people, a nation in fact, which a few

---

[18] «*...against the Saxons*»: Charles christened a great number of Saxon leaders, only to kill them off directly afterwards.

generations earlier had been very powerful. They had ruled widely in Scotland, yet at the beginning of the Viking Age they were on the verge of extinction. However, their exquisite aesthetics may have influenced the Norsemen.

The Runes

A thousand years of runic literature had existed in the North prior to the introduction of Christianity. The *Futhark,* the runic alphabet, was originally organized in three groups of eight letters, and each group was regarded as a family or clan and given its own name *(Freyr's clan, Hagal's clan, Tyr's clan)*. The oldest stage of runic script, the so-called *Elder Futhark*, was fitted to the ancient common Nordic language. This alphabet was in use approximately from the second century to the seventh. Inscriptions that have been discovered consist of mainly short messages on weaponry, jewelry, and on tools, rocks, stones and steles. The content of an inscription could simply be the name of the person who owned the object or that of the runic master. An inscription could also be made in memory of a relative or a comrade, and in some cases it could be an invocation of a god or of divine protection.

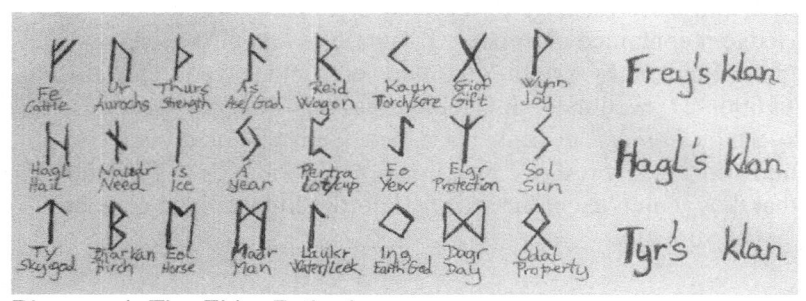

Diagram 1: The Elder Futhark

Later the runic alphabet underwent a radical change in the North. The Futhark was reduced from twenty-four to sixteen letters, and spelling no longer represented all the sounds of the language. What happened was that the number of runes in each family group was reduced. The first family in the new order retained six letters while the two others retained five letters each. Thus it was still possible to code a message – so-called 'hidden runes' – meaning that a rune (letter) may be designated by its family and position within the family. At the same time, the common Nordic language began to be split into several national variations, Old Norse being one of them. The words were then abridged, so that for instance the name *hariawalduR*, 'He who rules the army', was reduced to *Haraldr*, and *anulaibaR*, 'He who represents the ancestors', was reduced to *Ólafr*, by which process the names lost their meaning.

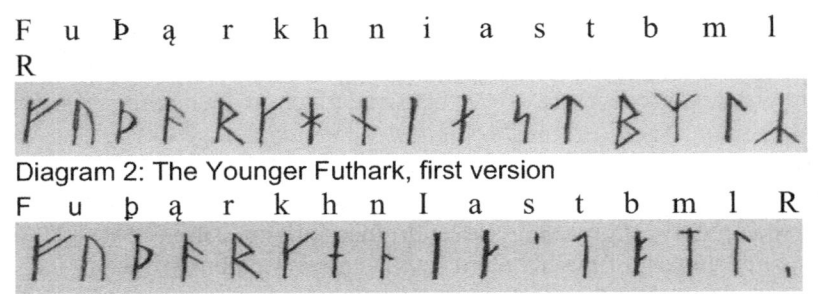

| F | u | Þ | ą | r | k | h | n | i | a | s | t | b | m | l |
| R | | | | | | | | | | | | | | |

ᚠᚢᚦᚨᚱᚴᚼᚾᛁᛆᛌᛐᛒᛦᛚ

Diagram 2: The Younger Futhark, first version

| F | u | þ | ą | r | k | h | n | I | a | s | t | b | m | l | R |

ᚠᚢᚦᚨᚱᚴᚼᚾᛁᛆᛌᛐᛒᛦᛚ

Diagram 3: The Younger Futhark, a later version with some letters further reduced

The last stage in the evolution of runic writing in Scandinavia occurred when the runes were rearranged in the order of the Roman alphabet, and when memory of the specific runic tradition and the knowledge it contained disappeared. The runes had also been brought to England by Anglo-Saxon invaders and stayed in use till about 1000 AD, eventually developing into a 28-letter alphabet, the Anglo-Saxon *Futhorc*, an alphabet which again accorded with pronunciation. A smart move by Christian missionaries to England was that they would use runic writing in order to fascilitate contact with pagan society.

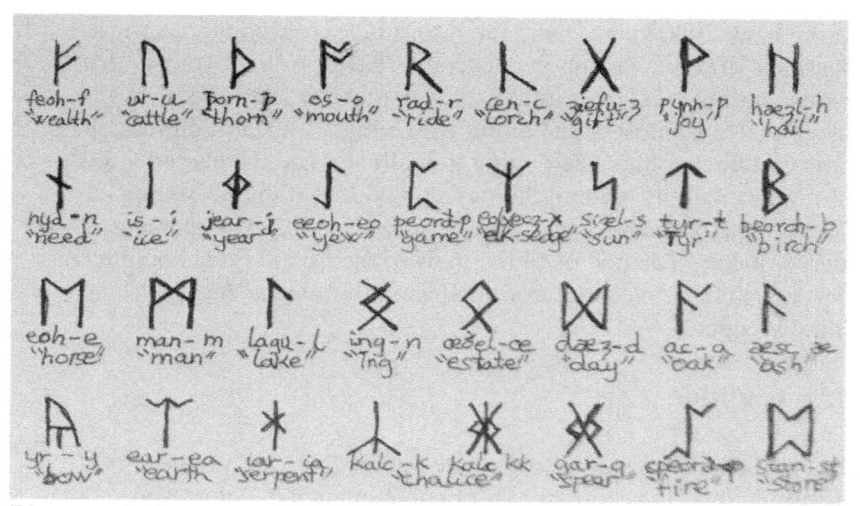

Diagram 4: The Anglo-Saxon Runes

Many runic inscriptions may be difficult to read, and even more difficult to interpret. Still, runic literature provides examples of Eddic metres and mythological fragments from the pre-Christian era. Christianity, the Religion of the Book, brought the art of writing on parchment with ink, using Roman letters. From the latter part of the 11th Century AD this art began to spread also in the North, and became widely used not only by the clergy, but also by the well to do. Several of Norway's leading families, especially from the West coast and the Trondheim area, had emigrated to Iceland because of king Harold Fairhair's usurpation of their lands. The cultural level of these families ensured that the art of reading and writing became spread outside of the monasteries. A famous example is the farm Oddi, where Snorri Sturluson was fostered. This farm is renowned for being a centre of learning, beginning with Saemundr the Learned (1056-1133).

As regards how long runes have been in use in Scandinavia, this question is difficult to assess. However, recent archeological findings show that their usage dates much further back in antiquity than what until now has been supposed. In 2021-22 a team of Norwegian archeaologists unearthed a stone with runic inscription dating back 2000 years[19], and the inscription is among the earliest examples of runic writing in existence. This proves, of course, that a corresponding level of culture had been reached at a far earlier age than hitherto supposed, and along with a higher level of culture one may assume that those belonging to it already had developed a form of religion with its own mythology and gods that they worshipped, – worshipped, probably with offerings and also with hymns, songs and … poems. The poems of the gods of the Poetic Edda could have their origin in a much earlier time than until now has been acknowledged.

Oral tradition

Oral tradition is a mystery to literate people. Nowadays it seems incredible that it was possible for people in ancient cultures to remember and preserve their legends throughout centuries and even millennia. In so doing, they relied on techniques that later were displaced by the written word, and from around the time of World War I oral culture became nearly extinct in the Western world. However, in recent times there has been a great revival of the forgotten art of story-telling. A main technique for memorizing a story is to envisage it as a pathway along which the images contained in the story appear as stations along the way.

In pre-literary society different categories of oral tradition were treated in different ways. It was important to keep stories of the gods and heroes as well as information about religion and legendary history as precise as possible for posterity. For that purpose these stories were delivered in a metrical form, as poetry. Poems of this kind were perhaps even sung, making them easier to recall. It was equally important for people to know their family history, and to keep track of family connections, cfr the great interest in these matters demonstrated by the sagas of the Icelanders. It became the task of the Nordic bard, the *skald*, to preserve family history of the

---

[19] *2000 year old runes found near Tyrifjorden in Norway*. See: https://www.theguardian.com/science/2023/jan/17/worlds-oldest-runestone-found-in-norway-archaeologists-say

kings and their deeds, in other words, history of national importance. The extremely formal metre *drottkvaett*[20] was preferred for this purpose. As regards the laws, which they also needed to remember precisely, it seems likely that many people knew them by heart, or at least were quite familiar with them.

There was sharp competition between bards to become the king's favorite skald, a person of significance at his court. We may assume that skaldic talent would be recognized in a child at an early age, and nurtured by people skilled in the art of skaldic poetry. Versatile and well informed, as confidants to the kings, the skalds could also function as ambassadors. In later times the skaldic poems came to be regarded as a primary source for the history of the kings. An example of this use of skaldic poetry is found in Snorri Sturluson's famous *Kringla heimsins*, his history of the Norwegian kings. It is known that some women were skalds, even among the best. One of them was Ragnhild Rolvsdaughter, the mother of Rollo (ON: *Gǫngu-Hrólfr*).[21] The Norwegian king Olav Kyrre had Vilborg as his court skald. Unfortunately none of her poems have been preserved, perhaps because Vilborg was a woman or because the king's long reign was a peaceful one. One of the most remarkable skalds of all times is Egill Skallagrimsson, who once saved his life by creating a poem in praise of his sworn enemy king Eiric Blood-axe, who had captured him. Since his poem *Hǫfuðlausn*, 'Head's Ransom',[22] was exceedingly well made, the king could not execute the poet. In addition to all the difficulties of the metre drottkvaett, Egill fitted end-rhyme between each pair of lines in his poem.

---

[20] *"... drottkvaett..."*:   ON Dróttkvætt, has 8 lines to the stanza, 3 stressed syllables to the line together with 3 or more unstressed ones. Inside of the lines – whose pairs are linked by traditional alliteration, like for instance in fornyrdislag – assonance was demanded too, a glide in vowel timbre, often acheived by splitting up compounds and creating a veritable puzzle-of-words. Late Latin hexametre from Merovingian circles seems to be a likely source of inspiration for the drottkvaett metrum.
[21] *Rollo*: Rollo (860-930 AD) was a Norwegian chieftain, who became the first duke of Normandy in France.
[22] In Egill's Saga, included in *The Saga of the Icelanders* (see Booklist), the poem is given in its entirely.

The Eddic tradition

Eddic poetry may be regarded as a monument to pagan society and culture, not only of the North, but even of the countless Germanic tribes which did not leave written records of their heathen past. A few examples of Germanic pagan legends outside of the Edda have survived. Worth mentioning is the Longobardian myth of origin from the 8th Century, where Frigg tricks Odin into granting victory to her own followers, the Longobards.[23] Germanic lore in an Eddic style is found in two heroic poems, the Anglo-Saxon *The Battle of Finnsburh* and the Old High German *Hildebrandslied*, whereas the concepts in the Anglo-Saxon *Beowulf* have been proven to be mainly Christian.[24] As to the Franks, their lore is largely lost to posterity, because Louis the Pious set fire to a whole library collected by his father, Charles the Great, containing their pagan songs and lore.

Eddic poems are all anonymous, they are composed in a simple metre and the subject matter is pagan mythology and stories of heroes. In contrast to *Beowulf* and *Hildebrandslied*, the Eddic poems are almost without exception divided into stanzas. Scholars have debated whether strophic organization was original, or whether it was a Nordic invention. Fredrik Paasche maintained that the flowing structure of *Beowulf* and *Hildebrandslied* was a literary phenomenon.[25] In contrast, the fact that the clauses and the division of stanzas coincide in the Nordic poems may indicate that this was original to oral tradition.

Edda in Old Norse is usually taken to mean 'Great-grandmother', cfr *The Tale of Rig*, which may point to its widespread familiarity

---

[23] «...*the Longobards*»: Paul the Deacan: *Historia Longobardorum*, «History of the Longobards», 8th C.
[24] «...*mainly Christian*»: It was a feat of J.R.R. Tolkien to demonstrate that *Beowulf* conformed with Christian concepts, and was not a product of pagan culture, contrary to German speculation.
[25] *Fredrik Paasche*: Bull og Paasche: 'Norsk Litteraturhistorie, Vol. I: Norges og Islands Litteratur', Kristiania 1924. Paasche was a noted scholar of Medieval Literature in Norway in the early twentieth century.

among common people. It may also indicate that these poems were considered to be very old and ancient indeed. In the first poem of our translation, *The Sibyl's Prophecy*, the speaker is a woman, which makes it not unreasonable to assume that the poem has been delivered from woman to woman throughout the generations. Another theory is that the name Edda simply means 'the book from Oddi', the famous Icelandic seat of learning. In any case, Edda was originally the name of Snorri Sturluson's textbook on poetry preserved, for instance, in the manuscript GKS 2367 4to. In 1643 the Icelandic bishop Brynjólfur Sveinsson discovered the manuscript later to be known as *Codex Regius* (GKS 2365 4to). In this manuscript he recognized poems that Snorri had quoted stanzas from in his textbook. Therefore he transferred the name Edda from Snorri's work to this newly found anthology, presuming that it had been put together at Oddi by Saemundr the Learned himself. In 1662 he sent the manuscript to the Danish king Fredrik III in Copenhagen, where it was catalogued, popularly called Codex Regius (CR) or Saemundaredda. This manuscript is the main source for Eddic poetry.

The Edda anthology presented in CR is divided into two parts. Ten poems relate the story of the gods and nineteen poems tell the stories of several heroes and their tribulations. In CR *Volundarkvida* is included among the poems about the gods, but it has become customary to place it among the heroic poems, as Volund is not a god. We have included seven poems from other sources than CR in our translation, six of which are Eddic. These poems are *Baldr's Dreams*, taken from the Arnamagnian Collection, manuscript no. 748 4°; *The Story of Rig* from the manuscript Codex Wormianus; *The Song of Hyndla* taken from the manuscript Flateyjarbók; *The Song of Grotti* from a manuscript of Snorri's Edda; *The Spells of Groa* and *The Tale of Fiolsvinn*, both taken from paper manuscripts. We have added *The Song of the Spear* (*Darraðarlióð*) from Njal's Saga, because of its mythological content.

All in all there are more than forty poems which may be called Eddic in a wide sense. CR contains twenty-nine poems in its present state, nineteen of which deal with heroes (if The Poem of Volund is counted among the heroic poems), although Gripir's Prophecy and

The Tale of Atli are often regarded as being inferior poems. Therefore the total number of poems in CR that may be counted as being genuine amounts to twenty-seven.[26] However some pages are missing from CR, indicating that an unknown number of verses have been lost to posterity. Depending upon the choice of guidelines, the catalogue of Eddic poetry will vary. One of our priorities has been to include poems where the main characters are women, because many interesting poems may have been too readily disregarded, since the focus in the years after the poems were written down has mainly been on men and their achievements. We follow the sequence of the mythological poems in the CR, and continue by following Sophus Bugge's edition: *Baldr's Dreams, The Story of Rig, The Song of Hyndla, The Song of Grotti, The Spells of Groa,* and *The Tale of Fiolsvinn*. We end with the somewhat skaldic poem *The Song of the Spear*.

Regarding the question of the origin of the Eddic poems, we believe that the conceptual core of many of the poems existed prior to the 9th century AD, in other words that they were in existence at the time of Iceland's settlement by Norwegian refugees, notably in an oral form and not in a written one. In the nineteenth century scholars tended to date these poems far back in pagan times. Scholars of the twentieth century, on the other hand, have tended to believe that they were composed at a much later date by placing many of them in the Christian era. Recently, Leiv Olsen has presented an investigation into linguistic criteria for dating the poems of CR, comparing well-chosen parameters.[27] According to his presentation the poems may be divided into three time periods, an older, a middle and a younger period. His conclusion ought to be considered by any reader of the Edda:

---

[26] «*...to twenty-seven.*»: See Appendix
[27] *Leiv Olsen*: «The Age of the Eddic Poems in *Codex Regius* – especially concerning the *of/um*-particle as a criterion for dating;" Master Thesis, Bergen University in Norway, 2019. *our trans.* (Norw. title: "Alderen til Eddakvada i *Codex Regius* – spesielt om of/um-partikkelen som daterings-kriterium." Masteroppgave ved Institutt for lingvistiske, litterære og estetiske studier ved Universitetet I Bergen, 2019.

> "The oldest layer of Eddic poems, in my estimation, must
> have been created before the 11th century and after 400-500
> AD, and rather in the beginning of this period than towards
> its end. It would not be a bad estimate to date them to 700-
> 800 AD with a margin of error of one hundred years both
> ways. Since the great majority of Eddic poems must have
> been created in pre-Christian times, and since nearly all the
> poems about the gods must be that old, we
> may safely assume that the concepts presented by these
> poems existed in the North in pagan times."
> (*our translation, authorized by L.O.*)

We concur with this conclusion, and see that it also reflects the views expressed by Fredrik Paasche.

In the High Middle Ages the aristocratic elite in Norway became influenced by new trends in culture, like for instance ballads, poetry of courtly love, and romances, which became very popular. One example of this type of literature is the story of Tristan and Isolde. The new medium of writing brought by Christianity – ink on parchment – afforded many and novel possibilities. Literature branched out in many categories. One of these was religious literature, like for instance the Old Norse Book of Homilies, a collection of sermons. Even the project of translating the Bible from Latin into Old Norse began promisingly, but it was never finished.[28] Another category was the collecting and unification of Norwegian law, culminating in Magnus Lawmender's *Law of the Realm*. Yet another was a kind of encyclopedia meant as an educational textbook for princes, *King's Mirror* (ON: Konungs Skuggsjá; L: Speculum regale). The result of all this was that Eddic poetry fell out of fashion.

In Iceland knowledge of the Eddic traditions and bardic skills were still kept up. Iceland became the center of collecting and editing Eddic poems and pagan lore. Even as late as in the 1380s the manuscript *Flateyjarbók* was created, containing for instance the

---

[28] *"...but never finished":* The Old Norse Bible, the fragments that were finished, is called 'Stjǫrn', meaning 'governance' or 'guidance'.

poem *The Song of Hyndla*. This book is the largest and most costly of the medieval Icelandic manuscripts, comprising 225 vellum leaves, richly illustrated. In 1402, a few years after the book was completed, the Black Death reached Iceland, causing a tremendous decline in the population and its resources. Old books became worn out, and though the practice of copying books continued, people could no longer afford the expensive vellum, and many errors eventually crept into the paper copies. Contact with Iceland's illustrious past slowly weakened.

In Norway the Black Death struck for the first time in 1349. After several waves of pestilence, the elite in Norway was drastically reduced. Their material resources dwindled as many farms lay barren due to lack of people who could work the lands. At the same time new types of sea-faring vessels had been developed in Northern Germany and Holland, against which the traditional viking ships could no longer hold their own, and the power of the Hanseatic League proved unstoppable. After having joined the Kalmar Union in 1397, Norway succumbed to Denmark along with the territories that were under her rule at that time: Iceland, Greenland and the Faeroe Islands.

Edda rediscovered

As already mentioned, the manuscript CR was rediscovered in 1643, and was eventually sent to Denmark where the first translations appeared in Latin in the years 1665 and 1667. Many translations followed, and parts of *The Tale of the High One* and *Baldr's Dreams* were published in French in 1756; a Danish translation appeared in 1783; *The Tale of Thrym*, *The Song of Hyndla* and other poems were published in German in 1789; in 1797 A.S. Cottle's *Icelandic Poetry or the Edda of Sæmundr* was published in Bristol in the style of Alexander Pope; a complete German version was presented by the Brothers Grimm in 1815. A number of English versions are listed in our Bibliography.

Our translation aims at rendering the Old Norse poetry into a modern vernacular which is easy to understand and yet conveys the meaning of the original text. At the same time we have tried to preserve poetic elements like verse rhythm and alliterative rhyme, as well as the division into stanzas according to metre. Whether the poems were sung, or in some special way recited, we do not know, yet there are indications that they were somehow sung. The name of the most cherished type of poem in praise of kings, *drápa*[29], has as its connotation 'to strike', namely to strike a string of an instrument in support of the recital of the poem.

Rhyme and metre

In order to do the Eddic poetry justice, we believe it essential to try also to deliver a notion of its spirit and power at the same time. We have found that this could best be achieved by keeping the original metrics in our present rendition. Eddic poetry is composed in two main metres, each of them having its specific variation. It is worth noting that the metres used in Edda are commonly fairly short, thereby producing a weighty or even terse impression.
Here follows a survey of these metres.

Fornyrdislag, ON: *fornyrðislag*, 'the ancient way of wording', is the story-telling metre. It has two stressed syllables (S) per line and a varying number of unstressed syllables (s); there are eight lines to the stanza, and the lines are joined in pairs by alliteration, as in big – bad or ever – open. Only stressed syllables carry the rhyme. Thus the first stressed syllable in line 2 decides the rhyme, and one or both of the stressed syllables in line 1 share it (The Sybil's Prophecy, stanza 1):

Old Norse		**Our translation**
S s S		S s S
Hlioðs bið ek	a	I bid you
S s S s		S s S s
allar kindir	b	all to listen,

---

[29] *Drápa*: See Cleasby/Vigfusson, *Icelandic-English Dictionary* drápa.

S s s S s		s S s s S s	
meiri ok **m**inni	c	both **h**igher and lower	
S s S s s		s S s S	
mǫgo Heimdallar;	d	of **H**eimdall's kin!	
S s s s S s		s s S s S s s	
Vildo at ek **V**alfǫðr	e	Would you **l**ike me, Valfather,	
S s S s		s s S s s S	
vel fyr telia	f	to de**l**iver to all	
S s S s		s S s S	
forn spiǫll **f**ira	g	the **o**ldest lore	
s s S s S		s S s S s	
þau er **f**remst um man.	h	that **I** remember?	

Most editors feel that the first pair of lines above (a – b) should be mended, because the metre here deviates from regular fornyrdislag and appears as *kviðuháttr* (a skaldic metre with three syllables to line one, and four syllables to line two). Most editors have chosen to exchange the first pair of lines from CR stanza 1 with lines from a younger version of this poem:

S s s S s		s s S s S	
Hlióðs bið ek allar	a	«I bid all to **h**ear	
S s S s		s S s S	
helgar kindir .....etc.	b	you **h**oly clans» ....etc.	

By so doing, the focus passes from the sibyl who speaks (stressed *I*, in CR) to the ones who might be hearing her opening words (*holy clans*, in the second example above). For this reason we prefer the Codex Regius (CR) version in this instance. In other places also throughout the Edda, the metre fornyrdislag may contain lines as short as three syllables.

Liodahatt, ON *lióðaháttr*, 'the metre of exchanging verse', is a six-liner used for dialogue and words of wisdom, its third and sixth line have three stressed syllables and internal alliteration, summing things up, as it were (The Tale of the High One, stanza 21)

Old Norse		**Our translation:**
S s s S s		s S s S
Hiarðir þat vito,	a	The flock can tell
s s S S s		s s S s s S
nær þær heim skolo,	b	when it's time to go home
s S s S s S s		s S s S S s
ok ganga þá af grasi;		and leave the lush meadows;
s S s S		S s S s
enn ósviðr maðr	d	but the nit-wit
s S s S		s S s S
kann ævagi	e	can never tell
S s S S s		s S s S s S
sins um mál maga.	f	the limits of his lust.

The number of unstressed syllables varies both in fornyrdislag and in liodahatt, which affords a rich variety of rhythm within the metrical pattern. In our translation we have taken certain liberties concerning the number of unstressed syllables, in order to obtain a rendition into English which sounds natural.

Malahatt, ON: *málaháttr* (the meaning is obscure), is a variation, an expansion of fornyrdislag, and has five stressed syllables to each pair of lines. This gives more space for embellishments.

Galdralag, ON: *galdralag*, 'the metre of spells', is a variation of liodahatt. The third line in any of the semi-stanzas is then doubled with a minor variation, cfr *The Tale of the High One*, first semistanza, lines a – c_2:

Every gateway,	a
when going through,	b
watch with utmost care,	c_1
watch with utmost caution;	c_2
for you don't know whether	d
enemies are seated	e
ahead of you in the hall.	f

Fornyrdislag, without division into stanzas, is used in the epic Beowulf. This metre is generally called *the long alliterative line*, and it also occurs in the Old High German Hildebrandslied.
As to end rhyme, Edda provides a few isolated instances. In one case, in The Sibyl's Prophecy, the end rhyme is onomatopoëtic. In another case, The Song of Thrym, it is impressionistic. Yet it was left to Egill Skallagrimsson, in his tributary poem to Eiric Blood-Axe, to give the end rhyme full play. Harbard's Contest is exceptional in that the metre is often irregular, containing also parts in prose. Taking Eddic poetry in a broader sense, we have chosen to include **The Song of the Spear**, ON: *Darradarlióð*, where twelve norns/valkyries weave life and death for those who take part in the Battle at Clontarf.

Heiti and Kennings

Besides metre and rhyme, Old Norse poetry also employed other poetic techniques. Two significant techniques should be mentioned. Certain poetical words which otherwise are not commonly used in everyday language are called **heiti**, ON: *heiti*. One example could be to call a woman 'bride'; another would be to call a son 'first-born'; yet another is to call the road 'the beaten track', as we have done in The Tale of Rig, stanza 26.

Kennings, ON: *kenningar*, are metaphors like 'sea-horse' for ship, 'hair-seat' for head and so on. The Tale of Hymir is particularly full of such kennings: 'goat-lord' for Thor, 'son of apes' for Hymir, and 'skid-horse' for a boat, etc. This technique creates an intellectual entertainment, firing the imagination of the listener. However, the use of kennings is rare in Eddic poetry, although the skalds excelled in it.

A few notes on the rules of the alliterative rhyme

Our translation is based on the actual pronunciation of English words. Thus *knave* rhymes alliteratively with *new*, not with *king*; *above* rhymes with *bring* and not with *all*, etc. As already mentioned, it is only stressed syllables that carry the rhyme. Consonants rhyme always with the same consonant. Some instances are: *high - heaven; pond – pig; lame – love*. However, the following three combinations only rhyme with themselves: *sk, sp* and *st* as in *spring – sprout; skimp – scan; stand – stick*. The vowel modifiers **Y** and **W** rhyme with themselves and with vowels: *year – yield; you – all; will – want; world – ill*. Any vowel rhymes with any other, except with itself: *owl – apple*, **not** *owl - out*.

About the Printing Practice

In medieval manuscripts, poetry is written without division into verse and often lacking separation between stanzas. It was important to make the most of the costly vellum. A recurring open space – a caesura – would therefore be a waste. We follow the common Scandinavian printing practice with one rhythmic entity to each line, as this provides an easier reading and sense of rythm.

BIBLIOGRAPHY

Text

Bugge, S.: *Norrœn Fornkvæði – Islandsk Samling af folkelige Oldtidsdigte om Nordens Guder og Heroer, almindelig kaldet Sæmundar Edda hins froda*, Christiania 1867, reprinted Oslo 1965

Dronke, U.: *The Poetic Edda I-II-III*, Oxford 1969-1997-2011

'Heimskringla', Old Norse-Icelandic texts at: <www.heimskringla.no/wiki/Main_Page>

Helgason, J. ed. *Eddadigte I. Vǫluspá, Hávamál*. Nordisk filologi A: Tekster. Stockholm, Copenhagen, Oslo 1964.

-- " -- *Eddadigte II. Gudedigte*, 1965.

Jónsson, F. ed.: *Sæmundar-Edda. Eddukvæði*. 2nd ed., Sigurður Kristjánsson, Reykjavík 1927

Neckel, G.: *Die Lieder des Codex Regius nebst verwandten Denkmälern*, revised by. H. Kuhn, 5th edition, Heidelberg 1983, searchable at <titus.uni-frankfurt.de/texte/ etcs/ germ/anord/edda/edda.htm>

Nordal, S. ed. *Vǫluspá*. Trans. Benedikz, B.S. and McKinnel, J., Durham and St. Andrews Medieval Texts, 1. Durham:

See, Klaus von, et al: Dept of English Language and Medieval Literature, 1978
Kommentar zu den Liedern der Edda, Heidelberg 1993-2019

Dictionaries
Barnhart, C.:   *The American College Dictionary*, New York 1947
Cleansby, R.:   *An Icelandic-English Dictionary*, revised, enlarged and completed by Gudbrand Vigfusson, Oxford University Press 1874, second edition by Sir W. A. Craigie, reprinted 1975
Egilsson, S.:   *Lexicon poëticum antiquae linguae septentrionalis*, Hafniae 1860, transl into Danish and enlarged by F. Jonsson, reprinted Copenhagen 1966
Farge, B. La & Tucker, J.:   *Glossary to the Poetic Edda*, transl. & enlarged from H. Kuhn, Kurzes Wörterbuch, Heidelberg, 1992
Fritzner, J.:   *Ordbog over det gamle norske Sprog 1-4*, Oslo 1973
Gering, H.:   *Vollständiges Wörterbuch der Edda,* Hildesheim 1971
Magnússon, Á. B.:   *Íslensk orðsifjabók, Orðabók Háskólans*, Stofnun Árna Magnússonar í íslenskum fræðum, 3. prentun 2008

Skeat, W. W.:	*An Etymological Dictionary of the English Language,* 4 vols, rev. ed. Oxford 1963
Vries, J. de:	*Altnordisches etymologisches Wörterbuch,* Leiden 1961

Translations

Auden, W.H. & Taylor, P. B.:	*Norse Poems* revised, London 1981
Bellows, H. A.:	*The Poetic Edda*, New York 1923
Bray, O.:	*The Elder or Poetic Edda*, London 1908
Cottle, A. S.:	*Icelandic Poetry, or the Edda of Sæmund*, Bristol 1797
Crawford, J.:	*The Poetic Edda*, Indianapolis 2015
Dronke, U.:	*The Poetic Edda II*, Mythological poems, Oxford 1997
-- " --	*The Poetic Edda III*, Mythological poems, Oxford 2011
Hollander, L. M.:	*The Poetic Edda,* Austin, TX, 16th reprint 2014
Holm-Olsen, L.:	*Edda-dikt*, Oslo 1975/1985
Larrington, C.:	*The Poetic Edda*, Oxford 1996
Mortensson-Egnund, I.:	*Eddakvæde*, Christiania 1907
Terry, P.:	*Poems of the Elder Edda*, reprinted Philadelphia 1990
Thorpe, B.:	*Edda Sæmundar hins froda*, 2 vols, London 1866
Vigfusson, G. & Powell, F. Y.:	*Corpus Poeticum Boreale*, The Poetry of the Old

Northern Tongue, 2 vols, reprinted New York 1965

Background

Allott, S.:	*Alcuin of York, his life and letters,* York 1974
Asbjörnsen, P.Chr. & Moe, J.:	*Popular Tales from the Norse,* translated by G. W. Dasent 1859, reprinted London 1969
Benedictow, O.J.:	*The Demography of the Viking Age and the High Middle Ages in the Nordic Countries*, Scandinavian Journal of History Vol 21, No 3, Scandinavian University Press 1996
Berlin, B. & Kay, P.:	*Basic color terms, their universality and evolution*, University of California Press 1969
Brodeur, A. G.:	*The Prose Edda,* New York 1916
Bruce-Mitford, R.:	*Aspects of Anglo-Saxon Archaeology. Sutton Hoo* London 1974
Butterworth, E. A. S.:	*The Tree at the Navel of the Earth*, Berlin 1970
Campbell, J. G.:	*Cultural Atlas of the Viking World*, London 1994
Christensen, A. S.:	*Casssiodorus, Jordanes and The History of the Goths – Studies in a Migration Myth,* Copenhagen 2002
Clunies Ross, M.:	*A History of Old Norse Poetry and Poetics,* Cambridge 2011
-- " --	*Prolonged Echoes. Old Norse myths in medieval Northern society. I: The myths,* The Viking

Davidson, H. R. Ellis: Collection, 7. Odense University Press, 1994
Saxo Grammaticus – The History of the Danes – Books I-IX, Cambridge 1998

-- " -- *Gods and Myths of Northern Europe,* Harmondsworth 1964

Eliade, M.: *Shamanism,* New York 1964

Elliott, R. W. V.: *Runes, an Introduction*, Manchester Univ Presss 1981

Enright, M.: *Lady with a mead cup. Ritual, prophecy and lordship in the European warband from la Tène to the Viking Age,* Dublin 1996

Faulkes, A.: *Edda,* (Snorri's Prose Edda), Everyman's Library 1995

Fitzhug, W. W. & Ward, E. I., eds.: *Vikings: The North Atlantic Saga,* Washington & London 2000

Frazer, J.: *The Golden Bough,* London 1930

Gibbon, E.: *The History of the Decline and Fall of the Roman Empire,* London 1994

Griffiths, D.: *Vikings of the Irish Sea,* Gloucestershire 2010

Hamel, G. von: *The Game of the Gods,* Arkiv for Nordisk Filologi 50, Lund 1934

Haywood, J.: *The Penguin Historical Atlas of the Vikings,* London 1995

Hedeager, L.: *Iron Age Society,* Oxford 1992

Hreinsson, V., ed.: *The Complete Sagas of Icelanders,* 5 vols, Reykjavik 1997-2019

Hulthén, B.: *On ceramic ware in Northern Scandinavia during the Neolithic, Bronze and Early Iron Age,*

Jerstad, M. & Harris, K.: Archeology and Environment 8, Umeå 1991

Jordanes: *Voluspå, gudinnene og verdens fremtid*, Saga Bok, Stavanger 2013
De origine actibusque Getarum, The Origin and Deeds of the Goths, transl. Merow, C.C., Princeton – Oxford 1915

Jørgensen, L. Bender: *North European Textiles until AD 1000*, Aarhus 1992

Kabell, A: *Balder und die Mistel*, Folklore Fellows Communications, 82:1, No 196, Helsingfors 1965

Kellogg, R. L.: *A Concordance to Eddic Poetry,* East Lancing, MI, 1988

Krause, W. & H. Jankuhn: *Die Runeninschriften im älteren Futhark I-II*, Göttingen 1966

Kristjánsson, J.: *Eddas and sagas. Iceland's medieval literature*, Reykjavík 1988

Leew, L. van der: *Phänomenologie der Religion*, Tübingen 1970

Lincoln, B.: *Myth, Cosmos and Society: Indo-European Themes of Creation and Destruction*, Harv Univ Press, London 1986

Lord, A.: *The Singer of Tales*, reprinted Cambridge 2003

Lund, N. ed.: *Two Voyagers at the Court of King Alfred. The ventures of Ohthere and Wulfstan together with the*

McEvedy, C.: *Description of Northern Europe from the Old English Orosius*, York 1984
The New Penguin Atlas of Medieval History, London 1992

McKinnell, J.: *Both One and Many. Essays on Change and Variety in Late Norse Heathenism*, Rome: Il Calamo, 1994

Morris, Richard L.: Runic and Mediterranean Epigraphy, John Benjamins Publ. Co.

Munch, Johansen and Roesdahl (eds): *Borg in Lofoten – A Chieftain's Farm in North Norway*, Trondheim 2006

Munch, P. A.: *Norse Mythology*, transl by S. B. Hustvedt, New York 1927

-- " -- *Norröne gude- og heltesagn*, rev. Anne Holtsmark, Oslo 1967

Olsen, L.: *Alderen til eddakvada i Codex Regius*, Master's treatise at Bergen University 2019

Orchard, A.: *Dictionary of Norse Myth and Legend*, London 2002

Quinn, J.: 'Editing the Edda; the case of *Vǫluspá*. Scripta Islandica'

--"-- 'The gýgr, the vǫlva, the ásynja and her lover: meetings with remarkable women in the eddic poems', in *The Treasures of the Elder Tongue. Fifty years of Old Norse in Melbourne.*

	Eds. Burge, K and Martin, J.S., Melbourne: The University of Melbourne, 1995
-- " --	*Vǫluspá and the composition of eddic verse'.* in *Poetry in the Scandinavian Middle Ages*, ed. Pàroli, T. Proceedings of the Seventh International Saga Conference. Spoleto: Centro Italiano di Studi sull'Alto Medioevo, 1990, *pages 303-20*
Rønne, P.:	*'Horg, hov and ve – a pre-Christian cult place at Ranheim in Trøndelag, Norway, in the 4th – 10th centuries AD',* http://www.rockartscandinavia.com/images/articles/preben_roenne_a11.pdf (http://www.transpersonlig.no/ranheim.pdf)
Sawyer, P.:	*The Oxford Illustrated History of Vikings*, London 1997
Saxo Grammaticus:	*History of the Danish People*, transl. Peter Fisher, Vol I-IX, Cambridge 1979
Simek, R.:	*Dictionary of Northern Mythology*, Cambridge 1993
Skeat, W. W.:	*The Concise Dictionary of English Etymology*, reprinted Wordsworth Reference 1993
Smiley, J.:	*Sagas of the Icelanders*, New York 2000

Snorri Sturluson:	*Heimskringla*, transl. L. M. Hollander, Texas 1999
-- " --	*The Prose Edda*, ed. Jessie Buock, London 2005
Steinsland, G.:	*Det hellige bryllup og norrøn kongeideologi. En analyse av hierogami-myten i Skírnismál, Ynglingatal, Háleygjatal og Hyndluljóð*, Oslo: Solum Forlag 1991
Steinsland, G.:	*Mytene som skapte Norge – Myter og makt fra vikingtid til middelalder*, Oslo 2012
Steinsland, G.:	*Norrøn religion: Myter, riter, samfunn*, Oslo 2005
-- " --	'*Giants as Recipients of Cult in the Viking Age?*' in *Words and Objects – towards a Dialogue Between Archaeology and Religion*, Oslo 1986, *pages 212-222*
Steinsland, G., ed.:	*Voluspå og andre norrøne helligtekster,* utvalg og innledende essay i *Verdens Hellige Skrifter,* ved Gro Steinsland, Oslo 2003
Steinsland, G. & Meulengracht-Sörensen, P.:	*Voluspå*, Oslo 1999
Ström, Å. V.:	'*Indogermanisches in der Völuspá*', Numen XIV, Brill 1967, *pages 167-208*
Ström, Å. V. and Biezais, H.:	*Germanische und Baltische Religion*, Berlin 1975
Swanton, M., transl and ed.:	*The Anglo-Saxon Chronicles*, London 2000
Tacitus, P. Cornelius:	*Agricola, Germania, Dialogus*, Loeb Classical

Titlestad, T.:	Library vol 35, Harvard Univ Press 2006 *Norge i vikingtid*, Stavanger 2012
-- " --	*Viking Norway – Personalities, Power and Politics*, Stavanger 2008
Turville-Petre, E. O. G.:	*Myth and Religion of the North*, London 1964
Vries, J. de:	*Altgermanische Religionsgeschichte I-II*, Berlin 1957
Weber, G. W.:	'*Intellegere historiam. Typological perspectives of Nordic Prehistory*', in *Tradition og historieskrivning. Kilderne til Nordens ældste historie*, eds.: Hastrup, K. and Meulengracht-Sørensen, P.: Acta Jutlandica LXIII: 2, Humanistisk Serie, Århus 1987, *pages 95-141*
Yates, F. A.:	*The Art of Memory*, London 1996
Ødegård, Knut	*Edda-dikt I-IV*, Oslo 2013-2016

The Sibyl's Prophecy
– VOLUSPÁ –

The Sibyl's Prophecy *is a visionary poem, which relates the world's creation, growth, conflicts, destruction and resurrection. It gives us a unique picture of North-Germanic mythology as seen through the eyes of a wise woman, an oracle. The poem is composed in the metre fornyrdislag, for which see our* Introduction *and* Appendix III. *For scholars the Sibyl's Prophecy has always been an important source of information.*

Two versions of this poem have been preserved, one in the manuscript Codex Regius (CR) from appr. 1270, while the other was added to the manuscript Hauksbók probably around 1340. Almost half of the stanzas are also quoted by Snorri Sturluson in his so-called "Younger Edda". In 1867 the Norwegian scholar Sophus Bugge published a reconstruction of the poem combining these two versions. Our translation relates largely to Bugge's version. In Appendix III *we give the two original texts, translated into English, together with a table of comparison.*

In the present rendering all the names of the dwarfs are translated into English, because we consider that they contain knowledge pertaining to human psychology. We give the original names in the margin and some further explanations in the Index of Mythological Names.

The Sibyl's Prophecy *is the first poem of the Eddic anthology. The main character of the poem is the sibyl. She is the narrator who starts by calling herself "I", and with emphasis on this word (in CR) she opens this first poem. The sibyl was an institution in her own right in pre-Christian society; she was highly esteemed and feared for her ability to foretell the future and to reveal things hidden.*

1.
I bid you
all to listen,[30]
both higher and lower
of Heimdall's kin! *'He who makes the world blossom'*
Would you like me, Valfather, *'Father of the fallen' = Odin*
to deliver to all
the oldest lore
that *I* remember?

2.
I recollect the giants,
born long ago,
in times gone by
they brought me up;
nine realms I know,
nine women in the tree, *female iotuns*
that noble measure *the World Tree*
beneath the ground.

3.
It was early in time[31]
when Ymir settled, *the primeval androgynous giant*
there was no sand, no sea,
nor soothing waves;
earth was not
nor any heaven;
Ginnunga-gap was – *the Universal Void*
and grass nowhere.

---

[30] *«I bid you all to listen...»:* We follow the CR version here, adding the same emphasis in the last line of the stanza.
[31] *"It was early in time..."*: Literally "early among the ages", implying a cyclic concept of history.

4.
Till Bur's sons let   *sons of the first god*
the lands rise up,
mighty Midgard   *Middle-earth*
was made by them;
Sun from the south
swept the hall's floor;
the ground was studded
with green leek.

5.
Sun[32] – Moon's friend –
from the south she came
and stretched her hand
toward heaven's gate;
Sun knew not where
her orbit lay,
the stars did not know
where to stay in the heavens,
Moon did not know
his might and force.

6.
The Governing Powers
gathered in council,
the most holy gods
met to decide:
Night and her kin
were named by them,
also Morning
and Mid-Day,
Afternoon and Evening –
the years were counted.

---

[32] *«Sun – Moon's friend...»*:   In Norse mythology the sun is feminine and the moon is Masculine, in contrast to the Classical concept.

7.
The aesir met   *the war gods*
at Idavoll,   *'Field of activity'*
they who timbered
temples and shrines;
they mounted anvils,
made riches,
they forged tongs
and tools aplenty.

8.
Playing board-games,
bristling with joy,
never they were
in want of gold;
until there entered
three iotun maidens,
all-overpowering,
from Iotunheim.   *the home of the giants*

9.
The Governing Powers
gathered in council,
the most holy gods
met to decide:
Who was to form
the family of dwarfs
from Brimir's blood   *Ymir's*
and Blaïn's legbones?   *Ymir's*

10.
Courage-Muncher   *Móðsognir*
was the mightiest one
among the dwarfs,
and Doorman was next;   *Durinn*

they made many
man-like figures
out of earth,
as ordered by Doorman.

11.

New Moon and Waning,	*Nýi, Niði*
North and South,	*Norðri, Suðri*
East and West,	*Austri, Vestri*
All-thief, Sleepy,	*Alþjófr, Dvalinn*
Corpse, Ghost	*Nár Náinn*
Clamper, Deceased	*Nípingr, Dáinn*
Shivering, Dithering,	*Bifurr, Báfurr*
Shorn and Bumbler,	*Nori, Bǫmburr*
Friend and Goodly,	*Ánn, Ánarr*
Great-grandfather, Meadwolf.	*Óinn, Mjóóðvitnir*

12.

Wall and Staff-elf,	*Veggr, Gandálfr*
Sturdy, Crooked-elf,	*Þorinn, Vindálfr*
Tough and Threatening	*Þrár ok Þráinn*
Trim, Glance and Wise,	*Þekkr, Litr ok Vitr*
New[33] and New-Counsel;	*Nýr ok Nýráðr,*
I name them all	
– Ruler and Quick-wit –	*Reginn, Ráðsvinnr*
I have reckoned the dwarfs.	

13.

Filer, Wedge,	*Fili, Kili*
Foundling, Skinny,	*Fundinn, Náli*
Handle, Will,	*Hepti, Vili*
Wastrel, Skilful,	*Svíurr, Hannarr*
Twin, Scowler,	*Billingr, Brúni*
Scalpel and Borne	*Bildr ok Buri*

---

[33] *New:* Nýr is our conjecture for nár, confer. stanza 11.

Fast and Horned,	*Frár, Hornbori*
Famed, Lingerer,	*Frægr ok Lóni*
Loam-heath, Edge,	*Aurvangr, Jari*
Eager-hothead.	*Eikinskjaldi*

14.
The tale of the dwarfs	
shall be told now	
from Sleepy's band	
and back to Thresher,	*Lofarr*
they who strove out	
from the stones of the hall[34]	
to Loam-heath's yard	*Aurvanga sjǫt*
and Edge's meadows.	*til Jǫruvalla*[35]

15.
There were Drop-maker	*Draupnir*
and Damager,	*Dólgþrasir*
Greyhair, Mound-stepper,	*Hár, Haugspori*
Glowing and Shelter-yard,	*Glóinn, Hlévangr*
Bodkin and Brawl,	*Dori, Ori*
Bobbing, Aware,	*Dúfr, Andvari*
Shearer, Turner,	*Skirfir, Virfir*
Shingle and Grandpa.	*Skafiðr, Áï*

16.
Elf and Spawny,	*Álf ok Yngvi*
Eager-hothead,	*Eikinskjaldi*
Concealer and Frosty,	*Fjalarr ok Frosti*
Deceiver and Gatherer;	*Ginnarr ok Finnr*
this list will last	

---

[34] *The stones of the hall:* When people arrived and built their houses, the dwarfs left for a more secluded place.

[35] *Aurvanga sjot til Jǫruvalla:* Double construction with accusative, implying the names *Aurvangr* and *Jari*.

as long as the world does:
the band of siblings
back to Thresher. *Lofarr*

17.
Until three entered
of that honoured kind
– fertile and loving –
along came the aesir.
On the beach they found,
fully powerless,
Ask and Embla[36] *'Ash' and 'Elm'*
without fate.

18.
They had no breath,
they had no brains,
nor heat nor voice
nor vivid colours.
Odin gave breath,
Hoenir gave brains,
Lodur gave heat
and lively colours.

19.
The ash stands there,
Yggdrasill, I know, *the World Tree*
this splendid tree,
splashed with white loam,
from there comes the dew
that drips in the valleys;
it always stands green
over Urd's well. *a norn, goddess of fate: the past*

---

[36] «*Ask and Embla...*»: Two logs, of ash and elm, seen as pieces of driftwood.

20.
The maidens came up
– wise and thoughtful –
three from the lake
below the tree;
the first is Urd,
the other, Verdandi   *a norn, goddess of fate: the present*
– they scratched on boards –
Skuld came third;   *a norn, goddess of fate: the future*
they laid down laws,
lives were ordered
for the children of men,
they chose their fate.

21.
She recalls that this war   *she = the sibyl*
between armies was the first,   *between the aesir and the vanir*
when Gullveig was spiked   *'Consecrated to gold', prob. Freyia*
with spears from all sides,
and in Odin's hall
they had her burned;
three times they burned her,
three times she was born,
often – not seldom –
yet she still lives.

22.
Heid they called her[37]   *'the Bright One'*
when she came to the farms,
the wise-telling sibyl
ordered her sticks;

---

[37] «*Heid they called her...*»: The sibyl speaks of herself in the third person and in the capcity of a local sibyl. It denotes a change of perspective which occurs quite frequently in mythological poems.

she performed magic
with her mind dancing,
she was always a joy
to the angry bride.[38]

23.
The Governing Powers
gathered in council,
the most holy gods
met to decide:
Should the aesir
own up to their debt,
or should all the gods
be given requital?

24.
Then Odin sped
his spear into the throng,
this war that happened
between armies was the first:
the wall was rent   *a palisade*
about the aesir's stronghold,   *Asgard, the home of the gods*
the vanir used their foresight *the vanir were fertility gods*
on the fields of battle.

25.
The Governing Powers
gathered in council,
the most holy gods
met to decide:

---

[38] *"...she was always a joy to the angry bride.":* This text has often been interpreted to mean *"evil women"*. Anger from dissatisfaction, especially concerning being forced into marriage, we find is a more plausible interpretation. The fact that both the sibyl and the powers of fate were female, would have helped to secure women's position in society.

Who had mixed the air
with wickedness,
and given Od's maiden   *Freyia, see index*
to the mighty giants?

26.
Thor was then seized   *the god of thunder*
with a searing rage,
seldom he sits
when such things are heard;
all promises perished
– pledges and oaths –
all mighty bonds
were broken then.

27.
She knows that Heimdall's   *she = the sibyl*
horn[39] lies covered
beneath the handsome
and holy tree;
she sees the white loam
lavishly poured on
from Valfather's wager.   *Odin's eye*
Do you know it *all* now, or what?

28.
She sat out in the open[40]
as the Old One came,   *Odin*
Yggiung of the aesir,   *Odin*
and eyed her sharply.

---

[39] *Horn:* The word in the original text is «Hlióðr», meaning both sound and hearing. Later in this poem we find Heimdall's horn mentioned. For this reason we have chosen here the rendering «horn» for the word «hlióðr».

[40] *"She sat out in the open...":* It was believed that sitting out in the open at night enabled you to perceive hidden realities, and to sense what was about to happen.

She said:
Why do you test me?
Why do you tempt me?
I know it all, Odin,
where your eye is hidden:
in the mighty
Mimir's well;
Mimir drinks his mead
each morning every day
from Odin's bail.
Do you know it *all* now, or what?

29.
War-father gave her   *Odin*
gold and jewels,
– wisely chosen –
and wands for prophecy;
she saw far and wide,
the worlds were uncovered.

30.
She saw valkyries   *war maidens, see 'Mythological Index'*
venturing from afar,
ready to fare
to the flock of gods;
Skuld held the shield
and Skogul another,
Gunn, Hild, Gondul
and Geirskogul
– now Herian's maidens   *Odin's maidens*
are mentioned, all –
the valkyries were ready
to ride to the battlefields.

31.
I saw fate hidden
for the fair Baldr,   *son of Frigg and Odin*
the wounded god

who was Odin's son;
higher than the field
and fully grown,
stood lovely and meek
the mistletoe.

32.
This twig[41], I think,
had turned into
a harmful weapon,
it was Hod who flung it.   *the blind god, Baldr's brother*
A brother was born   *Vidar*
to Baldr the fair,
and one night old
he went for Hod.

33.
He didn't wash his hands,   *He = Vidar*
his hair wasn't combed,
till he bore to the pyre
Baldr's enemy;   *Hod*
in Fensalir
Frigg bemoaned
the woe of Valhall.
Do you know it *all* now, or what?

[34.[42]
Then baneful straps
were brought by Vali,   *a son of Loki*
he forged them tightly
from taut guts.]

---

[41] *«This twig,...»:* The mistletoe transformed itself into an arrow.
[42] This stanza is taken from a younger version in *Hauk's Book*. It gives additional details to the capture of Loki. For the full version, see Snorri Sturlason's *"the Younger Edda"*.

35.
She saw him captured, *she = the sibyl; he = Loki*
under the cauldron-grove,
in the likeness of malice:
Loki in chains.
Sigyn sits there, *a goddess, Loki's wife*
but seldom her husband
pleases her well.
Do you know it *all* now, or what?

36.
It dives from the east
full of daggers and swords,
the river through Etherdales, *an ice cold cosmic place,*
its emblem is Sheath.

37.
Far to the north
on Nidavellir, *Dark Meadows*
stood a hall of gold,
held by the Sindri-clan; *Sindri, a dwarf and master-smith*
one other stood
at Okolnir, *a place where it never freezes*
it was the beer-hall
of Brimir the giant.

38.
She spied a hall
hidden from the sun
up on Nastrand, *the 'Beach of the Dead'*
to the north the doors faced;
drops of ether
slid down through the flue,
the walls were made out of
adders entwined[43].

---

[43] «*the walls...adders entwined*»: This refers to the ancient custom of building walls in wicker work.

39.
She saw them wading
through wild rapids:
breakers of oaths
and evil killers,
and the one who steals
another's sweetheart;
there Nidhogg sucked   *a serpent*
the naked corpses,
the wolf tore at the warriors.
Do you know it *all* now, or what?

40.
East in the Iron Woods
the Old One sat,   *the female iotun Angrboda, Loki's mate*
she brought forth the flock
of Fenrir there,   *a wolf, Loki's son*
out of this clan
one will appear   *one = a fierce wolf, Hati*
in the shape of a troll
to take the Moon.

41.
He drinks the life-force   *He = Fenrir*
of dying men,
he reddens the gods' seats
with gory slime;
the sunshine shall blacken
in summers to come,
the weather turns ill.
Do you know it *all* now, or what?

42.
Playing his harp,
on the hill sat Eggther,
the shepherd of the giantess,
he shone with glee;

above him a cock
crowed in the gallows-tree,
its feathers were red,
Fialar was its name.

43.
And Golden-Comb   *a cock in Valhall*
crowed for the aesir,
the one who awakens
warriors for Valfather;
another crows
beneath the earth,
a soot-red rooster
in the realm of Hel[44].

44.
Garm barks madly   *the Hel-hound*
at Gnipahellir,   *'Protruding rock'*
fetters shall weaken
and the wolf will run loose;   *Fenrir*
she wields wisdom   *she = the sibyl*
– wider I see –
of Ragnarok   *the end of the 'ruling*
powers'
for the raging gods.

45.
Brothers shall meet
in mortal combat,
siblings shall break
the bonds of kinship;

---

[44] *Hel:*   Daughter of Angrboda and Loki. She rules the realm of the dead.

harsh is the world,
whoredom reigns,
sword-age, axe-age
– shields break asunder –
wind-age, wolf-age,
before the world drowns;
no one shall spare
another being.

46.
Mim's sons shall fight,   *Mim, a iotun, see 'Mythological Index'*
fate will be told
by the grand, ancient
Giallarhorn;   *Heimdall's horn*
Heimdall blows hard,
his horn in the air,
Odin seeks help
from the head of Mim.

47.
Then Yggdrasill's
ash stands shivering,
the old tree whimpers,
the iotun cuts loose;   *Loki*
fear will strike all
on their way to Hel,
until Surt's kinsman   *Surt = a giant*
swallows everything.

48.
What is it with the aesir?
What is it with the elves?
Iotunheim groans,   *the home of the giants*
the gods are at the Thing;   *the Thing = the Assembly*

the dwarfs are moaning
behind doors of rock –
the watchmen of the mountains. *the dwarfs*
Do you know it *all* now, or what?

49.
Garm barks madly
at Gnipahellir,
fetters shall weaken
and the wolf will run loose;
she wields wisdom
– wider I see –
of Ragnarok
for the raging gods.

50.
Hrym from the east   *a age-old giant*
holds up his shield,
Iormungand jolts   *the World Serpent*
into a giant's mood:
the serpent kneads the waves,
the eagle screeches,
nicking at corpses,
soon Naglfar cuts loose.   *a ship of dead people*

51.
From the east Kioll sails   *'Keel', a ship from*
Muspelheim
with the sons of Muspell,
they cross the ocean,
the craft steered by Loki;
sordid ruffians
run with the wolf,
Byleist's brother   *Loki*
bands up with them.

52.
From the south comes Surt
with singeing flames,
his sword reflects
the sunlight of the war-gods;
the cliffs tumble
and the trolls fumble,
men hurry on Hel's path
and the heavens split open.

53.
Then Hlin's second   *Hlin = Frigg*
sorrow occurs
as Odin goes
against the scavenger,   *the wolf Fenrir*
the killer of Beli   *Freyr*
battles with Surt –
Frigg's beloved   *Odin*
shall fall there.

54.
Garm barks madly
at Gnipahellir,
fetters shall weaken
and the wolf will run loose;
she wields wisdom
– wider I see –
of Ragnarok
for the raging gods.

55.
Then comes Sigfather's   *Odin*
son Vidar,   *son of Odin and the giantess Grid*
ready to fight
the fierce scavenger;   *Fenrir*

with his sword to the hilt
in the heart of Fenrir
is his father then
fully revenged.

56.
Soon comes the strong
son of Hlodyn[45],   *Thor*
Odin's offspring,
to end the serpent.
Mightily he strikes then,
Midgard's ward,   *Thor*
– the heroes must abandon
their homesteads now –
Fiorgyn's son staggers   *Thor*
and steps nine paces,
spinning from the serpent,
no spite was uttered.

57.
The Earth sinks in the sea,
the Sun turns black,
the bright stars scramble
from the skies on down;
fumes rise up
with the feeder of life,   *the fire*
the roaring fire
rises to the heavens.

58.
Garm barks madly
at Gnipahellir,
fetters shall weaken
and the wolf will run loose;
she wields wisdom

---

[45] «...*Hlodyn*...»: Thor is son of the goddess Earth (Jǫrð), who has several names. Among them are Hlodyn and Fiorgyn; see Index.

– wider I see –
of Ragnarok
for the raging gods.

59.
She sees the Earth
a second time rise
up out of Aegir   *Aegir here means the sea*
forever green;
rapids well onward,
an eagle flies above,
he who hunts fish
in the high mountains.

60.
The aesir shall meet
at Idavoll   *'the Field of Action'*
and give their views
of the grand Earth-Belt; *the World Serpent*
they shall remember
the main feats of yore
and the former runes
of Fimbultyr.   *Odin*

61.
There they will find
in the fresh grass
wondrously grand
golden tablets,
those they had owned
in the early days.

62.
Green fields shall then
grow unsown,
Baldr will re-enter
and wounds shall heal;
Hod and Baldr shall rule
Hropt's fields-of-triumph, *Odin's*
well shall they live there.
Do you know it *all* now, or what?

63.
Then Hoenir shall choose
the Hallowed Tree;[46]
the brothers' sons
shall build their homes
throughout the wide world.
Do you know it *all* now, or what?

64.
She sees a hall standing
more striking than the sun,
thatched with gold
at Gimle, shimmering; *'Gleaming Shelter'*
there the worthy
shall always stay
and abide all their days
in bountiful joy.

---

[46] «...*Hallowed Tree*»:   We follow CR: *hlautvið*.

65.[47]
Then the ruler *an unknown character*
shall rise to power,
with might, from above,
he who masters all.

66.
There the dark dragon
comes down on his wings,
the glittering serpent
glides from Nidafell, *'the Shadowy Mountains'*
and holds in his feathers
– flying over meadows –
corpses, Nidhogg. *the serpent under Yggdrasill*
Now she may let go. *she = the sibyll*

---

[47] *St. 65:*   This stanza is not taken from CR, but from a younger MS, «Hauksbók».

The Tale of the High One
– *HÁVAMÁL* –

The poem The Tale of the High One *is a compilation of several individual poems which are composed in the metre liodahatt. The poem consists of seven parts:*

I.	The Wisdom	(st. 1-77)
II.	Odin's Story A	(st. 78-83)
	Odin's Story B	(st. 84-102)
III.	The Mead of the Skalds	(st. 103-110)
IV.	Advice to Loddfavnir	(st. 111-137)
V.	The Art of the Runes	(st. 138-145)
VI.	The Chants	(st. 146-163)
VII.	The End-Greeting	(st. 164)

The first part consists of words of wisdom, sayings and proverbs dealing with man and society. Man's survival before nations were consolidated in the north could often be precarious and needing caution at every turn. At the same time most people belonged to a larger family, a judiciary entity and a military system. For this reason the sayings in the present poem were important because they gave sound advice, teaching the individual how behave towards others.

The second part starts with Odin (the High One) giving further advice, especially as to what is untrustworthy, and continues with his account of an unsuccessful sexual adventure.

The third part is Odin's tale of how he acquired the skaldic mead by seducing the iotun woman Gunnlod, the daughter of the keeper of the mead.

The fourth part presents Odin's advice to an otherwise unknown mythological character, Loddfavnir.

The fifth part tells of how Odin came into possession of the runes.

The sixth part presents different chants which are used in love and war.

The whole compilation ends in a high-sounding stanza, no. 164, which constitutes an end-greeting.
Through this poem we become acquainted with the many-faceted god Odin.

I THE WISDOM

1.
Every gateway,
when going through,
watch with utmost care,
watch with utmost caution;
for you don't know where
enemies may be seated
ahead of you in the hall.

2.
Honour to the hosts!
Here is the guest,
shall he be shown a seat?
He will be cross
if he's to crouch on the woodpile
and yet deliver his errand.

3.
Fire is needed
by the newly arrived
who feels his knees are frozen;
food and woollens
are wanted by the one
who has made it over the mountains.

4.
Water is needed
when nearing the table,
a cloth and courtesy;
if he can find it,
friendliness,
amiable talk and attention.

5.
Wits are needed
when one wanders far,
it's always easy at home;
you meet with laughter
if you lack knowledge
yet walk among the wise.

6.
You should not boast
of your bright wits,
rather spare your speech;
when you enter
be wise and reticent,
then you seldom meet mischief;
no one can bring
a better friend
than supple common sense.

7.
The careful guest,
when he comes to the feast,
is modest and meek in speech;

his ears are open,
his eyes observe,
this is the way of the wise.

8.
Happy is the one
who harvests for himself
praise and a proud name;
it is never clear
what another makes of you,
for it is hidden in his heart.

9.
You will be happy
if you possess
worth and wit while you live;
for ill advice
often comes
out of another's bosom.

10.
Nothing better
can you bring along
than supple common sense;
in foreign abodes
it is better than wealth,
this is the poor man's pillar.

11.
Nothing better
can you bring along
than supple common sense;
you never set out
in a sadder way
than with too much beer in your belly.

12.
It's not so pleasant
as people say,
ale for the heirs of men;
you manage less,
the more you drink,
to keep your mind on course.

13.
The Heron of Oblivion
hovers over the binge,
he steals the minds of men;
in this bird's feathers
I was fettered once
within Gunnlod's yard.   *daughter of the giant Suttung*

14.
I was ale-drunk,
overly drunk,
when I sat with Fialar the Sage;   *a dwarf rel. to Suttung's mead*
the best thing with ale
is that afterwards
you always regain your wits.

15.
The son of a king
should be silent and mindful,
ready to brave the battle;
we should all appear
proper and merry
while we await our end.

16.
The listless man
thinks he'll live forever
if he backs away from battle,

and yet old age
yields him no peace
though he be spared the spear.

17.
The fool gapes
when he gathers with friends,
silly he sits and mumbles;
away his wits slip
as he swills down his beer,
then his folly is found out.

18.
He alone realizes
who roams the earth,
wandering far and wide,
how everyone
who has his wits about him,
knows how to rule his reason.

19.
Don't grab the dipper,
but drink with care,
speak your mind or spare it;
no grudge is borne
against the one
who went to bed early.

20.
The greedy man
with no aim in mind
eats to his own regret;
the clod's big belly
brings on laughter
when he waddles among the wise.

21.
The flock can tell
when it's time to go home
and leave the lush meadows;
but the nitwit
can never tell
the limits of his lust.

22.
The lowly pauper,
poorly endowed,
will mock everything he meets;
he doesn't know,
what he needs to fathom,
that faults are found with him too.

23.
The unwise man
lies awake all night
pondering every problem;
his mind is weary
when morning comes,
everything's a mess as always.

24.
The unwise man
thinks all are his friends
who smile when they get together;
he can never tell
that they're tripping him up,
when he sits among the sage.

25.
The unwise man
thinks all are his friends
who smile when they get together;

but he quickly finds
when he comes to the Thing   *the Assembly*
that sparse and few are his spokesmen.

26.
The unwise man
thinks all is clear
as long as he's safely seated,
though he's got no words
to give in reply
when others ask his opinion.

27.
The unwise man,
when others are around,
it's safer for him to be silent!
No one will find
that he knows but little,
unless he goes on gabbing;
the dim-witted man
does not know
that he shouldn't go on gabbing.

28.
He proves himself clever
who questions wisely
and also knows how to answer;
from another's hearing
you can hide nothing
once the word is out.

29.
If you're a noisy talker
and never keep silent,
your worthless words go wild;

untamed tongue
– and temperance gone –
creates its own calamity.

30.
A man ought not
to mock another
when he appears at a party;
he thinks he is clever
if questions aren't asked,
so he may sit secure and safe.

31.
He thinks he is smart
when he sneaks away,
the guest who has mocked a guest;
he's got no inkling
while gloating at dinner,
that guests may bear him a grudge.

32.
Many people
are perfect friends
until they brawl at the banquet;
the greatest evil
is always this:
guest who clashes with guest.

33.
You will always need
an early meal
– unless getting together with friends –
or you'll sit and sulk,
seeming hungry,
unable to utter a word.

34.
It's a long road
to a lousy friend
though he lives along your path;
but the going is easy
to a good friend,
although his dwelling be distant.

35.
Move along,
don't linger on
forever perched in one place;
pleasant turns paltry
if you depart too late,
outstaying your welcome.

36.
A dwelling is sweet
though small it may be,
at home each man is a hero;
with only two goats
and an awning for a roof,
it is still better than begging.

37.
A dwelling is sweet
though small it may be,
at home each man is a hero;
the heart will bleed
in him who must ask
for his meat at every meal.

38.
You should never walk away
from your weapons on the field,
not even an inch away!

For it is never certain
when the need will arise
for a man to lift his lance.

39.
No man is so mild
or more hospitable
that he doesn't fancy a favour,
nor so gracious
with gifts and treasures
that a reward isn't well received.

40.
His own wealth,
once acquired,
a man should have at hand;
a scoundrel may gain
what should be granted the worthy,
much ends worse than one wishes.

41.
Weapons and garments
gladly bestow,
gifts reflect the giver;
mutual givers
are granted friendship,
if fortune favours them.

42.
Toward a friend
be a friend always
and return a gift for a gift!
Laughter against spite
is a splendid remedy,
and lip service against a lie.

43.
Toward a friend
be a friend always,
to him and the friends of his;
but with a friend's enemy
one should never
foster the bonds of friendship

44.
Now, if you've got a friend
whom you firmly trust
and wish to gain some good:
Let your minds blend,
let both bring gifts,
go and greet him often.

45.
If you've got another
whom you greatly distrust,
yet still wish to gain some good,
you should speak honorably,
keeping ill thoughts hidden,
and return lip service for lies!

46.
About him you mistrust
one can tell even more,
when there's cause to doubt his candour:
You should speak to his liking
and laugh with him,
let gifts be equal to what's given.

47.
When I was young,
travelling all alone,
I lost my way before long;

I felt so rich
when I found someone else,
man is man's pleasure.

48.
Men live the best
when brave and generous,
seldom they breed sorrows;
but everything is dreaded
by an unwise man,
the prudish one fears presents.

49.
I gave my garments
on the grounds one time
to two men made of timber[48];
they felt so grand
with the gowns they wore;
you're blamed if your body is naked.

50.
The pine will rot
at a poor farm –
it will bear no needles nor bark;
it is like the one
who lacks friendship,
how can he live for long?

51.
Hotter than fire
and for five days will burn
delight with a faulty friend;
then it stops sizzling
on the sixth day,
all friendship becomes foul.

---

[48] «...*two men made of timber*...": May allude to statues of gods.

52.
All too much
a man shouldn't give,
a trifle may bring great return;
with half a loaf
and half a beaker
I found myself a friend.

53.
Small is the ebb tide,
small is the flood tide,
small, too, is the mind of man;
for all people
are not equally wise,
a lack will always linger.

54.
Medium-wise
one ought to be,
never overly wise;
living is happiest
for him who masters
just enough knowledge.

55.
Medium-wise
one ought to be,
never overly wise;
happiness is rare
in the heart of the wise,
if he who owns it knows all.

56.
Medium-wise
one ought to be,
never overly wise;

too soon should no one
see their own destiny,
then his mind will be more at ease.

57.
Blaze ignites blaze,
it keeps burning till the end,
flames will beget fire;
man taught by man
masters his speech,
if alone, he'll be lacking in wits.

58.
Early to rise!
if you want to gain
another man's life or belongings;
seldom does a sleeping wolf
snatch his lamb,
or the lazybones win his war.

59.
Early to rise!
if you own few servants,
but take yourself to your tasks;
things don't happen
for him who sleeps,
rapid is half-way rich.

60.
Dry boards for building
and bark for the roof,
a man knows the measure of this,
how much wood to gather
for a winter's need,
and also for thewhole year.

61.
Fed and ready
one should ride to the Thing,
although one's clothes be coarse;
you need not be ashamed
of your shoes or trousers
– nor of your horse neither –
even if it be not the best.

62.
Prowling and rummaging
as it reaches the sea's side:
an eagle at the ancient shore;
likewise is the fellow
who has few helpers
when he meets with many others.

63.
To question and answer
is the cunning man's way
if he wants to be counted as wise;
what one person knows
he should not tell another,
if three know it, everyone's wise.

64.
A person is wise
who applies his riches
in the right amount and measure;
among the bold
he is bound to discover
not one is the bravest of all.

65.[49]
- - - -   *missing lines*
- - - -   -- " --
- - - -   -- " --
every word
you award another
may put you deep in debt.

66.
I made it too early
to many a place,
and yet too late to others;
the beer was gone
or the brewing unfinished,
it's hard to hit the target.

67.
I was invited home
here and there,
if they found I didn't need food;
but two legs of mutton
my mate offered me
though I'd already eaten one.

68.
Fire is cherished
by the children of men,
and to have the sun in sight;
your own good health,
if you may have it,
helps you live a faultless life.

---

[49] The first half of the stanza is missing. It has been suggested that they were the same as in the previous stanza (st. 64). Some paper MSS give these verses: "Attentive and with a good memory/should each man be/and never too trusting towards friends."

69.
No man is all sorry
though he suffers in health;
some rejoice in sons,
some in their allies,
some in earnings they've made,
and some in work done well.

70.
It is better to be alive
than not to live anymore,
the quick one gets his cow;
I saw red fire
swallow a man's wealth,
and he lay dead at his door.

71.
Hobbling, you may ride,
you may herd with one arm,
deaf, you may do in battle;
it's better to be blind
than to be burned to ashes,
the dead are useless to all.

72.
A son is a boon,
though he be born late,
after the father has fallen;
rarely do steles
stand by the wayside
unless they're put up by an heir.

73.
With two in one army
the tongue may undo the head,
and every cloak
may hide a closed fist.

74.
The night is fair
when you have food enough
and the sails of your ship are short –
autumns are always unsteady;
loads of wind
is unleashed in five days
and even more in a month.

75.
He does not know,
who knows nothing at all,
that men are made monkeys for gold;
one gets rich,
the other gets poor,
let nobody bear any blame.

76.
Die cattle,
die kin,
you shall also die;
never shall fade
the fame of the one
who gained himself good renown.

77.
Die cattle
die kin,
you shall also die;
this I know
shall never die:
the judgment dealt to the dead.

II   ODIN's STORY: A

78.
I saw fields full of cattle
for the fitiung's sons –   *sons of an heir born out of wedlock*
they bear now the beggar's staff;
in the wink of an eye
wealth is gone,
it's a most faulty friend.

79.
The unwise one,
when he can get
wealth or women's lust,
he'll think he's well-off
though his wits are lacking,
and his folly grows to the full.

80.
This you will find,
when you ferret out runes
– those that are given by the gods,
made by the mighty powers,
painted by the peerless thulr[50] –
it's safest for you to keep silent.

81.
At night-fall praise the day,
when she's dead, the wife,
the broadsword when brandished,
the bride when married,
ice when crossed over,
ale when it's drunk.

---

[50] *"...painted by the peerless thulr"*:   (Orig.: 'Fimbul-thulr'). Painted by the 'mighty sacred orator at rituals', or Odin.

82.
In wind, chop wood,
row the waves when it's sunny,
in darkness, talk with your dear one
– the day has many eyes –
a ship should be fit to sail,
and a shield should protect you,
a sword is for swinging,
and a sweetheart is for kissing.

83.
By the fire-side drink ale,
and on the ice go skating,
buy the mare when slender
and the sword when filthy,
fatten the horse at home
and the dog out of doors.

II   ODIN's STORY: B

84.
Don't give any worth
to the words of a maiden,
nor to what a woman says;
for their hearts were wielded
on a wheel that was spinning,
and a breach was laid in their breast.

85.
A breaking bow,
a burning flame,
a cawing crow,
a crying wolf,
a ranting hog,
a rootless tree,
a waxing wave,
a welling kettle,

86.
a flying arrow,
a fierce wave,
ice one-night-old,
an adder coiled,
a bride's bed-speech
or a broken sword,
a royal prince
or a playful bear,

87.
a sick calf,
a self-willed thrall,
a babbling prophetess,
a brave just fallen,

88
a field sown too early
should a fellow not trust,
nor too soon a son;
the weather rules the field
and his wits the son,
both may bring danger,

89.
the slayer of your brother,
when you both meet,[51]
a half-burnt house,
and a horse all-speedy,
the foal is useless
when its foot is broken;
so safe should no one feel
that he fails to mind all this.

---

[51] *"...the slayer of your brother when you both meet"*: The rules governing blood vengeance demanded that one killed one's brother's murderer. He again would try to kill you first, knowing he would be in danger were you to meet each other. In other words, your brother's banesman would not be trustworthy.

90.
To enjoy a woman
who has wicked intent,
is like easing a horse
over ice, unshod
– a two-year-old bronco,
bucking and happy –
or like sailing without steering
in a strong wind,
or like herding deer
while hobbling on thawing ice!

91.
Now I'll speak bluntly,
for both sides are clear:
men's minds are warped as to women;
we speak most fairly
when falsehood governs us,
even the wise are won over.

92.
Speak graciously
and give presents,
if you want a lady's love;
praise the body
of the beautiful woman,
he will own her who woos her.

93.
No man should ever
think ill of another
for the love he has found in his life;
the wise may be struck
– though the stupid may not be –
by the looks of a lovely woman.

94.
No man should ever
think ill of another
for what happens to many a man:
a mighty lust often
makes it happen
that the wise become witless.

95.
The mind can tell
what's contained in the heart,
only you can ease your plight;
no curse is greater
for a clever man
than having no cause to care for.

96.
As I hid among the reeds
I realized this,
while longing for my beloved;
all body and heart
was the bright one to me,
still I could not keep her.

97.
I found a-bed
Billing's daughter, *the giant Billing, maybe Rind's father*
all asleep and sun-white;
an earl's favour
I found less worth
than living with this lady.

Billing's daughter said:
98.
"Towards evening,
Odin, you must come
if you wish to woo a maiden;

all will turn bad
if we both don't agree
to keep our caper secret."

99.
When I left her,   *Odin resumes his tale*
my love, I thought,
was beyond any measure;
this I wished:
to win for myself
all her love and longing.

100.
When next I got there
the guards were awake,
all were set to receive me;
with blazing torches
and bearing sticks,
they put me on a faulty path.

101.
In the morning
when I made it back,
the guards had gone to sleep;
I found a bitch
in the bright one's place,
she had bound it to her bed. *her: Billing's daughter*

102.
When you get to know
a good woman,
her mind is split toward men;
I learnt it when I tried
to lure her to disgrace,
that wise and shrewd woman;
hit by spite
from the head-strong one,
I never won her as wife.

III   THE MEAD OF THE SKALDS

103.
One should be giving toward guests
and glad when at home,
one ought to be keen and quick;
witty and word-strong
if you want to be clever,
and often give words of praise;
a fumbling fool
has few things to tell,
it clearly marks the moron.

104.
I sought out the old giant,
just now I'm back,
silence didn't serve me there;
not with few words
did I further my cause
when I came to the seat of Suttung[52].

105.
On a golden chair
Gunnlod offered me   *Gunnlod = Suttung's*
daughter
a drink of the dearest mead;
did I let her have
for her whole-heartedness,
for her sorrowful soul.

106.
Rati's mouth   *Rati =: Odin's drill*
made room for me,
gorging on the granite;
above and below
led the giants' pathways,
here I risked my head.

---

[52] *The giant's name is Suttung. He is keeper of the bardic mead.*

107.
Great was my enjoyment
and the gain I achieved,
little does the wise man lack;
for Odrerir[53]
has arrived now
to the seat of the ancient shrine.

108.
I doubt whether I'd managed
to make my way
back home from Iotunheim,   *the Realm of the giants*
had I not enjoyed Gunnlod,
that good-hearted woman,
I wrapped my arms around her.

109.
The ice-giants went
in the early morning
to ask the High One's[54] counsel
inside the High One's hall;
they asked if Bolverk   *a name for Odin,*
'Damager'
was back with the gods
or whether Suttung had slain him.

110.
The Oath of the Ring,
I think, Odin had sworn
– who can trust his talking? –
he betrayed Suttung,
he took his mead,
causing Gunnlod to cry.

---

[53] *Odrerir:*   The kettle containing the poetic mead, which Odin brought from Iotunheim to Asgard.
[54] *The High One (ON: Hávi)* : another name for Odin.

IV   ADVICE TO LODDFAVNIR

111.
Now is the time
to talk in the thul-chair[55]
close to Urd's[56] well;
I watched and kept silent,
I watched and I thought,
I listened to the tales that were told;
they left nothing unspoken,
the speech was of runes
at the High One's Hall,
in the High One's Hall,
I heard them speak thus:

112.
I counsel you, Loddfavnir,[57]
if listening suits you,
it's your wealth if you welcome it
and your gain if you grasp it:
Don't get up at night
if not to keep watch
or to enter into the outhouse[58].

113.
I counsel you, Loddfavnir,
if listening suits you,
it's your wealth if you welcome it
and your gain if you grasp it:

---

[55] «...*thul-chair*...»: The thulr had an official role in pagan ritual, and. He was a communicator of special knowledge.
[56] *Urd:* one of the three nornes in Norse mythology. Urd, refers to 'that which was'. The other two were Skuld: 'that which is to be'; and Verdandi: 'that which is happening now'.
[57] *Loddfavnir:* A figure in Norse mythology, whose identity is unknown.
[58] «...*the outhouse*. ...»: a place to go about one's business, a toilet.

Don't ever rest
in the arms of a sorceress,
in case her limbs enclose you.

114.
She will make it so
that you miss the Thing   *the Assembly*
and also the king's counsel;
you won't want food
nor fellowship,
you'll fall asleep in sorrow.

115.
I counsel you, Loddfavnir
if listening suits you,
it's your wealth if you welcome it
and your gain if you grasp it:
Never make
another's wife
become your favorite friend.

116.
I counsel you, Loddfavnir,
if listening suits you,
it's your wealth if you welcome it
and your gain if you grasp it:
Wherever you fare
on fiord or mountain,
bring with you enough to eat.

117.
I counsel you, Loddfavnir,
if listening suits you,
it's your wealth if you welcome it
and your gain if you grasp it:

Never let the wicked
ever discover
the mishaps you have met,
for from a wicked man
you will never
gain a good return.

118.
I saw a bloke
bitten severely
by a mean woman's words;
an evil tongue
put an end to him,
yet nothing true was told.

119.
I counsel you, Loddfavnir,
if listening suits you,
it's your wealth if you welcome it
and your gain if you grasp it:
If you have a friend
whom you fully trust
go and greet him often,
for bushes grow
and the grass gets tall
on tracks where no one treads.

120.
I counsel you, Loddfavnir,
if listening suits you,
it's your wealth if you welcome it
and your gain if you grasp it;
For runes of pleasure
you should pick a good man –
healing-spells learn while you live!

121.
I counsel you, Loddfavnir,
if listening suits you,
it's your wealth if you welcome it
and your gain if you grasp it:
With your comrade
don't come to be first
to break the bonds of friendship;
woes gnaw at your heart
if you never open
your soul completely to someone.

122.
I counsel you, Loddfavnir,
if listening suits you,
it's your wealth if you welcome it
and your gain if you grasp it:
Be wary enough
so you never quarrel
with a mindless monkey.

123.
For a wicked man
won't ever bring
a proper word of praise,
but a good man
may give to you
a mirror of your merit.

124.
Kinship awakens
when you open your mind
fully toward your friend;
all things are better
than being split,
he is no friend who flatters.

125.
I counsel you, Loddfavnir,
if listening suits you,
it's your wealth if you welcome it
and your gain if you grasp it:
Don't waste on a thug
three words in quarrel,
the better man bides his time,
while the scoundrel attacks with scorn.

126.
I counsel you, Loddfavnir,
if listening suits you,
it's your wealth if you welcome it
and your gain if you grasp it:
Do not be a shoemaker
nor a shaft-maker either
for others than your own self;
if the shoe doesn't fit
or the shaft is crooked,
then they'll harbour harm.

127.
I counsel you, Loddfavnir,
if listening suits you,
it's your wealth if you welcome it
and your gain if you grasp it:
If you sense harm
say it out loud,
and don't let your foes go free.

128.
I counsel you, Loddfavnir
if listening suits you,
it's your wealth if you welcome it
and your gain if you grasp it:

Do not enjoy
deeds that are evil,
open up to what is good.

129.
I counsel you, Loddfavnir,
if listening suits you,
it's your wealth if you welcome it
and your gain if you grasp it:
Do not look up
when in battle
– because all men may
go mad with fury –
if you wish to stay free and unfettered.

130.
I counsel you, Loddfavnir,
if listening suits you,
it's your wealth if you welcome it
and your gain if you grasp it:
If you want a good woman
and to win her favours
by employing runes of pleasure,
let your words be fair
and honestly kept –
few are grieved by gifts.

131.
I counsel you, Loddfavnir,
if listening suits you,
it's your wealth if you welcome it
and your gain if you grasp it:
You should be careful
but not overly careful,
most of all with ale
and with the wife of another,
and for the third:
keep thieves away.

132.
I counsel you, Loddfavnir,
if listening suits you,
it's your wealth if you welcome it
and your gain if you grasp it:
Don't ever mock
or meet with spite
a friend or travelling folk.

133.
Within the hall
it is hard to tell
what kind they are who have come;
no man is so good
that he's got no faults,
nor so nasty he's good for nothing.

134.
I counsel you, Loddfavnir,
if listening suits you,
it's your wealth if you welcome it
and your gain if you grasp it:
You should never grin
at the grey-haired thulr,
what the old ones say may be sound;
the words may be wise
that well from the dry pod –
he who hangs with the hides,
with sallow skins he rides,
dangling with dry guts besides.

135.
I counsel you, Loddfavnir,
if listening suits you,
it's your wealth if you welcome it
and your gain if you grasp it:

Don't bark at the guest
nor bid him leave,
treat the poor ones properly.

136.
May the pole be strong
which steadies the gate
that opens up to all;
you should offer gifts,
or else it may be
that hatred will grow against you.

137.
I counsel you, Loddfavnir,
if listening suits you,
it's your wealth if you welcome it
and your gain if you grasp it:
When you drink ale
let the earth give you strength,
for earth takes on ale,
against illness use fire,
oak takes on weakness,
against wizardry, a spike of barley,
elderberry against marital rows,
the moon against spells,
heather against bites,
against boils, runes,
soil soothes the fluids.

V   THE ART OF THE RUNES

138.
I know that I hung
in that harried tree
nine whole nights,
gashed by the spear,
given to Odin,
myself to me myself;
in that noble tree
of which none can find out
from where the roots run.

139.
They offered me no bread,
nor anything to drink;
I peered down,
I picked up runes,
I picked them up bellowing,
then I fell back from there.

140.
I got nine mighty spells
from the renowned son
of Bolthorn, Bestla's father,   *Odin's grandfather*
and they gave me a drink
of the dearest mead,
poured out of Odrerir.   *one of three vessel holding the*
                                               bardic mead

141.
I began to be fertile
and gain in wisdom,
I grew and prospered greatly;
one word sought another,
finding words for me,
one deed sought another,
finding deeds for me.

142.
You will light upon runes
and laden sticks,
very stout sticks,
very sturdy sticks,
painted by Fimbul-thulr,   *Odin*
forged by the great gods,
carved by the crafty Hroft;   *Odin*

143.
Odin carved for the aesir
for the elves Daïnn,
Dvalinn did so for the dwarfs,
and for the iotuns
Asvinn carved,
and some I carved myself.

144.
Do you know how to carve?
Do you know how to read?
Do you know how to paint?
Do you know how to test?
Do you know how to pray?
Do you know how to offer[59]?
Do you know how to send?
Do you know how to slay[60]?

---

[59] *Offer:* Litterally *'Bleed'* from ON *"blóta"*, meaning magical increase in strength through the smearing of blood onto objects, or the intake of it; to sacrifice, make an offering.
[60] *Slay:* Here we have used the word *'slay'* for the ON *"sóa"*: to sacrifice in the meaning of ritual killing in a   religious context.

145.
Better not to ask
than to offer too much,
a gift will want its gain;
better not to send
than to slay too much;
thus Thund carved   = *Odin*
before the coming of man,
where he got up,
where he again returned.

VI   THE CHANTS

146.
Two chants I know
that the chieftain's wife doesn't,
nor anyone's kith and kin;
the first is named Help,
it may help you
through causes and cares
and all kinds of troubles.

147.
The second I know,
which is needed by those
who hope to become healers:
- - - -   *missing verses*
- - - -
- - - -

148.
The third one I know,
if a need is pressing me,
to fetter my fiendish rivals:

I blunt the weapons
of my enemies,
sword and sorcery shall fail them.

149.
The fourth one I know,
if foes bring along
ropes to bind my body;
then I rant
so I may run free,
my feet are unfettered
my limbs are let loose.

150.
The fifth one I know,
if a fiendish arrow
I see aimed toward the army;
it won't fly so wildly
I'm not able to stop it
as soon as I have it in sight.

151.
The sixth one I know,
if someone harms me
with roots of raw wood,[61]
and if that man
means to curse me,
then harm eats him, not me.

152.
The seventh one I know,
if I see high flames
at the hall of my feasting friends,
it shan't burn so fiercely
that I fail to stem it,
then I shall choose to chant.

---

[61] *Raw wood:* Raw roots were regarded as magically potent and powerful.

153.
The eighth one I know,
that all may find
a useful treasure to obtain;
when hate grows
with high-born people,
swiftly I settle the score.

154.
The ninth one I know,
when the need looms before me
to keep my ferry afloat:
I still the storm
and stem the waves,
I calm the cutting seas.

155.
The tenth one I know,
if I notice iotuns
riding and romping aloft;
I fool them so
that they fare astray,
out of their own shapes –
out of their own minds.

156.
The eleventh one I know,
if I must lead into battle
my faithful bosom friends;
I chant under the shield
to shelter my warriors
– whole to the battle,
whole from the battle –
they'll return whole and healthy.

157.
The twelfth one I know,
if I notice in a tree
a dead man dangling;
I know how to carve
and to colour the runes,
so the fellow goes free
and tells me his tales.

158.
The thirteenth I know,
when I need to sprinkle
water upon the young one[62];
he shall not bend
on the battlefield,
he'll never sink under sword.

159.
The fourteenth I know,
when I need to speak
to a gathering about the gods;
aesir and elves,
I know all of them,
a numb-skull knows nothing of this.

160.
The fifteenth I know,
which was flung out by Thiodreyrir,
the dwarf at Delling's door;   *Delling = father of Day*
he sang force for the aesir,
fortune for the elves,
and reason for Hroptatyr.   *Odin*

---

[62] «... *to pour water onto the young one...*": A heathen initiation ritual.

161.
The sixteenth I know,
to win soul and heart
of a bright and wise woman;
I will bewitch
the white-armed maiden
and win her love and lust.

162.
The seventeenth I know,
so I never shall lose
this maiden of men's desire.
All of these chants,
you shall, Loddfavnir,
long live without;
it's your gain had you grasped them,
your wealth had you welcomed them,
fulfilment had you followed them.

163.
The eighteenth I know,
that I'll never reveal
to a woman or any man's wife;
all is better if only
one person knows it,
– now the chants are over and ended –
unless I tell it to the one
whose arms embrace me,
or to my own sister herself.

VII THE END-GREETING

164.
Now the High One's speech
is spoken in the High One's Hall,
may it be good for the children of men,
may it be gall for the children of giants.
Health[63] to the one who chanted!
Health to the one who knows!
Gain to the one who grasps it!
Health to all who have heard it!

---

[63] *Health:*   ON Heill implies health and prosperity

The Tale of Vavthrudnir
– *VAFÞRÚÐNISMÁL* –

This poem, in the metre of liodahatt, is a contest of wits between the iotun Vavthrudnir, 'he who tightens the web', and Odin disguised as Gagnrad *(gagnrad: useful advice). The race of giants/iotuns was regarded as the first race in existence, and therefore it was considered that they knew everything that had ever happened. It was dangerous to approach a iotun since they were huge and generally cruel, selfish, ill-tempered and angry. In a contest of wits like this one, there would always be a price to pay for the one who lost, and commonly the price would be one's head. Another poem in the Edda with a similar structure is* The Tale of Alviss, *where a dwarf loses his life.*

Odin said:
1.
"I want some advice, Frigg,   *Odin's wife*
for I wish to go
and visit Vavthrudnir;
I want to possess
the ancient knowledge
of that wise old giant."

Frigg said:
2.
"I'd rather you stay here,
Heriafather,   *'Father of the army' =*
Odin
at home with the good gods;
for no iotun
is equally as rough
as Vavthrudnir, I think."

Odin said:
3.
"Much have I travelled,
much have I tried,
much have I proved the Powers;
I wish to learn
how that iotun lives,
and what his hearth and home are like."

Frigg said:
4.
"May you fare safely!
may you safely return!
may your sojourn be safe!
May your spirit steady you,
when you start, Allfather,   *Odin*
to juggle words with the giant."

5.
Then Odin travelled
to test the knowledge
of the crusty old iotun;
he entered the hall
owned by Im's father;   *Im = a giant, son of Vavthrudnir*
there Ygg went in.   *Odin*

Odin said:
6.
"Hail to you, Vavthrudnir,
here I have come
to see what you're like for myself;
I'm eager to discover
if you are able and smart
and also whether you're wise."

Vavthrudnir said:
7.
"What sort of man
has entered here
hurling his words at my head?
You will never leave
alive from this place
unless you're the wiser of us."

Odin said:
8.
"In truth, I'm Gagnrad,
travelling made me thirsty,
here I have come to your hall;
I need your welcome
– I've wandered long –
and your gentle care, giant."

Vavthrudnir said:
9.
"But why then, Gagnrad,
do you garble while you stand?
Find yourself a seat!
Then we shall see,
who's the sagest of us,
you or the old thulr."   *a thulr was a chanter at rituals*

Odin said:
10.
"The poor man
who meets with a rich one,
should never say more than what's needed;
too many words
will cause ill for a man
when he meets with cool cunning."

Vavthrudnir said:
11.
"Tell me, Gagnrad,
since you're trying to state
your cause while still standing:
What's the horse called
that keeps on dragging
the light of day over the living?"

Odin said:
12.
"Skinfaxi is the name   *'Shining mane'*
of the noble horse
that drags light over the living;
this horse is best,
the Hreidgoths think,   *a clan of mythol. warriors*
the mane of that good horse glitters."

Vavthrudnir said:
13.
"Tell me, Gagnrad,
since you're trying to state
your cause while still standing:
What's the horse called
that hauls the night
from east to west over the gods?"

Odin said:
14.
"He's named Hrimfaxi,   *'Frosty mane'*
who hauls the night
over the able gods;
from his muzzle saliva
each morning drips,
that's why there's dew in the dales."

Vavthrudnir said:
15.
"Tell me, Gagnrad,
since you're trying to state
your cause while still standing:
What is that river called
that runs between
the aesir and the iotuns' sons?"

Odin said:
16.
"The river is called Iving   *'the turbulent one'*
that runs between
the aesir and the iotuns' sons;
she flows easily
till the end of time;
she'll never be iced over."

Vavthrudnir said:
17.
"Tell me, Gagnrad,
since you're trying to state
your cause while still standing:
What is that field called
where they fight the battle
between Surt and the good gods?"   *Surt, fire demon*

Odin said:
18.
"Vigrid is that field
where they fight the battle
between Surt and the good gods;
a hundred rests[64]
it reaches both ways,
that field which awaits the foes."

---

[64] «...*a hundred rests*»:   A 'rest' is the distance one travels between each time one needs to rest.

Vavthrudnir said:
19.
"How wise you are, guest!
Welcome and be seated!
Let the two of us talk together,
here in this hall
our heads are at stake,
we'll see who's most sharp and shrewd."

Odin said:
20.
"First tell me one thing,
if your wits are about you
and you, Vavthrudnir, are awake:
How was the earth made
or the mighty heavens
in the beginning, wise iotun?"

Vavthrudnir said:
21.
"The earth was shaped
out of Ymir's flesh,
and from his bones came the boulders,
heaven from the ice-cold
head of that giant,
and out of his sweat the seas."[65]

Odin said:
22.
"Tell me secondly,
if you're served by your wits,
and you, Vavthrudnir, are awake:

---

[65] «*...out of his sweat the seas.*»: In another tradition the seas come from his blood.

From where did the moon come
that wanders above people,
and the same with the sun as well?"

Vavthrudnir said:
23.
"Mundilfari is the name   *'He who moves in*
intervals'
of the Moon's father
and also the Sun's as well;
across the sky
they shall skip each day
for men to tell the time."

Odin said:
24.
"Tell me thirdly,
if you thrive by your wits,
and you, Vavthrudnir, are awake:
How did Day arise,
that dawns upon men,
and Night with the New Moon?"

Vavthrudnir said:
25.
"He is called Delling,
who is Day's father,
and Night was born to Norr;
Waxing and Waning
were wielded by the gods
for men to tell the time."

Odin said:
26.
"Tell me the fourth,
since you affirm you are wise,
and you, Vavthrudnir, are awake:
How did Winter arise,
or the warm Summer,
among the mighty gods?"

Vavthrudnir:
27.
"Wind-cool is the source
and sire of Winter,
as Sweet One is of Summer."

- - - - -
- - - - -
- - - - -

ON: 'Vindsval'

ON: 'Svasud' is father of Summer
missing verses
-- " --
-- " --

Odin said:
28.
"Tell me the fifth,
since you affirm you are wise,
and you, Vavthrudnir, are awake:
Which came first,
the family of the aesir
or of Ymir, in the days of old?"

Vavthrudnir said:
29.
"Many winters
before Earth was created,
Bergelmir was born,
Thrudgelmir
begot him then,
Aurgelmir was his grandfather."

'Roaring bear'
'the Mighty roarer'

'the Loam-roarer' = Ymir

Odin said:
30.
"Tell me the sixth,
if you are smart and able,
and you, Vavthrudnir, are wise:
How was Aurgelmir
of the iotuns' clan
fathered first of all?"

Vavthrudnir said:
31.
"Out of Elivagar   *'waves of icy showers'*
came etherdrops,
they increased and became the giant;   = *Ymir*
all of our clans
have come from this,
that's why we are so wicked."

Odin said:
32.
"Tell me the seventh,
if you are smart and able,
and you, Vavthrudnir, are wise:
How did the iotun
have offspring then,
when he had no woman to woo?"

Vavthrudnir said:
33.
"From under his arms
– the ice-giants said –
female and male were made,
his two feet sired
a six-headed boy
for the fully wise iotun."

Odin said:
34.
"Tell me the eighth,
since you're ever so quick,
and you, Vavthrudnir, are wise:
What is the first thing
called forth by your memory,
you all-wise iotun?"

Vavthrudnir said:
35.
"Numberless winters
before Earth was,
Bergelmir was born;
the first I recall
of this crafty giant
is that they closed the lid of his coffin."

Odin said:
36.
"Tell me the ninth
since you know it all,
and you, Vavthrudnir, are wise:
What causes the wind
that wanders over the seas,
but is seldom seen by any?"

Vavthrudnir said:
37.
"Hraesvelg sits   *'Corpse-swallower'*
at Heaven's end,
a iotun in eagle's feathers;
they say that his wings
make the wind arise
which moves over men and women."

Odin said:
38.
"Tell me the tenth,
the tale of the gods,
if you, Vavthrudnir, are wise:
How did Niord come   *Lord of the sea, see Index*
to the clan of the aesir,
he has a wealth
of alters and temples,
and yet was born elsewhere?"

Vavthrudnir said:
39.
"In Vanaheim   *home of the fertility gods, see Index*
the High Powers made him,
he was given as hostage to the gods;   *gods = aesir*
at the end of time
he'll return once more
home to the venerable vanir."   *the vanir = the fertility gods*

Odin said:
40.
"Tell me the eleventh,
where lies the yard
where lads fight the livelong day?
They kill a good score
and scurry home,
and settled they sit through the night[66]."

---

[66] «...*settled they sit...*»: Each night the dead revive and feast with their adversaries.

Vavthrudnir said:
41.
"All the warriors
on Odin's field
draw their swords each day,
they kill a good score
and scurry home,
and settled they sit through the night."

Odin said:
42.
"Tell me the twelfth,
the tale of the gods,
if you, Vavthrudnir, are wise:
About the runes of the iotuns
and of all the gods
you will tell me the truth,
you all-wise giant!"

Vavthrudnir said:
43.
"About the runes of the iotuns *runes, see Index*
and of all the gods
I can tell you the truth;
I have been to each
and every realm,
there are nine in all
under Nivlhel, *nebulous realm of the dead*
where dead men from Hel go to die."

Odin said:
44.
"Much have I travelled,
much have I tried,
much have I proved the Powers:

Who shall survive
when hit by the mouth
and freezing Fimbul-winter?" *extreme winter, lasting three years*

Vavthrudnir said:
45.
"Liv and Livthrasir *'Life' and 'Life-striver'*
alive and well,
will hide in Hoddmimir's grove[67];
their meal will be
the morning dew,
mankind will be made from them."

Odin said:
46.
"Much have I travelled,
much have I tried,
much have I proved the Powers:
What happens with the Sun
on heaven's sheet,
when Fenrir has fed on her?" *a wolf, son of Loki and Angrboda*

Vavthrudnir said:
47.
"One will be born,
Alvrodul's daughter, *Alvrodul = 'Elf-Blush', the Sun*
before Fenrir eats her up;
the daughter shall ride
after the death of the gods,
and tread on her mother's trail."

---

[67] *Hoddmimir's grove:*   A skaldic expression for 'at the World Tree'.

Odin said: and
48.
"Much have I travelled,
much have I tried,
much have I proved the Powers:
Who are the wenches,
so wise mindful,
who cross the wide ocean?"

Vavthrudnir said:
49.
"Three mighty rapids
rush through the farm
of Mogthrasir's maidens[68];
each are disguised
when they enter this world,
for they grew up with the iotuns."

Odin said:
50.
"Much have I travelled,
much have I tried,
much have I proved the Powers:
What shall the aesir
own and govern
when Surt's blaze has burned?"

Vavthrudnir said:
51.
"Vidar shall own   *'He of the woods', son of Odin*
the aesir's shrines
with Vali when the blaze has burned;   *son of Odin*

---

[68] *Mogthrasir's maidens:* Rivers were perceived as female iotuns, perhaps thought to be daughters of Ymir;
  Mogthrasir: He who strives to have children, alias Ymir.

Modi shall have Miollnir[69]　　　*Modi = 'Raging', son of Thor*
– and Magni shall too –　　　　　*'Strong', son of Thor*
when Thor's battles are through."

Odin said:
52.
"Much have I travelled,
much have I tried,
much have I proved the Powers:
How will Odin
end his life,
when the Powers are torn apart?"

Vavthrudnir said:
53.
"The wolf will swallow　　　　　*Fenrir*
Aldafather,　　　　　　　　　　*Odin*
Vidar will wreak revenge;
he will cleave
its cold jowls
as he catches and kills the wolf."

Odin said:
54.
"Much have I travelled,
much have I tried,
much have I proved the Powers:
What did Odin speak
in the ear of his son　　　　　　*Odin's son Baldr*
before he was placed on the pyre?"

---

[69] *Miollnir:*　　'the Crusher' = Thor's hammer.

Vavthrudnir said:
55.
"Nobody witnessed
what you whispered that time
into your son's ear;
death is the reward
for my ancient runes
and the tale of Ragnarok. *the End of the Gods*
Now I have shared
my shrewd words with Odin;
you are the wisest of the wise."

The Tale of Grimnir
– *GRÍMNISMÁL* –

This poem is about Odin who suffers at the hands of his sometime protégé Geirrad. Starving and in pain, Odin tells of his visions of the gods' dwellings and of mythological geography. He also reveals many of his own secret names.

The topic of gods having special favourites or protégés is one that is found in several other sources, for instance the Langobardian 'Myth of Origin' by Jordanes (Historia gothorum). *Like so many poems of wisdom, The* Tale of Griminir *is in the metre of liodahatt.*

King Raudung had two sons, one was called Agnar and the other Geirrad. Agnar was ten winters old and Geirrad eight. Together the two of them rowed out in a boat with their trawling line to catch small fry. The wind took them out to sea. In the darkness of night they struck land and went ashore. There they met a crofter and stayed with him through the winter. His wife cared for Agnar, while he himself took care of Geirrad, giving him advice. When spring came, the crofter gave them a boat. But when the wife and her husband followed them to the sea-shore, the crofter spoke in private with Geirrad.

The wind was favourable and they reached their father's pier. Geirrad was in the bow of the boat; he leapt ashore and shoved the boat back out again, saying:

"Be gone with you, and may the trolls take you!"

The ship drifted out to sea, but Geirrad went up to the farm and was well received. By then his father had died, so Geirrad was made king, and became a very renowned man.

Odin and Frigg were seated in Hlidskialf looking outwards into all the worlds. Odin said:

"Can you see Agnar, your favourite, how he is breeding children with a iotun woman in a cave? But Geirrad, my favourite, is king and rules his land!" Frigg says:

"He is such a food-miser[70] that he strangles his guests if he thinks too many have come." Odin says: "That is the biggest lie!"

Then they made a wager about this. Frigg sent her chambermaid Fulla to Geirrad, to warn him against letting the magician, who had recently arrived in his kingdom, cast a spell on him; the magician could be recognized by this: no dog would be fierce enough to dare to attack him.

But it was just a big lie that King Geirrad didn't wish to feed his guests. Even so, Geirrad had that man arrested, whom the dogs would not attack. His fur coat was black and he called himself Grimnir. He told them nothing more about himself, even though they asked him many questions. The king wanted to force him to talk, so he made him sit between two fires. There he sat for eight nights.

King Geirrad had a son who was ten winters old and who was named Agnar after Geirrad's brother. Agnar approached Grimnir and gave him a full horn to drink, telling him that the king had acted badly and was mistreating him without cause. Grimnir drank from the horn; the fire had come so close now that his coat had caught fire.

Grimnir said:
1.
"Hot you are, Hasty! *Hasty = the fire*
Your heat is too strong,
leave me alone, flame!
My fur coat is singed
though I've flung it up,
now the fleece has caught fire!

2.
"Eight nights I sat
between sizzling fires,
and no one fetched me any food

---

[70] *food-miser:* To be a food-miser was looked down upon in the Viking era. To share your food and drink with your guests was what one was supposed to do.

except Agnar,
the one who shall rule
the land of the Goths[71] alone.

3.
"I greet you, Agnar!
Grimnir[72] bids you
be alive, whole and healthy;
not one drink is found
that ever will bring you
a gain greater than this!

4.
"The land is holy
that lies before me,
close to the aesir and elves;
but in Thrudheim   *Thor's home: 'Home of Strength'*
Thor shall have his seat
till the order of gods go under.

5.
"It's called Ydalir   *'the valleys of the yew tree'*
where Ull once built
a high hall for himself;
and to Freyr the gods
have given Alvheim   *Freyr's home: 'Home of elves'*
long ago as a tooth-gift.

6.
"The third house
the happy gods
have thatched with solid silver;

---

[71] *«...the land of the Goths...»:*   A mythical land of warriors; Goths being warriors.
[72] *Grimnir*:   For the sake of the rhyme, we have used the name Grimnir for Odin instead of Veratyr. Both names are aliases for Odin.

it's called Valaskialv,   *'Seat of Vali', Odin's son*
crafted by a god
in ancient days of yore.

7.
"The fourth is Sokkvabekk,   *'treasure chest beneath the ocean'*
where the soothing waves
spread their splendid light;
there Odin and Saga
every day drink
their mead from golden goblets.

8.
"The fifth is Gladsheim,   *'Home of joy'*
where the golden-bright
Valhall was raised and roosts;   *'Hall of the fallen warriors'*
every day there,
Odin chooses
who are to be killed in combat.

9.
"It is easy for those
who enter Valhall
to grasp where they have got to:

Spears space the walls,
shields are used for shingles,
armour brightens the benches.

10.
"It's easy for those
who enter Valhall
to grasp where they have got to:

A wolf is hanging
west of the gate,
and an eagle hovers over.

11.
"The sixth is Thrymheim,   *'Home of strength*
where Thiatzi lived,
that eager and strong iotun;
now Skadi has got it
– the gods' fair bride –
her father owned it before her.

12.
"The seventh is Breidablikk   *'Wide View'*
where Baldr has made
himself a hall and homestead;
I know that there
you'll never find
hurting and harmful runes.

13.
"The eighth is Himinbiorg,   *'Heaven's mountain'*
where Heimdall lives
and rules the sacred sites;
there the watchman
of the worthy gods
merrily drinks his mead.

14.
"The ninth is Folkvang,   *'the Army's field'*
where Freyia places
her guests and rules the roost;
she picks half of the soldiers
that are slaughtered each day,
and Odin gets the others.

15.
"The tenth is Glitnir   *'the Glittering'*
with golden columns,
its roof is wrapped in silver;
most of his days
this dwelling is Forseti's,   *son of Nanna and Baldr*
where he settles every suit.

16.
"The eleventh is Noatun,   *'Shipyard'*
where Niord has got
himself a hall and homestead;
he is the chieftain of men,
no malice clings to him,
he rules the open altar.[73]

17.
"The straw grows high
and the grass is tall
in Vidar's land Vidi;   *Vidi = 'the Wide'*
there he avowed
to avenge his father,
while seated in his saddle.

18.
"In Eldhrimnir   *'Sooting Flame'*
Andhrimnir lets   *a giant*
Saehrimnir seethe and boil   *Saehrimnir is a mythological pig*
– the finest pork –
yet few can tell
what Odin's warriors[74] eat!

---

[73] *Open alter:*   The ON word translated here is *'horg'*. The Germanic tribes were known to worship their gods out in the open, at sacred sites called *'horg'* which contained an outdoor altar.

[74] *Odin's warriors:* The ON word is *'einheriar'*, pl. of *'einheri'*, meaning a warrior who is an entire army in himself. *'Einheriar'* were thought to continue living in Valhall, Odin's hall, after having died in battle.

19.
"Geri and Freki   *both are wolves*
are fed by the proud
and weapon-wise Heriafather;   *'Father of armies' = Odin*
yet wine alone
keeps the well-armed god
Odin fit and fed.

20.
"Huginn and Muninn   *Odin's ravens, 'Mind' and 'Memory'*
make their flight
each day over the wide world;
I worry about Huginn,
whether he'll return,
yet I'm more afraid for Muninn.

21.
"Thund swells   *a mythological river*
and Thiodvitnir's fish[75]   *the World Serpent*
wallows in the waves of the river;
it seems too strong,
the stream of Valglaumir,   *a mythol. river*
for any warrior to wade.

22.
"Valgrind is found   *'Gate of the dead'*
standing firmly on the plain,
holy at holy posts;
age-old is that gate,
and yet few know
how it is bolted and barred.

---

[75] *Thiodvitnir*:   a kenning for the Fenriswolf, brother of the World Serpent, son of Loki and Angrboda.

23.
"Five hundred doors
and forty, I think,
open to Odin's hall;
eight hundred warriors
go out through each door
when they want to fight the wolf.   *the wolf Fenrir*

24.
"Five hundred floors
and forty, I think,
are built in Bilskirnir;   *Thor's hall at Thrudvang*
of all the cabins
that are covered with roofs,
the largest belongs to my son.   *Thor*

25.
"On the gable of Valhall
stands the goat Heidrun,
biting on Lerad's branches;   *maybe an alias for Yggdrasil*
she fills the cauldron
with a clear drink,
a mead which is never diminished.

26.
"On top of the hall   *Valhall*
stands the hart Eikthyrnir,
biting on Lerad's branches;
from his antlers drip
drops into Hvergelmir   *'Seething cauldron'*
from whence all waters flow.

27.

[76] "Sid and Vid,   *mythological rivers:*   *'Long' and 'Wide'*
Sekin and Eikin,   *'Guilty' and 'Aroused'*
Svol and Gunnthra,   *'Cool' and 'Longing for Battle'*
Fiorm and Fimbulthulr,   *'Busy' and 'Mighty roarer'*
Rin and Rennandi,   *'Flow' (the Rhine?) and 'Running'*
Gipul and Gopul,   *'Snatcher' and 'Gaper'*
Gomul and Geirvimul   *'Old' and 'Spear-shaker'*
– they dive around the gods' dwellings –
Thyn and Vin,   *'Torment' and 'Desire'*
Tholl and Holl,   *'Toil' and 'Swelling'*
Grad and Gunnthorin.   *'Greedy' and 'Battle-eager'*

28.

"Vina is one,   *mythol. rivers: perhaps Dvina?*
another Vegsvinn,   *'Quick-passage'*
the third Thiodnuma,   *'People-grabber'*
Nyt and Naut,   *'Receiver' and 'Sacrifice'*
Nonn and Hronn,   *'Woman' and 'She who grunts'*
Slid and Hrid,   *'Sheath' and 'Strife'*
Sylgr and Ylgr,   *'Swallower' and 'She-wolf'*
Vid and Van,   *'Wide' and 'Wish'*
Vond and Strond,   *'Troublesome' and 'Shore'*
Gioll and Leift;   *'Roar' and 'Glittering'*
they glide past men,
and from here they fall to Hel.

29.

"Kormt and Ormt   *mythol. rivers: 'Framed' and 'Heated'*
and Kerlaugar, the twins,   *'Water-bowls'*
Thor shall wade them all
every day
to act as judge
by the ash Yggdrasil;

---

[76] *The mythological rivers:* They are all named after iotun women.

for the bridge of the aesir   *the bridge = the rainbow*
is all a-flame
and the sacred waters are seething.

30.
"Gladr and Gyllir,   *mythol. horses: 'Happy' and 'Golden'*
Gler and Skeidbrimir,   *'Shiny' and 'Foamer'*
Silvrintopp and Sinir,   *'Silver-top' and 'Sinewy'*
Gisl and Falhovnir,   *'Bolt' and 'Speedy-hoof'*
Gulltopp and Lettfeti –   *'Golden-top' and 'Lightfoot'*

the aesir are carried by these colts
every day
to act as judges
by the ash Yggdrasil.

31.
"Three roots grow
in three directions
under the ash Yggdrasil;
Hel lives under one,
under the other the frost-giants,
men thrive under the third.

32.
"Ratatosk is the squirrel,
who runs up and down
the ash Yggdrasil;
he shall fetch the words
of the eagle from above
and deliver them to Nidhogg below.   *the snake gnawing*
     at Yggdrasil's roots

33.
"There are four harts,
they feed on the buds,
nibling with their necks thrown back:
Dainn and Dvalinn,   *'Ghost' and*
'Somnambulent'
Duneyr and Durathror.   *'Downy-eared' and 'Slumberer'*

34.
"More snakes lie under   *Mythological snakes:*
the ash Yggdrasil
than any numb-skull may know:
Goinn and Moinn   *'Crawler' and 'Moor-creeper'*
– the sons of Gravvitnir –   *'Grave-dweller'*
Grabak and Gravvollud,   *'Gray-back'; 'Grave-ruler'*
Ovnir and Svavnir,   *'Exciter' and 'Calmer'*
will always, I think,
gnaw at the twigs of the tree.

35.
"The tree Yggdrasil
takes more strife
than men may ever imagine:
the hart chews its top,
the tree-trunk rots,
and Nidhogg gnaws at its roots.

                                    Valkyries,
36.   *female deities:*
"Hrist and Mist   *'Shaker' and 'Dimmer'*
bring mead to Odin,
Skeggiold and Skogul,   *'Axe-age' and 'Attacker'*
Hildr and Thrudr,   *'Fight' and 'Might'*
Hlokk and Herfiotur,   *'Racket'; 'Spell-binder of armies'*
Goll and Geironul,   *'Yeller' and 'Spear-fencer'*

Randgrid and Radgrid   *'Shield-ready' and 'Ready-to-rule'*
and Reginleiv,   *'Daughter of the Powers'*
they carry beer to the brave.

37.
"Arvak and Alsvinn,   *mythol. horses:*
watchful and slender,   *'Wide-awake' and 'All-quick'*
haul the Sun up from here;
the gods have bound
about their flanks
cold iron to cool them.

38.
"Svalinn is the one   *a shield called 'Cool'*
that the Sun is covered by,
the shield before the shining goddess;
mountain and brine
will burn, I know,
if it ever should fail and falter.

39.
"Skoll is the wolf   *'the Scolder'*
that scampers after the bright
goddess to the forest that guards her,
another is Hati,   *'Hatred'*
he is Hrodvitnir's son,   *Hrodvitnir = Loki*
who rounds up heaven's relish.   *= the Moon*

40.
"From Ymir's flesh
the earth was made,
and from his sweat the sea,
rock from his skeleton,
from his scalp the trees,
and from his skull the sky.

41.
"From his eyebrows
the eager gods
built Midgard for the sons of men,
and from his brain
they brought forth
the dark and dreadful clouds.

42.[77]
"*He* has good will
from Ull and the gods,
who first touches the flame;
all worlds open
for the aesir's sons
when the kettles are hauled from the heat.

43.
"In the early days
the Ivaldi-sons   *dwarfs*
had built Skidbladnir,
the finest of ships
for Freyr, the pure
and noble son of Niord.

44.
"The ash Yggdrasil
is the utmost of trees,
and Skidbladnir of schooners,
Odin of the high ones,
and of horses Sleipnir,
of bridges Bivrost,   *the rainbow*
and Bragi of poets,

---

[77] *Stanza 42:*   The whole stanza tells about a pagan ritual. *Ull* was an ancient god. Touching his ring at the temple would grant a person asylum. *The kettles* probably contained meat prepared for the sacred meal.

of hawks Habrok,   *'Short-pants'*
and of hounds Garm.   *'Noisy'*

45.
"I've given my glimpses
to the gods' favourites,   *his listeneres at Agnar's court?*
bringing the aid that's wanted;
the high aesir, too,
shall hear of this
when they enter to sit with Aegir,
when they want to drink with Aegir.

46.   *various names for Odin:*
"I call myself Grim,   *Grim = 'Masked'*
I call myself Gangleri,   *'Tired-of-walking'*
Herian and Hialmberi,   *'War-god' and 'Helmet-bearer'*
Thekk and Thridi,   *'Dashing' and 'the Third'*
Thund and Unn,   *'Archer' and 'Winner'*
Helblindi and Har.   *'the One who blinds'; 'the Gray One'*

47.
"Sann and Svipall   *'True' and 'Fast'*
and Sanngetall,   *'Guessing-the-Truth'*
Herteit and Hnikar,   *'Happy-in-the-Army' and 'Exciter'*
Bileyg, Baleyg,   *'Cock-eyed' and 'Flaming-Eye'*
Bolverk, Fiolnir,   *'Damage-monger' and 'Knowing'*
Grim and Grimnir,   *'Mask' and 'Masker'*
Glapsvinn and Fiolsvinn; *'Impish' and 'Quick-witted'*

48.
"Sidhott, Sidskegg,   *'Brim-Hat' and 'Long-Beard'*
Sigfodr, Hnikur,   *'Father-of-Victory' and 'Exciter'*
Alfodr, Valfodr,   *'Allfather' and 'Corpse-Father'*
Atrid and Farmatyr;   *'Attacker' and 'God-of-Commerce'*
I have never used
just one name
when I began to mingle with men.

49.
"They called me Grimnir   *'Masker'*
at Geirrad's place,
and Ialk at Asmund's dwelling,   *'Gelding'*
and later Kialar   *'Sleigh-driver'*
when I lugged the sleigh,
Thror at the Thing,   *'Thriving'*
Vidur when at war,   *'Weather-beaten'*
Oski and Omi,   *'Wish' and 'Roar'*
Iavnhar and Bivlindi,   *'Equal-in-Height'; 'Shield-shaker'*
Gondlir and Harbard with the gods.   *'Rod-handler' and 'Greybeard'*

50.
"As Svidur and Svidrir   *'Whirling' and 'Whirler'*
Sokkmimir knew me,
I fooled the foul old giant;
alone I became
the killer of Midvitnir,   *'Mead-Wolf'(Suttung?)?*
that big and sturdy brute.

51.
"You're drunk, Geirrad,
you've had a drink too many,
you totter and toss about
since you've left me
and the leading warriors,
you've lost Odin's favour as well.   *Odin speaks of himself*

52.
"Much I told you,
you took in little,
now your friends are your foes;
I see it now:
the sword of my friend   *Odin means Geirrad*
lying all bathed in blood.

53.
"Ygg must now have						*Odin as 'the Frightening'*
a hacked up corpse,
your life, I know, is lost;
the disir are angry,						*the goddesses*
watch Odin now,
come close to me, if you can!

54.
"I call myself Odin,
I was Ygg before,
before that, even, Thund,				*'Archer'*
Vak and Skilving,					*'Awake' and 'Heir-of-Skiolvir'*[78]
Vavud and Hroptatyr,					*'Woven' and 'Screaming-God'*
Gaut and Ialk with the gods,				*Gaut: maybe 'Father of the Goths'*
Ovnir and Svavnir –					*'Exciter' and 'Calmer'*
all of them, I think,
came alive by me alone."

King Geirrad was sitting with his sword half-drawn across his knees. But when he heard that Odin had come, he got up wishing to pull him away from the fire. The sword slipped from his hand and fell to the ground, the hilt pointing downwards. The king tripped and fell forward so that the sword penetrated his body and he died. Then Odin vanished. Geirrad's son Agnar became king and ruled the land a long time.

---

[78] *Skiolver:* Legendary ancestor to a Swedish royal family, 'the Skilvingar'.

The Tale of Skirnir
– SKÍRNISMÁL –

This is the story of how the god of fertility, Freyr, gains the love of his life by the aid of his servant, Skirnir. While seated on Odin's magical throne Hlidskialv, Freyr catches sight of Gerd, daughter of the iotun Gymir, and falls deeply in love with her. The contents of this poem has been interpreted in many ways. Among others as a myth representing winter melting into spring. Freyr's parents were Niord, himself a god of fertility (a vani) and the iotun woman Skadi. This poem demonstrates the the use of the powerful runes. The Tale of Skirnir *is in the metre of liodahatt.*

Freyr, son of Niord, was seated on Hlidskialv, looking into all the worlds. He looked into Iotunheim and there he saw a lovely maiden walking from her father's hall towards her bower. This made him lovesick. Skirnir a man was called. He was Freyr's servant. Niord asked him to go and speak with Freyr. Then Skadi said:

1.
"Get up, Skirnir!
Go to our son,
ask him to answer this question;
you have to find out
who it may be
that our wise heir is angry with."

Skirnir said:
2.
"I rather fear
his wrathful speech
if I go to see your son,

and have to question
who it may be
that your wise heir is angry with."

Skirnir said to Freyr:
3.
"Listen to me, Freyr,
you Leader of the Army,
for this I need to know:
Why do you sit alone
and languish in the hall,
Sire, each single day?"

Freyr said:
4.
"Why should I tell *you*,
who are young and healthy,
about this misery of mine?
Even though Alvrodul   *'Elf's blush' = the sun*
always shines,
it never lightens my needs."

Skirnir:
5.
"To me your needs
are not so great
that you must keep them from your comrade;
in the early days
we were young together,
let us still be faithful friends."

Freyr said:
6.
"In Gymir's garden
the girl was walking,
the lady that I lust for;

her arms were shining
and all was bright,
both air and water glistened.

7.
"More than any man
has ever loved
I long for this wonderful lady!
But the aesir and elves
won't ever allow
that we two walk together."

Skirnir said:
8.
"Give me your horse,
it will get me through darkness
and scary, flickering flames,
and your sword, too,
that swings by itself
and can cleave the clan of giants."

Freyr said:
9.
"I'll give you my horse,
that will get you through darkness
and scary, flickering flames,
and my sword, too,
that swings by itself,
if the one who holds it can handle it."

Skirnir said to the horse:
10.
"It's dark outside,
let us dare to set out
over the wet mountains,
over the iotun people;

we'll both arrive
or we'll both be taken
by the all-powerful iotun."   *Gerd's father Gymir*

Skirnir rode into Iotunheim, and arrived at Gymir's farm. Angry dogs were tied to the gate in the fence surrounding the hall where Gerd lived. Skirnir rode up to the shepherd who sat on a mound there, and spoke to him thus:

11.
"Tell me, shepherd,
from your tall mound,
you who watch in all directions:
How can I meet
the maiden of the house
and dodge Gymir' dogs?"

The shepherd said:
12.
"Do you wish to die,
or are you dead already?
- - - - -   *missing line*
There is no way
that you'll ever meet her,
this good maiden of Gymir's."

Skirnir said:
13.
"Rather than fret
I prefer this course:
I shall try to give it a go!
In one single day
my destiny was shaped,
this life has been planned all along."
this life has been planned all along." [79]

---

[79] *"...this life has been planned all along"*: It was believed that every newborn baby was visited by the nornes, the goddesses of fate, who determined their future at birth.

152

Gerd said:
14.
"What horrible noise
do I hear now
thundering through the house?
The earth is shaking,
and a shivering is felt
all throughout Gymir's garden."

A slave woman said:
15.
"There's a man here,
who has dismounted his horse
and left it to graze on the grounds."
-- -- --   *missing verses*

Gerd spoke:
16.
"Ask him to step
into the hall
and drink a draught of our mead;
though I do fear
that you'll find outside
the banesman of my dear brother.[80]"

Gerd spoke to Freyr:
17.
"Do you belong to the elves,
or the aesir's sons,
or to the clever vanir's clan?
Why do you come alone
over the wild flames,
here to my hall and yard?"

---

[80] *"...the banesman of my dear brother"*: Freyr, not Skirnir, is otherwise called "the Bane of Beli", Beli is probably Gerd's brother.

Skirnir said:
18.
"I'm not of the elves
nor the aesir's sons,
nor of the clever vanir's clan;
I've come all alone
over the wild flames,
here to your hall and yard.

19.
"Eleven apples,
they are all of gold,
I would like to give you, Gerd,
to purchase peace
and your promise, in return,
of full-hearted love for Freyr."

Gerd said:
20.
"I will never allow
your eleven apples
to be payment for a lout's lust;
neither shall Freyr
find favour with me;
we shall never lie next to each other."

Skirnir said:
21.
"Then I offer the ring
that once was burned
with the young son of Odin;   *Baldr*
eight equal rings,
arise from it
every ninth night."

Gerd said:
22.
"I don't fancy your ring
although flames have burned it
with the young son of Odin;
in Gymir's garden
I have gold enough,
I rule my father's riches!"

Skirnir said:
23.
"See this sword,
supple and handsome,
I hold it here in my hand;
I'll cleave your head
clear off your shoulders,
if you dare to turn down my terms."

Gerd said:
24.
"I shall never be
a needy victim
of any lout's lust;
it seems to me
if you meet with Gymir,
that a fatal fight will follow."

Skirnir said:
25.
"See this sword,
supple and handsome,
I hold it here in my hand;
its edge will make
the iotun kneel,
your father will face his death.

26.
"Bright One, I'll whip you,
I'll break you in,
you'll soften to my desire!
You shall limp
where no living being
will ever be able to see you.

27.
"Early each morning
from the eagle's nest
you'll be staring out of this world,
you'll be hankering toward Hel;
food will seem to you
fouler than an adder
that slithers among men.

28.
"You'll be a spectacle
if you're spotted outdoors,
Hrimnir[81] will stare,
everyone shall glare;
more well-known
than the watchman of the gods,   *Heimdall*
you'll be glowering from behind your grating.

29.   Magic runes, spells that bode ill:
"Folly and Limbo,   *Tópi and Ópi*
Lust and Obsession,   *Tiosull and Óþoli*
tears shall follow upon torment!

---

[81] *Hrimnir:*   The father of the valkyrie Liod. His name means soot-black, in other words, he is very ugly. The threat here is that she will be made to look even worse than him.

Sit down and listen
for I will say this now:
one Powerful Passion   *Súsbrekka*
and two times an Anguish!   *Trega*

30.
"Iotuns shall arouse you
every day
within the giants' yards;
each day you shall
wobble without aim,
wobble wanting an aim
to the fort of the Frost-Giants;
what you shall gain
is not gaiety but tears,
weeping, you shall suffer your sorrows.

31.
"With a three-headed iotun
you shall always dwell,
or else you shall lack a lover;
may your wits be bound,
may you be weakened by your fate!
Be like the thistle,
thrust to the ground
when the harvest is all ended!

32.
"I took to the forest,
a tree I chose,
to get me a good wand,   *magical wand*
I got me a good wand!

33.
"Odin is angry with you,
and the Aesir's Pride too,   *Thor*
Freyr shall be your foe;

you wicked bitch!
All you will gain
is the great wrath of the gods.

34.
"Listen all iotuns,
listen you frost giants,
heirs of Suttung,
the aesir also:
how I denounce you,
how I deny you
a maiden's delight in a man,
a maiden's joy in a man.

35.
"Hrimgrimnir he is called   *'Sooty mask', a nasty giant*
who shall have you now
down by the Gates of Death;
at the roots of the tree
trolls are waiting
to give you goat's piss;
you shall never enjoy
a nobler drink
wench, by your will,
wench, by my will!

36.
"Thurs I carve for you   *Thurs, a name of the rune þ = Iotun*
and three runes:
Perversion, Sordidness   *Ergi, Oedi*
and Obsession;   *Óthola*
I may carve it off
as I carved it on,
should ever the need come up."

Gerd said:
37.
"Come, youth, good cheer,
this chalice I give you
full of mellow mead;
though I thought I knew
that I never would want
to give love and delight to a vani."   *She means Freyr, see Index*

Skirnir said:
38.
"I need to find out
if my errand's fulfilled
before I bid you goodbye;
when is it you mean
to meet with him,
that noble son of Niord?"

Gerd said:
39.
"Barri, it is called,   *"budding trees"*
as we both well know,
a calm and quiet grove;
when nine nights are gone,
then Gerd will serve
the son of Niord his desire."

Then Skirnir rode home. Freyr stood outside, waiting to hear what had happened:

40.
"Before you unsaddle,
say it now, Skirnir,
don't make another move!
What did you arrange
in Iotunheim,   *the Home of the giants*
to your gain or to my own good?"

Skirnir said:
41.
"Barri it is called,
as we both well know,
a calm and quiet grove;
when nine nights are gone,
then Gerd will serve
the son of Niord his desire."

Freyr said:
42.
"Long is the night,
still longer are two,
three are unthinkable!
A month seems shorter
than for me to linger
by myself in the high seat![82]"   *there awaiting his bride*

---

[82] *High seat*:   Gro Steinsland's interpretation: *Det hellige bryllup og norrøn kongeideologi,* Oslo 1991; p. 84-86

The Song of Harbard
– *HÁRBARÐSLJÓÐ* –

The motif in this poem, a son who meets his father without recognizing him and the battle ensuing between them, is reminiscent of the Old High German Hildebrandslied. *In* The Song of Harbard *Thor, who according to Snorri is Odin's son, meets the ferryman Harbard (Greybeard), who is Odin in disguise. A terrible row develops in which there is no limit to the insults that they hurl at each other.*
Metrical inconsistencies in our text follow the original.

Thor returned from his travels in the East and reached a sound. On the other shore was the ferryman with his boat. Thor shouted to him:

1.
"Who is that little lad,
I see lurking across the sound?"

The ferryman answered:
2.
"Who is that sturdy stud,
who stands there shouting?»

Thor said:
3.
"Ferry me over the sound,
and I'll feed you tomorrow;
on my back I've a rucksack,
no better food's to be had;

before I set out
I ate in comfort
herring and oats,
I've had my fill."

The ferryman said:
4.
"You boast of having
breakfasted early –
you don't know much, do you,
your folks back home are sad,
I fear your mother is dead."

Thor said:
5.
"What you mention now
is what most people
would dread to hear of:
the death of my mother." *Thor's mother is the Earth*

The ferryman said:
6.
"I barely think
you have three good ranches;
in your bare feet you stand,
stashed out like a tramp –
not even a pair of pants!"

Thor said:
7.
"I'll show you where to dock,
row your dinghy over here!
But who owns the boat
that you have in your keep?"

The ferryman said:
8.
"Hildolf is the name   *another name for himself, Harbard*
of him who owns my boat,
that quick-witted warrior
who camps in Radsey-sound;
he told me not to help
horse-thieves and pickpockets,
only good people
that I get to know;
tell me who you are
if you wish to cross the sound."

Thor said:
9.
"Even if I were outlawed,
I'd be open about my name
and about my kin to boot:
I am Odin's son;
I am Meili's brother
and Magni's father,
the mighty among the gods,
mind you speak with Thor!
I want to ask you now
what you call yourself."

The ferryman said:
10.
"My name is Harbard,
I hide it seldom."

Thor said:
11.
"Why hide your name
when you have no lawsuits?"

Harbard said:
12.
" I can hold my own,
even if I'm guilty,
against a dude like you,
unless death were my fate."

Thor said:
13.
"To cross the bay
will cause me harm,
the wading will make me wet!
I'll repay you, suckling,
for your insulting words,
if I manage to come across."

Harbard said:
14.
"Here I'll stand
and stay till you come;
since Hrungnir toppled,   *a giant, felled by Thor*
a tougher guy you never saw!"

Thor said:
15.
"So you want to talk about this,
how I tussled with Hrungnir,
that haughty giant
whose head was of stone!
I made him fall,
he fell down before me.
And what were you up to then, Harbard?"

Harbard said:
16.
"I stayed with Fiolvar   *a giant*
five whole winters
on that island,
Allgreen it's called;
there we fought for real,
we ravished people;
we were tested enough,
we tried many women."

Thor said:
17.
"How did it turn out for you,
with your women?"

Harbard said:
18.
"Had they only been willing,
the women had been frisky;
they would have been wise,
had they wanted to love us;
they braided ribbons   *female giants shaping the landscape*
out of bare sand,
they dug out earth,
made deep valleys;
but I was way smarter
than any of them,
I rested with seven sisters,
I had their favours and fondness!
And what were you up to then, Thor?"

Thor said:
19.
"I destroyed Thiatzi,
that sturdy giant,
I cast the eyes
of Alvaldi's son   *Thiatzi is Alvaldi's son*
up to high heaven;
they mark best
my mighty works,
there they are for all to see.
What were you up to then, Harbard?"

Harbard said:
20.
I used love charms
to lure the night-riders,   *female giants or witches*
hustling them from their husbands;
I thought that Hlebard
was a harsh giant,
he made me a magic wand,
yet I brought him out of his wits."

Thor said:
21.
"Then you were wicked
when thus you repayed
such a gracious gift."

Harbard said:
22.
"An oak will keep
what it carves from another,
all look out for their own.
What were you up to then, Thor?"

Thor said:
23.
"In the East I waged
war on the giants,
brimful of menace
they were mountain-women;
the clan of giants will grow
if they get to live,
and there'll be no place
for people in Midgard.
What were you up to then, Harbard?"

Harbard said:
24.
"I went to Valland   *France*
to watch the battles,
I owned the mighty,
I made no peace;
in war Odin
gets the earls who die,
but Thor, he gets the thralls."

Thor said:
25.
"You'd deal out unevenly
the dead amongst the gods,
if you had as much power as you pleased."

Harbard said:
26.
Thor has much power
but his punch is lacking:
Out of fear and faint heart
you found your way into the glove[83],

---

[83] «*...you found your way into the glove*»:   Refers to Snorre's story in 'Skaldskaparmál' about a trip that Thor made to Utgarda-Loki.

then you didn't think you were Thor;
you did not dare
through dread and fright
to sneeze or fart,
in case Fialar would hear you." *alias the giant Utgard-Loki*

Thor said:
27.
"Harbard, you queer!
I'll kill you right now,
if I can only cross over the bay."

Harbard said:
28.
"Why come across
when no cause divides us?
What were you up to then, Thor?"

Thor said:
29.
"I had gone to the East
to guard the river,
when Svarang's sons *a clan of giants*
sought me out;
they hurled rocks at me,
it helped them little,
they were the first to plead
for peace and safety.
What were you up to then, Harbard?"

Harbard said:
30.
"I'd gone to the East
to woo a lady,
I toyed with the linen-white one
and made love to her in secret,

the gold-glimmering one,
she gave me pleasure."

Thor said:
31.
"So they treated you well, the women there."

Harbard said:
32.
"I had needed your help, Thor,
to hold and to keep
the linen-white lassie."

Thor said:
33.
" I would have given it you,
if I'd only got there."

Harbard said:
34.
"I would have believed you,
if you had let me trust you."

Thor said:
35.
"I don't bite at the heel
like a hardened shoe in springtime!"

Harbard said:
36.
"What were you up to then, Thor?"

Thor said:
37.
"At Hlesey I battled
with berserk women;
they knew best
how to bother people."

Harbard said:
38.
"It's paltry work, Thor,
to give women beatings."

Thor said:
39.
"They were she-wolves
and surely not women,
they sattered my ship
when I had shoved it on land,
they threatened me with clubs
and Thialvi shrank from fear. *Thor's 'servant'*
What were you up to then, Harbard?"

Harbard said:
40.
"I was in the army
on its way to this place,
waving the war-banners,
our weapons were reddened."

Thor said:
41.
" What you're hinting at now
is that you're here to kill us ."

Harbard said
42.
"I'll make it up to you
by means of the ring,   *an insinuation of homosexuality*
like the judges would order
to equal the score."

Thor said:
43.
"Where do you get
these insults from?
I've never in my life
heard such belittling words!"

Harbard said:
44.
"I get the words from the men,
the age-old ones,   *the deceased*
who dwell in the hillocks back home."   *the burial mounds*

Thor said:
45.
"You surely give
the graves a good name,
when you call them the hillocks back home."

Harbard said:
46.
"This is how I think
about that kind of journey."

Thor said:
47.
"Your sordid words
will serve you poorly,
if I could only wade these waters!
I think your shrieks
will be sharper than the wolf's,
if you're ever hit by my hammer."

Harbard said:
48.
"Siv has a lover at home,   *Siv = Thor's wife*
he is the one you should meet;
for you to endure that fight,
that will befit you better!"

Thor said:
49.
"Yours words are mindless,
meant to taunt me,
you low-down bloke,
you are lying like crazy."

Harbard said:
50.
"I'm telling you the truth:
You travel slowly,
you'd have done far better
if daylight had guided your journey."

Thor said:
51.
"Harbard, you faggot,
you've held me up here!"

Harbard said:
52.
"I don't think a herdsman
could hold back Thor,
that mighty one, with mumbling."

Thor said:
53.
"I'll try to give you counsel,
let's cut out arguing,
row your boat across the firth,
then the father of Magni shall greet you."

Harbard said:
54.
"Get away from the firth,
I refuse you passage!"

Thor said:
55.
"Well, show me the way
if you won't ferry me."

Harbard said:
56.
"It's easy for me to refuse you,
it's a far walk for you:
A stretch to the foot-bridge,
then further to the landing,
take the road to the left
till you reach Verland;
there will Fiorgyn   *Thor's mother = Earth*
find her son Thor,
and she'll show him the clan's roads
to the countries of Odin."

Thor said:
57.
"Can I get there today?"

Harbard said:
58.
"With guts and cunning
you'll get there by sun-rise,
and I think, when the ice thaws."

Thor said:
59.
"Our talk will be short now,
since you shower me with abuse;
I'll repay you for denying me
if our paths should cross again."

Harbard said:
60.
"Be gone with you now,
where the trolls may get at you!"

The Poem of Hymir
– *HYMISKVIÐA* –

This poem, although in fornyrdislag, is among the most artful of the Edda poems. This is due to an excessive use of kennings, similes on a guesswork basis. For instance the giants' griefgiver *means Thor. The poem is also probably one of the most recent ones of the anthology. It is composed of three separate stories, one embedded in the next.*
The outer story, about Ægir being obliged to throw a party for the gods, leads directly to the next poem in the Edda anthology: Loki's Quarrel.

The middle story in The Poem of Hymir *tells of the aesir Thor and Tyr visiting Tyr's father, the iotun Hymir, in order to borrow his giant brewing kettle for their big party. The third and perhaps most spectacular story tells of Thor competing with Hymir and winning the cauldron.*

1.
Once the war-gods
were eating their game,
and being thirsty
for a thorough spree,
they shook their twigs
to tell the pattern,   *the practice of divination*
and found there were countless
of cauldrons at Aegir's.

2.
There sat the giant,   *Aegir*
jolly as a child,
looking just like
the lad of Miskorblindi's: *a name for Aegir's father?*

Ygg's son stared him
straight in the face:
"Begin brewing
a bout for the gods!"

Odin's son; Thor

3.
The word-strong fellow,
forced him to toil;
revengeful feelings
filled the giant,
he called to Siv's husband:
"A cauldron is needed,
bring me one big enough
to brew all your ale!"

Thor

Aegir
Siv = Thor's wife

4.
This kind of kettle
was quite unknown
to the mighty aesir,
the all-powerful,
until, in trust,
Tyr gave Hlorridi
welcome advice
with words like these:

Hlorridi = Thor

5.
"He lives east
of Elivagar
where heaven ends,
Hymir the Cunning;
my father owns
an ample pot,
a mighty cauldron,
it is miles deep."

Tyr's father, a giant

Thor said:
6.
"May we borrow
this brewing vat?"
  Tyr said:
"Yes, my friend,
if we use cunning."

7.
Then they travelled
the entire day
away from Asgard
to Egil's farm,[84]
he herded the rams
whose horns were renowned;
they left for the hall   *Thor and Tyr*
that Hymir owned.

8.
The son found Grandma   *the son = Tyr*
grim indeed,
she had nine hundred
heads in all;
another one came,   *Tyr's mother*
covered in gold
and fair-browed, she offered
ale to the son:

9.
"Heir of the giants!
I want you both,
though full of daring,
to duck under the kettles,

---

[84] *...to Egil's farm:* Thor leaves his rams with the iotun Egil, who herds them while he is gone. Egil is a farmer who is the father of Thialvi and Roskva, and lives at the border of the giants' realm.

for many a day
my dear one has   *Hymir, her husband*
been mean toward guests
and mightily ill-tempered."

10.
Late from the hunt
came the horrible one,
tough as nails,
the testy Hymir;
he was gleaming with icicles
as he entered the hall,
the bushes on his cheek   *bushes = beard*
were chilled with frost.

The mistress said:
11.
"Hail to you, Hymir!
I hope you feel well!
Your son has come home
to your hall and realm,
the one we have longed for
from lands far away;
you'll find he has come
with the famous enemy,   *Thor*
mankind's comrade,
they call him Véurr.   *Thor as temple guardian*

12.
"Look where they sit,
slouched in the corner,
they have hidden themselves
behind the pillar."
When the giant peered,
the pillar was split,
and the beam as well
broke in two parts.

13.
Eight tumbled down
yet one remained
— a hard-forged cauldron —
whole and unscathed;
then they stood up
and the sturdy giant
eyed his enemy,
watched him closely.

eight cauldrons

Thor

14.
He sensed trouble
when he saw that Thor,
the giants' grief-giver,
had entered the hall;
then three oxen
were offered up for slaughter,
the giant ordered them
all to be boiled.

Hymir

15.
They chopped the heads off
from the oxen's bodies,
then they carried the bulls
to be boiled in pots;
Siv's husband ate,
— all by himself
before going to bed —
two bulls of Hymir's.

They, the servants

16.
The grey-haired Hymir,
Hrungnir's friend,
found Hlorridi had eaten
a heap of a meal:

"Tomorrow evening,
if we want our supper,
we three need to go
together and fish."

17.
Véurr was ready
to row the waves
if only he got bait
from the bold giant.
    Hymir said:
"Then, off to my herd,
if what you desire
is to hunt up bait,
you basher of Rock-Danes!   *'rock-soldiers' = the giants*

18.
"I hardly expect you
to have the strength
to use my bulls
as bait for fishing."
Then the skillful fellow   *Thor*
scurried to the woods,
and there stood the bull,
it was black as night.

19
The troll's death-tutor   *Thor*
tore from the bull
the high farm-yard   *the bull's head*
where its horns rested.
    Hymir said:
"The deed you've done now
seems damnable to me,
you keel-ruler,   *Thor*
you could have left it!"

20.
The goat-lord said   *Thor*
to the son of apes: *Hymir*
"Row the skid-horse further   *the boat*
afloat on the sea!"
But Hymir said
that he himself
didn't feel like taking
any further action.

21.
The renowned Hymir
hauled up fiercely
two whales from the sea
all in one go;
aft in the stern
Odin's kin, Véurr,
got a bait prepared
with proper skill.

22.
Men's safe-keeper   *Thor*
– the serpent-slayer –
used for bait
the bull's head;
the gods' enemy,   *the World Serpent*
engirdling all lands,
rushed toward the lure
from his low dwelling.

23.
The valiant Thor
adventurously hauled
the venom-coloured adder   *the World Serpent*
up to the gunwale;

with his hammer he hit
the hair's summit   *the serpent's head*
– freakish and ugly –
of the wolf's brother.   *the wolf is Fenrir, brother*
                                     of the World Serpent

24.
The ground moaned
when the monster shrieked,   *the World Serpent*
the earth shuddered
altogether;
the fish then sank,   *the World Serpent*
floundering in the sea.

25.
The iotun Hymir
wasn't pleased
as they rowed away,
not a word he spoke,
but struggled with the oars,
first one, then the next.

Hymir said:
25.
"Will you lend me a hand,
go half-and-half?
You may haul the whales
up to the house,
or you may fasten
our float-ram tightly."   *ship*

26.
Hlorridi got going,
he grabbed the stern,
mastered the sea-horse   *ship*
full of murky bilge-water
all by himself
with oars and bailers;

to the giant's quarters
he carried the surf-swine,   *ship*
he carried it straight
through stretches of forest.

27.
But the quarrelsome iotun
still wished to jostle
and struggle with Thor
so the strongest might win:
"Although he can row,
he's really not strong
– though he rows forcefully –
unless he fractures my beaker!"

28.
But when he held it,   *it = Hymir's beaker*
Hlorridi
straightway struck it
'gainst the steep rock beside him;   *steep rock =*
column/pillar
seated, he thrust it
through the pillars;
still it was whole
when Hymir retrieved it.

29.
Then the lovely
lady offered
useful advice
that only she knew:
"Use the skull of Hymir,
it is harder still
– the food-craver's –   *Hymir's*
than any cup on earth."

30.
The lord of rams   *Thor*
rose to his knees,
he mustered all
his might and power;
the giant's helmet-seat   *the giant's head*
stayed whole all the same,
but the round beaker
rent asunder.

Hymir said:
31.
"I think of my life's
lost treasures
as I see the cup
lying crushed on the floor."
The guy then added: *Hymir*
"Never again shall I
be able to say,
ale, now you're ready!

32.
"If you can bring it about,
it shall be like this:
Out of my house
you may haul the beer-kettle."
Tyr tried to move it
two times in all;
both times the cauldron
didn't budge an inch.

33.
Then Modi's father   *Thor*
took a firm grip,
heavily he stomped
through the hall's floor;

Siv's husband
heaved the cauldron,
and at his heels
the handles clattered.

34.
They hadn't gone far[85]
before Thor started
for the first time
to turn and look back:
Hymir from the East
came out of the scree,
and many-headed iotuns
made his army swell large.

35.
Thor stood firmly,
he flung down the cauldron,
he swung Miollnir
murderously forward,
thus killing off
all the rock-whales.   *giants*

36.
[86]They hadn't gone far   *Thor and Tyr*
before they saw
that one of Thor's rams
was rendered half-dead;
the shaft-horse was injured   *one of Thor's rams*
in one of its legs,
and that was the mark
of the mean Loki.

---

[85] *«They hadn't gone far...etc. ...»:* We have added the negation, for the sake of logic.

[86] *«They hadn't gone far...etc. ...»:* Apparently a few stanzas are missing here. However, in 'Gylvaginning' Snorri Sturluson tells the missing part, that they had already collected Thor's rams at Egil's.

37.
As you have heard[87]
– anyone who knows
the tale of the gods
can give you the story –
the rock-dweller   *the farmer Egil*
had to right the error[88]
by giving Thor as servants
his son and his daughter.

38.
Returning to the Thing
Thor, the unstoppable,
carried with him
the cauldron of Hymir;
now each of the gods
could eagerly enjoy
a beer-bash at Aegir's
after the flax-harvest.

---

[87] «*As you have heard…*»: Addressing the public in this fashion is unusual in Eddic poetry.
[88] «*…had to right it…*»:   According to Snorri, Thor's rams could be eaten at night and be revived the next day, as long as all their bones were gathered in their hides. Loki had tempted Thialvi to split one of the legbones of Thor's rams to get at the marrow. This caused the ram to limp, but Thor made it well again.

Loki's Quarrel
– LOKASENNA –

In this poem the envious and amoral Loki tries to put everybody down by revealing their faults. He expertly belittles their virtues by scandalous slander, thus violating the peace at this sacred gathering of the gods, a symposion. The poem is in liodahatt.

Aegir, also known as Gymir, had invited the aesir to his home for a drinking bout, as he had got hold of the great cauldron we have just heard of. To this party came Odin and his wife Frigg. Thor did not come, because he was in the East. Siv, his wife, was present, Bragi and his wife Idunn as well. Tyr was there. He had only one hand, since the wolf Fenrir had torn his other hand off when he was fettered. There was Niord and his wife Skadi, Freyr and Freyia, and Odin's son Vidar. Loki was there and Freyr's servants, Byggvir and Beyla. Many aesir and elves were present. Aegir had two servants, Fimafeng and Eldir. They used shining gold to light up the place. The beer was carried around by itself. It was a holy place, consecrated to peace. The guests praised highly how competent Aegir's servants were. Loki could not stand to hear this, so he killed Fimafeng. Then the gods shook their shields and screamed at him, and chased him into the woods, whereupon they went back to their drinking. Loki turned back too and outside he met Eldir.

Loki spoke to him thus:
1.
"Stay where you are,
Eldir, tell me this
before you make another move:
What is the topic
of the talk inside
 amongst the mighty gods?"

Eldir said:
2.
"The talk is
 of weapons
and warriors' victories
amongst the mighty gods
of all the aesir
and the elves, too,
few of them call you their friend."

Loki said:
3.
"Let me enter!
I want to see
what Aegir offers his guests;
I'll bully them
with brawl and trouble,
and mix their drink with damage!"

Eldir said:
4.
"If you enter
into Aegir's halls
to watch what he offers his guests,

and pour onto the gods
gall and blame,
they'll wipe it off on you."

Loki said:
5.
"Listen here, Eldir,
if ever we two
should have it out in words,
I'll truly know
how to talk back
if you risk raising your voice."

Then Loki stepped into the hall. And when they saw
who it was that had entered, they immediately fell silent.

Loki said:
6.
"I was thirsty
when I entered this hall,
Loft, from his long journey,   *Loft = Loki*
to ask the aesir
if one of you will give me
a measure of the precious mead.

7.
"Why are you aesir
so uneasy and silent
that you do not utter a word?
You will either stand me
a stoup and a seat   *a stoup is a drinking*
vessel
or ban me from the banquet!"

Bragi said: *the god of poetry*
8.
"We will neither stand you
a stoup or a seat,
any one of us aesir;
for the gods know well
who they wish to have
as guests at their merry gathering."

Loki said:
9.
"In the days of yore,
Odin, do you remember
that we mingled our blood as brothers?

You swore you would never
swallow beer
unless it was bidden us both!"

Odin said:
10.
"Look out, Vidar,   *son of Odin*
let the wolf's father
join in our jubilant feast,
or Loki shall speak
spiteful words
here in Aegir's hall."

Then Vidar got up and poured Loki a drink.
But before he drank, Loki addressed the aesir:

11.
"Hail to you, aesir,
hail to you, asynior,   *the goddesses*
and to the great and holy gods –
except the one
in the inmost corner
Bragi on the benches!"

Bragi said:
12.
"Horse and sword
I swear to give you
– thus Bragi makes amends –
so you won't offer the gods   *the aesir*
your envious plots,
calling forth the aesir's anger."

Loki said:
13.
"You shall always
want in vain
both horse and bracelet, Bragi;   *bracelet = golden armring*
of all the aesir
and elves, here, too,
you are the biggest wimp,
forever shy of arrows!"

Bragi said:
14.
"Had I been outside
and not seated like now
here in Aegir's hall,
I would carry your head
in my hands, be you sure!
That's little to pay for your lie."

Loki said:
15.
"You know how to talk,
but you never act,
you, Bragi Benchpride!
If you're so angry,
go on and fight,
a brave man fears no battle!"

Idunn said: *one of the asynior, Bragi's wife*
16.
"I bid you, Bragi,
bear in mind
our kith and all our kin,
don't tease Loki
with taunting words
here in Aegir's hall."

Loki said:
17.
"Keep quiet, Idunn!
Among all women
you are the most man-crazed;
you put your arms
eagerly around
your own brother's bansman."

Idunn said:
18.
"I won't tease you, Loki,
with taunting words
here in Aegir's hall;
I wish to calm Bragi,
beer made him drunk,
I don't want a furious fight."

Gevion said: *one of the asynior, 'giver of gifts'*
19.
"How come that you two
should quarrel here
with wounding, spiteful words?
It's known that Loki
is light-headed,
so he's loved by the lot of you."

Loki said:
20.
"Keep quiet Gevion,
I quite remember
the time you were won over
by the pale guy   *a dwarf*
who gave you the jewel,
and you threw your thighs around him."

Odin said:
21.
"You are witless,
it's an error, Loki,
to make Gevion mad;
for she knows in full
the fate of all men
just as well as I."

Loki said:
22.
"Be quiet, Odin,
you could never
choose which warriors should win;
victory you often
offered to dullards,
you should never have given those gifts."

Odin said:
23.
"I shouldn't have given
what I gave away,
victory to dim dullards,
but you spent eight years
in the earth's bosom
as a dairy-maid and damsel;
there you gave birth
to beastly offspring,
I think you're a pure pervert!"

Loki said:
24.
"One time on Samsey,   *Samsey, a Danish island*
in a trance and haze,
like a sibyl you tapped the tom-tom;
just like a witch
you whisked through the air
I think you're a pure pervert!"

Frigg said: *Frigg, Odin's wife, addresses them both*
25.
"What you've needed to do,
I hope it never will
be mentioned to the common man;
what you two aesir
did earlier on
let never men remember!"

Loki said:
26.
"Be quiet Frigg,
you are Fiorgyn's daughter,   *Fiorgyn = Earth, Thor's mother*
you're always looking for lovers;
you let Vidrir's brothers   *alias Odin, see Index*
both embrace you,
even though you were his wife."

Frigg said:
27.
"If only I possessed
in Aegir's hall
a son like beaming Baldr,
you would never get away
from the aesir's sons,
but angrily be driven to your death."

Loki said:
28.
"I can go on further,
 Frigg, if you like,
to speak even more words of spite!
You can blame it on me
that Baldr shall never
wind up in Aegir's hall."

Freyia said: *goddess of love, life and death, see Index*
29.
"You're brain-sick, Loki,
when you boast of this,
and speak such words of spite;
Frigg knows, I think,
the fate of all,
and yet she always keeps silent."

Loki said:
30.
"Be quiet, Freyia,
I've figured you out,
your flaws aren't hard to find:
the aesir and elves
inside these walls,
they've all been in bed with you."

Freyia said:
31.
"Your tongue is flawed!
In future, I think,
it will talk you into trouble!
The aesir are angry
and the asynior too,
when you leave here you'll wallow in worry."

Loki said:
32.
"Be quiet, Freyia,
you're a fiend to me,
and *you* are thoroughly wicked;
when the gods found you
together with your brother,
remember, Freyia, you farted!"

Niord said: *one of the vanir, god of the Sea*
33.
"Who would care
if it comes to pass
that a lass gains a husband or lover?
The surprise indeed
is that a pervert has come,   *Loki*
who himself has even born off-spring!"

Loki said:
34.
"Be quiet, Niord,
we know you were sent
as a handy hostage for the gods;
the daughters of Hymir
had you for a chamber pot
and wee'd in your open mouth."

Niord said:
35.
"I'll admit I was
sent away to serve
as a handy hostage for the gods,
but I've a lovely son   *Freyr*
who is loathed by no one,
he is given to support the gods."

Loki said:
36.
"Halt now, Niord,
get a hold of yourself!
Just let me tell you this tale:
Your sister is even
your son's mother –
it's no worse than one expects."

Tyr said: *an ancient god of war and justice*
37.
"Of all the brave ones,
the best is Freyr
within the aesir's yards;
he makes no maiden
or madame cry,
he breaks the chains of bondage."

Loki said:
38.
"Be quiet, Tyr!
Could you ever
make peace between people?
your right hand,
if I correctly remember,
Fenrir forced from you."

Tyr said:
39.
"I may lack a hand,
but you've lost Grey-leg,   *the wolf Fenrir*
damage is done to us both!
Fenrir suffers,
fettered in chains
he must linger till Ragnarok."

Loki said:
40.
"Be quiet, Tyr!
It turned out your wife
had a son who was sired by me;
when did *you* ever get
garment or coin
in repayment, you lousy pauper!"

Freyr said:
41.
"By the river's outlet
I see the wolf lying
till the gods begin their battle;
you're next in line
– unless you keep silent –
to be tied up, you tattle-tale."

Loki said:
42.
"You needed gold
to buy Gymir's daughter,
you even sold your sword;
when Muspel's sons
cross Murky Woods[89],
then how will you fight, you fool?"

Byggvir said:	*barley*
43.	
"If I were as wealthy	
as Ingunar-Freyr	*Freyr*
and had as lucky a lot,	
more mellow than marrow	
would I mash this vermin	*vermin = Loki*
and tear him limb from limb."	

Loki said:
44.
"What's this tiny one?
I see his tail wagging,
eagerly wanting a tidbit!

---

[89] *Murky Woods:* A mythological forrest between the Huns and the Goths in the heroic poem 'Atlakviða'.

he is clinging
close to Freyr's ears[90]
and mumbling under the millstone."

Byggvir said:
45.
"They say I'm quick,
they call me Byggvir,
both gods and good people;
it makes me feel honoured
that Odin's sons,
all of them, drink their ale."

Loki said:
46.
"Be quiet, Byggvir!
You could never
serve food fairly among men!
In the straw on the bench
you bury yourself
when fit guys start to fight."

Heimdall said: *watchman of the gods,*
47.   *mankind's father*
"Your senses have left you,
Loki, you are drunk,
do calm down, Loki!
Too much to drink
will make anybody
talk a mile a minute."

---

[90] «...*You're constantly clinging close to Freyr's ears,...*": Freyr was a god of fertility, and as such statues of him were probably adorned with wreaths of ripe barley.

Loki said:
48.
"Stop talking, Heimdall!
In times long gone
your lousy fate was laid;
your back is wet
as it will always stay;
thus you stand guard for the gods ."[91]

Skadi said:
49.
"It's easy now, Loki,
but it'll be over shortly
that you wag your tail in the air!
You'll be fettered to sword points
with your frosty sons' guts,   *Narfi*
the gods will tie you up tightly."

Loki said:
50.
"If I'm fettered to sword points
with my frosty sons' guts
and the gods tie me up tightly,
don't forget I was head
of the horde of gods
when we caught and killed Thiatzi.   *Skadi's father*

Skadi said:
51.
"If you were the head
of the horde of gods
who caught and killed Thiatzi,
from my holy sites
and sacred shrines
cold spells will always catch you."

---

[91] «*...your back is wet...etc.*»: Loki insinuates that Heimdall is a homosexual, a 'queen'.

Loki said:
52.
"You spoke more softly
to the son of Lauvey   *Lauvey was Loki's mother*
when you bade me come to your bed;
let's add this
to the list of our faults,
if we need to make them known."

Then Siv approached and poured mead
into the crystal chalice for Loki, and said:

53.
"Hail to you, Loki,
and have this cup,
a measure of age-old mead;
let *me* be the one
among the gods
whom you find to be without fault."

He took the horn and drank.

Loki said:
54.
"You may be the one,
if you are indeed,
who proves to be proper and noble;
although I know one,
and that's for sure,
who bedded Hlorridi's bride,   *Siv, Thor's wife*
and that was the low-down Loki!"

Beyla said: *wife of Byggvir*
55.
"The mountains shake,
I mean to sense
that Hlorridi soon will be here;

he shall take in hand
the harmful offender
of gods and good people."

Loki said:
56.
"Be quiet, Beyla,
you are Byggvir's wife
you're mixed with plenty of malice;
a greater freak
the gods never saw,
you dung-covered dairy-maid!"

Then Thor came and said:
57.
"Be quiet, you faggot,
my forceful hammer
Miollnir shall make you mute;   *Thor's hammer*
I'll sever your noggin
from your neck in a minute,
and that's how your life will leave you."

Loki said:
58.
"The son of Earth   *Thor*
has entered here,
but why do you threaten me, Thor?
You won't be so brave
when you battle with the wolf,
and he eats up Odin completely."

Thor said:
59.
"Stop your talk, pervert!
I'll strike you dumb
with my mighty hammer Miollnir;

I'll throw you in the air,
to the East and further,
and then you'll be gone for good."

Loki said:
60.
"Stop talking about
your trips in the East
in front of fearless people!
In the thumb of the glove
the great one crawled;   *Thor*
did you think you were Thor, then?"

Thor said:
61.
"Stop your talk, pervert!
I'll strike you dumb
with my mighty hammer Miollnir;
my right hand will hit you
with Hrungnir's bane,   *Miollnir*
so all your bones will be broken."

Loki said:
62.
"I intend to live
for a long time,
though you hound me with your hammer;
tough were the knots
that were tied by Skrymir,   *alias the giant Utgard-Loki*
you failed to get at the food,
hunger held you in its grip."

63 *Thor said:.*
"Stop your talk, pervert!
I'll strike you dumb
with my mighty hammer Miollnir;
you'll be taken to Hel   *goddess of the Realm of the Dead*
by Hrungnir's bane,
down past the Gate of the Dead."

Loki said:
64.
"I told the aesir
and I told their sons
whatever entered my mind.
For you alone
I will leave this place,
I am quite sure that you'll kill me!

65.
"You made ale, Aegir,
but *you* will never
again have guests in your hall:
Over and above
all your belongings
flames will rise and flare,
and then they'll burn your back."

But afterwards Loki hid in the waterfall Franangr in the shape of a salmon. There the aesir caught him. He was bound with the guts of his son Nari, while his son Narvi had become a wolf. Skadi attached an adder above Loki's face. Venom dripped from it. Sigyn, Loki's wife, sat by and held a cup to catch the venom. But when the cup was full, she carried the cup with the poison away, and in the meantime the venom dripped on Loki. Then he would struggle so hard that all the earth shook.
This is what we now call earthquakes.

The Poem of Thrym
– ÞRYMSKVIÐA –

In this humorous poem Thor's hammer has gone missing, and this is a great calamity for the gods, since it means that they have lost their major defense against the iotuns. This tragic situation is turned into a comic one when Thor dresses up in bridal costume in order to retrieve his hammer from the thief, who is no other than Thrym, king of the iotuns. The poem is in fornyrdislag.

1.
Wingthor was angry   *Thor*
as he awakened,
and found that his hammer
had been taken,
his hair billowed,
his beard shook,
the son of Earth   *the goddess Earth was Thor's mother*
had searched in vain.

2.
These are the words
he uttered first:
"Listen here, Loki!
Let me tell you
what no one knows
neither on earth
nor in heaven:
this god's hammer is stolen!"[92]

---

[92] «*Listen here, Loki...*»: All the aesir know that Loki is the likely culprit. That is why Loki later on volunteers to go with Thor to help him retrieve the hammer, probably saving his own hide in so doing.

3.
They went to the fair
Freyia's hall,
and these are the words
he uttered first: *Thor*
"Lend me, Freyia,
your feathered cloak[93]
so that I may retrieve
my trusted hammer!"

Freyia said:
4.
"Were it of gold
I would give it you,
and pass it to you
were it pure silver."

5.
Then Loki flew
– feathers whizzing –
until he had come
from the court of the aesir,   *Asgard*
until he had reached
the realm of the giants.   *Iotunheim*

6.
Thrym sits on the mound,
the thane of the giants,
braids leashes of gold
for his greyhounds,
brushing the manes
of his mares gently.

---

[93] «... *your feathered cloak,...*": A magical cloak which made its bearer able to fly like a bird.

Thrym spoke:
7.
"What is it with the aesir?
What is it with the elves?
Why do you rush
to the realm of the giants?"
    Loki said:
"It looks ill for the aesir,
it looks ill for the elves!
Hlorridi's hammer!
Have you hidden it, Thrym?"

Thrym said:
8.
"Hlorridi's hammer
has been hidden by me,
it lies eight miles deep
under the ground.
No man shall bring
back the hammer,
unless he fetches me
Freyia for wife."

9.
Then Loki flew
– feathers whizzing –
until he had raced
from the realm of the giants,
until he had come
to the court of the aesir;
he was met by Thor
in the middle of the yard,
and these are the words
he uttered first: *Thor*

10.
"Have your pains now
payed off at all?
Before you land,
deliver your news!
A fellow at ease
will often gab,
and a guy who lies down
is engulfed in fibs."

Loki said:
11.
"I have had pains
and profit, too:
Thrym has your hammer,
the head of the giants!
No one can bring
back your hammer,
unless he fetches him
Freyia for wife."

12.
They went to find
Freyia, the lovely,
and these are the words
he uttered first: *Thor*
"Freyia, you must bring
your bridal costume,
we two shall journey
to the giants' realm."

13.
Freyia was angry,
she fumed and raged,
the aesir's hall
heaved and shook,

the jewel Brisinga
burst from her chest:
"They'll call me man-crazed,
can't you see that,
if I join you on your trip
to the giants' realm!"

14.
Later the aesir
all went to the Thing,
also the asynior,
they argued fervently;
they met to decide
– the mighty gods –
how to get Hlorridi's
hammer back safely.

15.
Then Heimdall uttered,
the whitest of gods,
he divined the future
as vanir do:
"In bridal costume
we'll clothe Thor,
and embellish him with
the Brisinga-gem.

16.
"From his belt we'll hang
blinking keys,
we'll let skirts billow
about his knees!
On his broad chest
we'll bind stones,
and daintily
we'll do his hair."

17.
Then Thor stated,
the strong god:
"They will call me
a queer if they ever
find that I'm clothed
in the costume of a bride!"[94]

18.
Then Loki said,
Lauvey's off-spring:
"Keep quiet, Thor,
with your thoughtless words!
The giants will own
Asgard shortly,
if you don't get hold of
your hammer again!"

19.
Then in bridal costume
they clothed Thor,
adorned him with the brilliant
Brisinga-gem,
they hung from his belt
blinking keys,
the skirts billowed
about his knees,
on his broad chest
they bound stones,
and daintily
they did his hair.

---

[94] *«...in the costume of a bride!»:* For a man to dress and act as a woman was taboo for the people of the North.

20.
Then Loki said,
Lauvey's off-spring:
"I'll come with you
as your courtly maid,
as women we shall journey
to the giants' realm."

21.
The goats were then herded
home from the fields,
and fastened to the chariot
they charged ahead:
With the earth ablaze
and with bursting mountains,
Odin's son went
to Iotunheim.

22.
Then Thrym said,
the thane of the giants:
"Arise all iotuns,
make ready the benches!
Now they bring me
the bride Freyia,
daughter of Niord
from Noatun.

23.
"Here cows abound,
their horns are golden,
I'm filled with joy
at my jet-black oxen;
I have buckets of gold
and barrels of gems,
now all I lust for
is the lovely Freyia."

24.
That very evening
they all gathered,
ale was brought
to the eager giants –   *One: Thor, dressed as Freyia*
One ate an ox,
eight salmons,
and the giblets meant for
the giants' women;
Siv's husband imbibed
three barrels of mead.

25.
Then Thrym said,
the thane of the giants:
"Have you ever witnessed
a woman eat more?
I never saw a bride
gorge beef like this,
nor a courtly maiden
drink mead by the bucket!"

26.
Now the sly maid   *Loki, dressed as maid*
who sat there also,
found these words
to face the giant:
"Freyia hasn't eaten
in eight whole days,
all she longed for
was to leave for Iotunheim."

27.
Thrym lifted the veil
lusting for a kiss,
but he darted back
down through the hall:
"Why are they so evil,
the eyes of Freyia,
they seem to be filled
with fire and rage?"

28.
Now the sly maid
who sat there also,
found these words
to face the giant:
"She hasn't slept a wink
in eight days,
all she longed for
was to leave for Iotunhem."

29.
The giants' sister
then slunk in,
daring to beg for
a bridal gift:
"Let drop from your wrists
the rings of gold,
if you wish to gain
my good love,
my good love
and gracious favours."

30.
Then Thrym said,
thane of the giants:
"Let's bless the bride,
bring in the hammer!
Place Miollnir
in the maiden's lap,
and happily wed us
by the hand of Var."   *goddess of promises and alliances*

31.
Then Hlorridi's heart
heaved in his chest,
as the stubborn god
gripped his hammer;
first he slayed Thrym,
thane of the giants,
then he killed
the kinfolk of the giant.

32.
He slayed the old
sister of the giant,
the one who had begged
for bridal gifts;
instead of a gift
she got a beating,
and a rap of the hammer,
not rings of gold.
Thus Odin's son
saved his hammer.

The Tale of Alviss

– ALVÍSSMÁL –

Like The Tale of Vavthrudnir, *this poem is a contest of wits. The dwarf Alviss ('All Wise') approaches Asgard to fetch himself a bride. Thor does not like this alliance with his daughter Thrud, and challenges Alviss to a battle of wits. The topic is again the secrets contained in mythological knowledge, especially concerning names given to natural phenomena in each and every realm of existence. The poem is in liodahatt.*

Alviss said:
1.
"Prepare the benches,
for the bride shall now
be fetched to follow me home;
everyone thinks
that I'm wise to make haste,
there's no reason to rest at home."

Thor said:
2.
"What creature are you
with a countenance so pale!
Did you cradle a corpse last night?
You look like an awful
iotun to me;
you are not born for this bride."

Alviss:
3.
"My name is Alviss,
I live under the ground,
I stay underneath the stones;
the Lord of the Wagon   *Thor*
is who I want to see,
he shan't pass up on his promise!"

Thor:
4.
"I may break it,
for being her father
I crave the right to give counsel;
I was away
when this oath was made,
and I am the one to make it."

Alviss:
5.
"Who is this fellow
who feels it's his right
to govern this golden maiden?
You fleeting rambler,
there are few who know you,
so who can vouch for your valour?"

Thor:
6.
"I am called Wing-Thor,
widely I've travelled,
I am the son of Sidgrani;   *Sidgrani = Odin*
it is against my will
that you get this maiden
and win consent to wed her!"

Alviss:
7.
"I'll soon get you
to agree with me,
I'll win consent to wed her;
I'd rather own her
than want in vain
this fair and flour-white maiden."

Thor:
8.
"You shall not forfeit
the favours of this maiden,
my wise guest, if you want them:
Can you answer me
all I wish to know
about each and every realm?

9.
"Tell me now, Alviss,
I am testing you
about everyone's fate and future:
What is Earth called
by all who live
in each and every realm?"

Alviss:
10.
"People call it *Earth*
the aesir call it *Soil*,
and the worthy vanir the *Ways*,
iotuns *Evergreen*,
the elves *Growing*
the high lords call it *Loam*."

Thor:
11.
"Tell me now, Alviss,
I am testing you
about everyone's fate and future:
What is heaven called,
that hovers above us,
in each and every realm?"

Alviss:
12.
"People call it *Heaven*
High Arch, the gods,
the vanir call it *Wind-woven,*
the iotuns *the World Above,*
the elves *Fair Ceiling,*
the dwarfs call it *Dripping Hall.*"

Thor:
13.
"Tell me now, Alviss,
I am testing you
about everyone's fate and future:
What is Moon called
that men can see,
in each and every realm?"

Alviss:
14.
"People call it *Moon,*
Diminished, the gods,
with Hel *the Whirling Wheel,*   with Hel = *'in death's realm'*
the iotuns *Shover,*
Shine the dwarfs,
the elves call it *Year-Teller.*"

Thor:
15.
"Tell me now, Alviss,
I am testing you
about everyone's fate and future:
What is Sun called,
that is seen by all
in each and every realm?"

Alviss:
16.
"People call it *Sun*,
Solar, the gods,
the dwarfs call it *Dvalin's Rival*,
the iotuns *Ever-Glow*,
the elves *Pretty Wheel*,
the aesir call it *All-Clear*."

Thor:
17.
"Tell me now, Alviss,
I am testing you
about everyone's fate and future:
What is the cloud called
that carries the showers
in each and every realm?"

Alviss:
18.
"People call it *Cloud*,
Promise-of-Rain, the gods,
the worthy vanir *Wind-Flow*,
the iotuns *Drizzle-Hope*,
the elves *Heavy Weather*,
with Hel it's called *Hiding-Helmet*."

Thor:
19.
"Tell me now, Alviss,
I am testing you
about everyone's fate and future:
What is the wind called
that widely travels
through each and every realm?"

Alviss:
20.
"People call it *Wind*,
Waver, the gods,
the noble lords *the Neigher*,   *the noble lords*, here: *the vanir*
the iotuns *Cryer*,
the elves *Rumble-Carrier*,
with Hel it's called *Howling Gale*."

Thor:
21.
"Tell me now, Alviss,
I am testing you
about everyone's fate and future:
What is the calm called
that camps throughout
each and every realm?"

Alviss:
22.
"People call it *Calm*,
Quiet, the gods,
the vanir name it *No-Wind,*
the iotuns *Warm Shelter,*
the elves *Day's Length,*
the dwarfs call it *Day's Dwelling*."

Thor:
23.
"Tell me now, Alviss,
I am testing you
about everyone's fate and future:
What is the sea called
that is sailed by men
in each and every realm?"

Alviss:
24.
"People call it *Sea*,
Silence, the gods,
the vanir *Vaulting Wave*[95],
the iotuns *Home of Eels*,
the elves *Mash-Staff*[96],
the dwarfs call it *Deep Waters*."

Thor:
25.
"Tell me now, Alviss,
I am testing you
about everyone's fate and future:
Whatever is fire called
by all who live
in each and every realm?"

Alviss:
26.
"People call it *Fire*,
Flames, the aesir,
the vanir call it *Vaulting Wave,*

---

[95] *Vaulting Wave:* The same name is given by the vanir for *'fire'* in st. 26.
[96] *Mash-Staff:* A brewing tool. It seems to give little meaning. *'Mash'* alone would have been a better simile for *'Sea'*.

the iotuns *Desirous*,
the dwarfs *Burner*,
with Hel it is called *the Hasty*."

Thor:
27.
"Tell me now, Alviss,
I am testing you
about everyone's fate and future:
What do you call the forests
that are found where men walk
in each and every realm?"

Alviss:
28.
"People call it *the Woods*,
Pasture's Mane, the gods,
with Hel it's called *Hill's Kelp*,
the iotuns *Firewood*,
the elves *Lovely Branch*,
the wise vanir call it *Wand.*"

Thor:
29.
"Tell me now, Alviss,
I am testing you
about everyone's fate and future:
What is Night called
– Norr's daughter –
in each and every realm?"

Alviss:
30.
"People call it *Night*,
Nebulous, the gods,
the mighty lords call it *Mask*,   *mighty lords,* here: *vanir*
the iotuns *Non-Light*,
the elves *Sleep's Joy*,
the dwarfs call it *Goddess of Dreams*."

Thor:
31.
"Tell me now, Alviss,
I am testing you
about everyone's fate and future:
What is the seed called
that sons of men plant
in each and every realm?"

Alviss:
32.
"People call it *Barley*,
Prickly, the gods,
the good vanir call it *Growth*,
the iotuns *Mush*,
the elves *Mash-Staff*,
with Hel it's called *Head-Hanging*."

Thor:
33.
"Tell me now, Alviss,
I am testing you
about everyone's fate and future:
What is the mead called
that men enjoy
in each and every realm?"

Alviss:
34.
"People call it *Ale*,
the aesir *Beer*,
the vanir call it *Viscous*,
the iotuns clear *Water*,
Mead only with Hel,
it's *Binge* with the sons of Suttung."

Thor:
35.
"Not once have I met
in one and the same being
such wealth of ancient lore!
Treacherous treason
I will treat you to now:
Daylight hits you, dwarf,
The Sun's rays fill the room! "[97]

---

[97]*«Daylight hits you...»*: Thor has kept the conversation going until sunrise, and the dwarf turns to stone when the sun's rays hit him.

Baldr's Dreams
– *BALDRS DRAUMAR* –

This poem tells about Odin's investigation of the omens foretelling the death of his son Baldr. It is one of several examples of Odin consulting female oracles. In this case he has to awaken her from the dead.

The text is taken from Arnamagnean collection Codex 748[4to,] and the poem is composed in fornyrdislag.

1.
Later the aesir
all went to the Thing,
also the asynior,
and argued fervently;
the mighty gods
met to find out
why Baldr was haunted
by bad dreams.

2.
Odin got up,
the ancient god,
he fastened the saddle
on Sleipnir's back;
then he rode down
to the depths of Nivlhel,
a hound from Hel
headed towards him.

3.
Its breast was covered
in blood all over,
the father of spells   *Odin*
spun his magic;
Odin rode forth,
the earth resounded,
till he came to the home
of Hel, the mighty.

4.
Odin rode on
east of the door,
where he knew for certain
a sibyl rested;
he went to chant
over the wise lady's corpse,
she spoke as follows
when he forced her to rise:

5.
"Who is this man
– to me unknown –
who has made me take
such a troublesome road?
I lay snuggled in snow
and slapped by rain,
I was bedecked with dew,
I was dead a long time."

Odin said:
6.
"I call myself Vegtam,   *'Weary-of-Travel'*
I am Valtam's son;   *'Weary-of-Battle'*
give me news of the dead,
for I know about the living:

For whom are the benches
brightened with rings   *rings of gold*
and the seats garnished
with a golden stream?"

The sibyl said:
7.
"It is for Baldr
they have brewed this mead,
it is clear and pure
and covered by a shield;
worry weighs heavily
on the aesir's sons.
I've been forced to talk,
I will tell you no more."

Odin said:
8.
«Keep going, sibyl!
I seek to find out
the full knowledge,
nothing but the truth:
Who is it that will be
Baldr's killer
and steal the years
from Odin's son?"

The sibyl said:
9.
"Hod brings us the tall
tree of honour,   *kenning for Baldr*
and he will be   *he: Hod*
Baldr's killer

and steal the years
from Odin's son.
I've been forced to talk,
I will tell you no more."

Odin said:
10.
«Keep going, sibyl!
I seek to find out
the full knowledge,
nothing but the truth:
Who will avenge
Hod's ill deed
and bear to the bonfire
Baldr's enemy?"

The sibyl said:
11.
"Rind begets Vali   *Rind: an asynia, mistress of Odin*
in the Realm of the West,
he'll kill, one night old,
Odin's son, Hod;
he won't clean his fists
nor comb his hair,
till he bears to the bonfire
Baldr's enemy.
I've been forced to talk,
I will tell you no more."

Odin said:
12.
«Keep going, sibyl!
I seek to find out
the full knowledge,
nothing but the truth:

Who are the maidens
that will moan and weep
and toss their scarves
toward the heavens?"

The sibyl said:
13.
"You're not Vegtam,
as *I* have thought,rather you're Odin,
you age-old god!"
Odin said:
"And you're not a sibyl
nor a sage woman,
rather you're the mother
of three monstrous children!"[98]

*He implies that
she is Angrboda*

The sibyl said:
14.
"Ride home, Odin,
your honour has grown!May no one ever
wish to visit me
till Loki loosens
his limbs from bondage
and Ragnarok
rages ahead."

---

[98] «*...mother of three monstrous children!*»:   Angrboda, Loki's mistress. The three monsters are their offspring, namely: The World Serpent, the wolf Fenrir, and Hel.

The Story of Rig
– *RIGSÞULA* –

This poem tells how Heimdall, alias Rig, fathers the three social classes of society. Tripartition is a familiar motif in many Indo-European traditions. The Story of Rig has a unique suggestive power due to its many and unusual repetitions. Unfortunately, the end of the poem has been lost, though it is however evident that Kin Young ("King") is destined for both a priestly and a royal function.
The metre is fornyrdislag.

In ancient sagas men tell that one of the aesir, whose name was Heimdall, once, as he was travelling, passed along the sea-shore. He came to a farm where he called himself Rig. From that story this poem was made:

1.
It is said he walked
across open fields,
the skillful god,
he was great and strong,
Rig approached,
powerful and swift.

2.
He made his way
in the middle of the road,
the door was closed
as he came to the house;
the fire was lit
as he let himself in;

a couple was hovering,
hoary, by the fire,
Aï and Edda,   *Great-grandpa and Great-grandma*
who were old and grey.

3.
Rig knew how
to hand them advice;
in the middle of the bench
he bent to sit down,
the man and the woman
on either side.

4.
Great-grandma brought   *Edda*
bread to the table,
the loaf was heavy
and laden with groats;
on a large plate
she placed the bread,
there was soup in the bowl
which she set on the table,
[it was boiled veal,
the best of tidbits.]⁹⁹

5.
Rig knew how
to hand them advice;
he arose from the table
and got ready for bed,

---

[99] *[it was boiled veal, the best of tidbits.]*: Unlikely food for such poor people.

he lay down on the mat
in the middle of the bunk,
the man and the woman
on either side.

6.
He stayed on through
three whole nights,
then he kept on marching
down the middle of the road;
then nine months went
after he left.

7.
Then Edda had a child,
they poured water over him;
- - - -   *missing lines*
his skin was black,
a boy called Thrall.

8.
He started to grow,
greatly thriving,
his hands were covered
with coarse skin,
his knuckles bony,
- - - -   *missing line*
his fingers huge,
his face was ugly,
he stooped when he walked
on his stubby legs.

9.
He didn't stop growing,
he gained in strength:
he carried burdens,
he bound ropes,
he hauled twigs back
each bitter day.

10.
She came to the farm
her feet were bare,
her heels were soiled,
sun-burned her arms,
her nose was flat:
she named herself Maid.

11.
Then Maid sat down
in the middle of the bench,
beside her sat
the son of the house;
they talked and had fun,
they tumbled into bed,
Thrall and Maid
had much to do.

12.
They bred children
— they built and loved —
I think these were called
Cryer and Stable-boy,
Coarse and Hairy,
Clinging, Soiler,
Churl and Dumpy,
Drab and Tubby,

Bent and Long-legs;
they laid out fences,
manured the fields
and fed the swine,
herded the goats
and heaved up turf.

13.
Their daughters were
Dumpy and Clumsy,
one was called Ham-calved,
others were: Hook-nose
and Chatterbox,
Bawler and Helper,
Clad-in-Tatters
and Crane-legs too;
from these came forth
the families of thralls.

14.
On the beaten track
Rig trampled along,
the door was not closed
as he came to a home,
and the fire was lit
as he let himself in,
a couple was at home,
their hands were busy.

15.
The man was carving
a cross-beam out of wood,
his hair cut with bangs,
his beard was trimmed,
his shirt was well-fitted,
on the floor stood a chest.

16.
There sat the woman,
she was whirling her distaff
and measuring wool
for weaving cloth;
a headdress on her braids,
on her bosom she wore a smock,
a kerchief around the neck,
a clasp at each shoulder;
Avi and Amma,   *Grandpa and Grandma*
they owned the hall.

17.
Rig knew how
to hand them advice;
in the middle of the bench
he bent to sit down,
- - - -   *missing lines*

18.
Then Amma took
- - - -   *missing lines*

19.
- - - -   *missing lines*
- - - -   *missing lines*
he arose from the table
and got ready for bed,
he lay down on the mat
in the middle of the bunk,
the man and the woman
on either side.

20.
He stayed on through
three whole nights,
then he kept on marching
down the middle of the road;
then nine months went
after he left.

21.
Then Amma had a child,
they poured water over him,
they called him Carl,
in cloth she swaddled him;
red-headed, bouncing,
bright were his eyes.

22.
He started to grow,
greatly thriving,
he mastered oxen,
and made ploughshares,
he raised barns,
he built houses,
he made trolleys
and tilled the soil.

23.
They brought a bride
back again to Carl,
she carried keys   *meaning she was head of the household*
and a cloak of goatskin,
She was called Snor,   *daughter-in-law*
she sat beneath the veil;   *she got married*

the couple settled
and swapped rings,
they spread the sheets
and shared a home.

24.
They bred children,
– they built and loved –
Fellow and Youth,
Owner, Dean and Smith,
also Beard-in-braids,
Broad and Farmer,
Yeoman, Brother,
Big-Guy and Short-beard.

25.
And other names
were also given:
Quick, Bride, Rapid,
Beauty, Noble,
Lively, Spunky, Enshrouded,
Shy and Furrow;
from them the families
of farmers have come.

26.
On the beaten track
Rig trampled along,
he got to a hall,
the gates faced southward,
the door was open,
adorned by a ring.

27.
He strode on in,
straw was on the floor,
a couple was seated,
courting each other,
Father and Mother,
they were full of joy.

28.
The husband took to
twisting a bow-string,
the bow was tightened,
he attached the arrowheads;
the lady of the house
looked down her arms,
stroked her dress,
and straightened her sleeves.

29.
With a broach on her bosom
her bonnet was mounted,
her gown was long,
her garment blue;
her brows were brighter
and breast paler,
her neck was fairer
than sifted flour.

30.
Rig knew how
to hand them advice;
in the middle of the bench
he bent to sit down,
the man and the woman
on either side.

31.
Then Mother took
a table-cloth, embroidered,
white and of linen,
and laid it on the table;
she brought thin loaves
of bread to the table,
of wheat, white and pure,
and placed them on the cloth.

32.
Then in she brought
bowls, overflowing
and trimmed with silver,
- - - -   on the table,   *missing half-line*
tidbits and bacon,
and braised fowl;
wine was in the pitcher,
they had precious cups;
till the day was done
they drank and talked.

33.
Rig knew how
to hand them advice;
he arose from the table
and got ready for bed,
he stayed on through
three whole nights;
then he kept on marching
down the middle of the road,
then nine months went
after he left.

34.
Then Mother had a son,
in silk she dressed him,
they poured water over him,
Earl he was called;
his hair was blond,
beautiful were his cheeks,
his eyes were piercing
like poisonous snakes.

35.
There he grew up,
Earl, in that place,
he learnt to twist strings
and strike the shields,
he bent elm-bows,
and arrows he hafted,
he learnt to fling spears
and flourish halberds,
to fight with swords,
and swim across straits,
he rode horses
and hounds he trained.

36. Out of the thicket
Rig came walking,
Rig came walking,
he taught the runes;
he told who he was
and that he owned the son;   *the son = Earl*
he urged him to acquire
open freeholds,
open freeholds,
and ancient burrows.

37.
He rode ahead   *Earl*
through rough woodlands,
over icy mountains
till he made it to a hall;
his spear began shaking,
the shield quivered,
the horse leapt to,
he heaved up his sword;
then he waged war,
the wide field reddened,
the warriors fell
as he won the land.

38.
Eighteen ranches
he ruled alone,
he shared his wealth
among all his folk,
– gifts and gold
and grand mares –
he shed riches
and rent his arm-ring.[100]

39.
Messengers travelled
along moist pathways,
they came to the hall
where Hersir resided;   *'Leader'*
he had a daughter
– her hands were soft –
fair-skinned and wise,
Erna was her name.   *'Eagle'*

---

[100] «*...and rent his arm-ring*: Arm-rings of gold were used as money. One would cut off a part of the arm-ring to pay for services rendered or for merchandise. Each piece of an arm-ring would be weighed and valued.

40.
Then they proposed   *they: his deputies*
and parted for home;
she was married to Earl,
she went under the veil;   *part of the marital rites*
they lived together,
loving each other,
their family flourished,
they found happiness.

41.
Born was the eldest,
and Baby came next,
Given and Able,
then Heir and Boy,
Kith and Kinsman
came to practice
– Son and Youth also –
swimming and board-games,
one was called High-Born,
the youngest was Kin.

42.
There they grew up,
Earl's many children,
they managed horses
and they made shields,
they whittled shafts
and they shook spears.

43.
Now Kin Young[101]
knew his runs,
runes everlasting,
the runes of life;
besides, he knew
how to save his men,
to blunt the swords, *the swords of his enemies*
and to soothe the waves.

44.
He knew bird-talk,
abated fires,
lightened sorrows
and soothed the waves;
he had eight men's
might and power.

45.
He wrestled with Earl Rig
in rune-knowledge,
he held him at bay
with his better grasp;
he gained in wisdom
and got the right
to be named Rig *Ruler, King*
and rune-master.

46.
Then Kin Young rode
through rough woodlands,
he shot his bolts
so the birds fell silent. *meaning he hunted birds*

---

[101] *Kin young:* 'Kin young' contracts as king. In ON 'Kon ungr' contracts as konungr, meaning king.

47.
Then a lone crow said,
sitting on a branch:
"Why is it, Kin Young,
that you kill the birds?
Rather you ought to
ride your horses,
- - - -   *missing line*
and wreck armies!

48.
"Dan and Danp own   *legendary kings of the Danes*
wondrous strongholds,
you, sir, have got
no greater treasures;
they know rightly
how to ride the waves,
to use the sword
and wound their foes."

The Song of Hyndla
– HYNDLULJÓÐ –

One motif in Nordic lore was obtaining wisdom by raising someone from her grave. In this poem the goddess Freyia awakens the sibyl Hyndla, and calls her 'Sister'. Freyia has brought along her lover, Ottar, whom she has changed into a wild boar, and she is riding on him when she goes to meet Hyndla.
Stanzas 29 – 35 are traditionally called The Short Sibyl's Prophecy. *This poem is preserved in* Flateyjarbók. *Fornyrdislag is the metre.*

Freyia said:
1.
"Maiden of maidens,
my mate wake up!
Hyndla, my sister,
whose home is in a cave;
in the dusk of dusks
we shall dash away
to high Valhall
and to the holy shrine.

2.
"Let us ask Warfather[102]   *Odin*
to welcome us,
the one who gives
gold to his darlings;

---

[102] *Warfather:*   We have translated *Heriafather* ('Father of the Army') to *Warfather*.

he gave Hermod *son of Odin*
a helmet and mail-coat,
and to Sigmund *son of Odin*
a sword was given.

3.
"Some gain wealth,
others get victory,
some get glib speech
and gain in man-wit;
he fills the sails,
gives songs to bards
and manliness
to many a warrior.

4.
"She'll bring offerings to Thor, *Freyia speaks about herself*
she must ask of him this,
that he always will act
well toward you –
yet to Valhall he rarely
invites the giants.

5.
"Now bring out one
of your wolves from the stable,
and let him run
along with my boar."
Hyndla said:
"Your hog's too slow
on the highway to the gods,
I don't want my horse *her wolf*
so heavily burdened.

6.
"Freyia, you lie
since you lead me on thus,
casting your eyes
in our direction;
you've brought your lover
along to Valhall,
that young Ottar,
Innstein's son!

Freyia said:
7.
"You're thick, Hyndla,
you have to be dreaming
if you think that my love
has come along to Valhall;
it's my golden hog,
this is Gullinbusti,
the battle-swine,
brought to me
by the skillful dwarfs
Dainn and Nabbi.

8.
"We'll get out of the saddle,
let us sit on the ground!
We'll reflect upon
the families
of the princely studs
who stem from the gods.

9.
"They have made a wager
in ore from Valland,   *gold from western France*
Ottar the young
and Angantyr;

for the young warrior
my aid is needed,
so he could get the legacy
left him by his kin.

10.
"He laid out altars
loaded with stones[103],   *marble; ON 'griot' = 'stone,*
this marble has now
melted into glass;
he colored the altars
with cattle's blood,
the asynior were always
the ones Ottar trusted.

11.
"Let the ancient
lineages then
be brought to mind,
man's ancestry:
Who are the Skioldungs,
who are the Skilvings,
who are the Audlings,
who are the Ylvings,
who are the yeoman-born,
who are the highborn;
the choicest of men
in Midgard's realm?"

Hyndla said: *Hyndla is speaking to Ottar*
12.
"To Innstein, Ottar,
you were born,
and to Alf the Old
Innstein was born,

---

[103] *Loaded with stones:*   An ancient custom of building outdoor altars.

he was Ulf's son,
Ulf was son of Sævari,
and Sævari was son
of Swan the Red.

13.
"Your father's mother
had many jewels,
people called her
the priestess of Hledis; *Hledis = Freyia*
Frodi was her father
and Friund her mother;
this whole line
belonged to the best.

14.
"In days of old
Ali was the strongest,
the highest of the Skioldungs,
and Halfdan came next;
the battles were famous
that were fought by this hero, *Ali*
throughout the world
his work was renowned.

15.
"He fought Eymund,
the finest of men,
and he killed Sigtrygg
with cold iron,
he married Almveig,
of women the choicest,
and eighteen boys
were born to them.

16.
"Hence the Skioldungs
hence the Skilvings,
hence the Audlings,
hence the Ynglings,
hence the yeoman-born,
hence the highborn,
– the best of men
in Midgard's realm –
all are your family,
Ottar Homebody!

17.
"Then Hildigunn
got Almveig,
she was daughter of Svava
and a sea king;
all are your family,
Ottar Homebody.
Do you want to go on?
It is well that you know this!

18.
"Thora, Dag's wife,
had wiry sons,
in that family were born
the best of warriors:
Fradmar and Gyrd
and Frekar twice,
Am and Iosumar,
Alf the grey one.
Do you want to go on?
It is well that you know this!

19.
"Ketil was their friend,
he was Klypp's heir,
he was the mother's father
of your mother as well;
then came Frodi
– before Kari –
Alf was the eldest
off-spring he had.

20.
"Nanna was next,
Nokkva's daughter,
her son was married
to the sister of your father;
these forebears were forgotten,
further I will tell you:
I knew them both,
Brodd and Horvir;
all are your family,
Ottar Homebody.

21.
"Isolf and Asolf,
Olmod's sons
and Skurhild's,
Skekkil's daughter,
– here you must add
warriors aplenty –
all are your family,
Ottar Homebody.

22.
"Gunnar the Beam,
Grim the Ploughshare,
Thor Iron-shield,
Ulf the Gaper,

23.
"[Hervard, Hiorvard,
Hrani, Angantyr],   *inserted from another manuscript*
Bui and Brami,
Barri and Reivnir,
Tind and Tyrving,
and twice Hadding;
all are your family,
Ottar Homebody.

24.
"Ani and Omi
entered next,
sons to Arngrim
and Eyfura;
the berserks raged,
ravaging where they came,
the land and sea
they saddled with flames;
all are your family,
Ottar Homebody.

25.
"I knew them both,
Brodd and Horvir,
they were in the army
with the age-old Hrolf;
they all descended
from Iormunrek,
in-laws of Sigurd
– my saga tells you –
that fierce folk,
Favnir's destroyers.

26.
"He was the valiant,
from Volsung descended,
and Hiordis
from Hraudung,
and Eylimi
from the Audlings;   *a family line*
all are your family,
Ottar Homebody.

27.
"Gunnar and Hogni,
were Giuki's heirs,
and Gudrun also
was their sister;
Guthorm was not
of Giuki's kin,
though he was brother
to both of them;
all are your family,
Ottar Homebody.

28.
"Harold Battle-tusk   *'Harald Hilditann'*
was Hrorek's son,
the ring-slinger[104],
who was son of Aud,
– Aud the Deep-minded –
Ivar's daughter,   *Ivar Vidfarnir, 't he widely travelled'*
and Radbard was
Randver's father;

---

[104] *Ring-slinger:* Harald Hilditann was a great hero from the legendary past. When it is said that he was a ring-slinger, it means he was extremely generous to his men, giving them golden armrings.

these valiant men
were devoted to the gods;
all are your family,
Ottar Homebody.

29.
"The aesir were eleven
in all when counted,
as Baldr was put
upon his death-bed;
to wreak vengeance
Vali was born,
and to avenge his brother
he beat Hod to death.
All are your family,
Ottar Homebody.

30.
"Baldr's father
was Bur's heir,
Freyr married Gerd,
Gymi's daughter
– of the iotun clan –
and Aurboda's;
and the old Thiatzi
was their kinsman,
the wanton giant,
his heiress was Skadi.

31.
"Much we tell you,
and more we will tell.
Do you want to go on?
It is well that you know this!

32.
"Haki was the best
of Hvedna's sons,
and Hiorvard was
Hvedna's father;
Heid and Hrossthiov
were Hrimnir's children.

33.
"All the sibyls
descend from Vidolv,
and all the sorcerers
descend from Vilmeid,
those stiff with magic
stem from Svarthovdi,
and all the iotuns
are Ymir's family.

34.
"Much we tell you,
and more we will tell.
Do you want to go on?
It is well that you know this!

35.
"One was born then   *Heimdall*
in the early days,
this child of the gods
was given great powers;
nine bore him
– they nailed magic to him[105] –
iotun maidens,
at the edge of the earth.

---

[105] «*...they nailed magic to him...*»: It was a custom to nail metal studs into statues and statuettes to give them magical powers.

36.
"Much we tell you,
and more we will tell.
Do you want to go on?
It is well that you know this!

37.
"Giolp bore him,   *Heimdall's nine mothers, see Index*
Greip bore him,
also Eistla
and Eyrgiava,
Ulvrun bore him,
and Angeyia,
Imd and Atla
and Iarnsaxa.

38.
"Strong he was made
by the might of the earth,
by the cold ocean
and the offering of blood.   *blood of a boar*

39. "Much we tell you,
and more we will tell.
Do you want to go on?
It is well that you know this!

40.
"Loki got a wolf
with Angrboda,
and he had Sleipnir
with Svadilfari;

and yet another
evil creature   *the World Serpent*
was born to the brother
of Byleist before this.   *Loki is brother to Byleist*

41.
"Once Loki found
a woman's heart[106],
half-way fried
on a fire of linden-wood;
by this wicked woman
he waxed with child,
he became the mother
to all monsters on earth.

42.
"In rage the seas
rose to the sky,
flooded the earth,
the air gave way,
hence came the snows
and howling winds
till fate ordered
the fall of the gods.

43.
"One was born,
better than the rest,
he was made strong
by the might of the earth;

he is the richest

---

[106] *a woman's heart:*   The original has *'hugstein'* for heart. *'Steinn'* means stone; and *'Hugr'* indicates an essential human drive, an interest arising from the heart rather than from the mind. The shape of the heart is perceived as that of a stone.

among rulers, they say,
he was related
to the leading families.

44.
"Then another will come,
even more powerful,
I don't have the courage
to call out his name.
There are few who can see
further ahead
than to the moment when Odin
meets the scavenger."   *the wolf Fenrir*

Freyia said:
45.
"Bring in the memory-mead
to this man who's my guest,
and make him able
to remember fully
on the third morning
this mighty tale,
and to reckon the lineages
when he lines up with Angantyr!"

Hyndla said:
46.
"Get away from here!
I wish to sleep,
there's not much good
you may get from me,
you roaming bitch,
you run each night,
like Heidrun tumbles
and tosses with billy-goats!

47.
"You ran to Od,
always lusting,
many have skirmished
up your skirts and frocks;
you roaming bitch,
you run each night
like Heidrun tumbles
and tosses with billy-goats!"

Freyia said:
48.
"At you, hag,
I will hurl fire,
so you won't be able
to get away from here."
- - - -   *missing lines*
- - - -   *missing lines*

Hyndla said:
49.
"I see flames grow
from the ground on up,
we all must face
that our forces dwindle;
bring to Ottar
some beer to drink –
and blend it with poison
for bad fortune,
you roaming bitch,
you run each night
like Heidrun tumbles
and tosses with billy-goats!"

Freyia said:
50.
"These good words
won't ever harm him,
even though, iotun,
you wield your damage;
he shall drink
the deerest mead,
I bid the gods
to guard Ottar!"

The Song of Grotti
– *GROTTASǪNGR* –

This poem tells of two iotun women, the sisters Fenia and Menia, who had somehow been captured in Sweden and then bought by the Danish king Frodi. He forced them to work at a mill, which they had produced themselves and brought with them into the human realm. However, his greed allows them no rest or respite, which results in them debating whether they should continue to grind health and happiness for Frodi or death and disaster instead.

The Song of Grotti *is found in a manuscript of Snorri's Edda, and as an epic poem its metre is fornyrdislag.*

Skiold was the son of Odin, and from him came all the Skioldungs. He dwelt in and ruled the land which is now called Denmark but which was then called Gotland. Skiold had a son whose name was Fridleif and who ruled the country after him. The son of Fridleif was Frodi. He ruled the kingdom after his father at that time when Augustus Cæsar made peace in all the world. Then Christ was born. And because Frodi was the mightiest king in the North, this peace was known under his name by all who spoke the Danish language, and the Norwegians called it Frodi's Peace. No man harmed another even if he met the murderer of his father or brother walking freely or in chains. During that period there were neither thieves nor robbers, so that a golden ring could be left out in the open at Ialang Heath for a long time. King Frodi was invited by king Fiolnir to a celebration in Sweden. There he bought two female servants who were called Fenia and Menia. They were big and strong. In Denmark at that time there were two millstones so huge, that no man was able to turn them. And the nature of these millstones was such that they could grind whatever you wished for. The mill was called Grotti. They say it was Hengikiopt[107] who had given the mill to king Frodi.

King Frodi let his two servants be brought to the mill, and ordered them to grind gold and peace and happiness for him. But he did not let them rest longer than the cuckoo stayed silent or it took to sing a song. It is told that they then sang a song which is called "The Grottasong". Before the song had ended, they had ground an army against Frodi, and in that night the sea-king Mysing came and killed Frodi and took a large booty as well. That was the end of Frodi's Peace.

Mysing carried away with him the mill Grotti, and Fenia and Menia too. He bade them grind white salt, and at midnight they asked if Mysing now didn't have enough. He told them to keep on grinding. They continued to grind a while longer until they had sunk the ship.

There is now an undertow at that spot, where the water rushes into the eye of the millstone.[108] That is why the sea is salt.

1.
Now there have come
to the king's house
two women of foresight,
Fenia and Menia;
they're kept as servants
with the son of Fridleif
– these fearless girls –
with Frodi the king.

---

[107] *Hengikiopt:* 'Hang-Jaw', maybe a name for Odin.
[108] *There is now an undertow...:* Two such maelstroms exist in the north of Norway. "Saltstraumen" is the most powerful maelstrom in the world. The name translates into "the Salty Stream". "Mokstraumen" is the most famous maelstrom and the second largest in the world; it lies in Lofoten in northern Norway.

2.
They were brought to the mill,
both of them,
and told to grind
with the grey stones;
he never allowed them
to leave their work
until he heard
their harsh complaints.

3.
They began to grind,
the grey stones shrieking.
Fenia said:
"Let us put down the log   *the mill's handle*
and let the mill rest!"
Still he told them
to continue grinding.

4.
They sang and swayed
while swinging the stone,
till most of Frodi's
maids fell asleep;
then said Menia,
still minding her work:

5.
"We'll grind gold,
we'll grind happiness
and wealth for Frodi
at the wishing-mill;
may he ride on gold,
may he rest on down,
may he wake up happy!
Then it's well ground!

6.
"Here shall no one
harm another,
nor damages devise,
nor death prepare;
nor kill the culprit
with the cutting sword,
though you see your brother's
banesman in chains."

7.
Frodi held his tongue
until he said:
"You'll stay calm no longer
than the cuckoo on the rooftop,
nor the time it takes me
to twitter a song!"

Fenia said:
8.
"Frodi, your thinking
was faulty enough,
you slick-talking man,
when you made us your servants;
you judged us by our power
and apparent skills,
but forgot to figure
on our family and clan.

9.
"Hrungnir was just as
hard as his father,
and Thiatzi was even
worse than them;

Idi and Aurnir
are our relations,
these iotun brothers
are both our fathers.

10.
"Grotti just couldn't
have come out of rock,
nor the base-stone
be brought from the earth,
nor could we girls
be grinding flour
without us knowing
the workings of the mill.

11.
"For nine long winters
we went on playing,
beneath the ground
we gained in strength;
we maidens took on
a mighty task:
we pushed the boulder
from its place ourselves.

12.
"We rolled the rock
from the realm of the giants,
the ground beneath
began to tremble;
the two of us hurled
the heavy boulder
– the spinning slab –
so someone could catch it.

13.
"We two, later,
over in Sweden,
busted the army
– wise and prescient –
we cut up mails,
we crushed shields,
we went against
the grey-clad people[109].

14.
"We brought down a prince,
we supported another,
and we gave aid
to Guthorm's men;
there was no calm
until Knui fell.

15.
"We kept on going
for a good while
until fighting made us
famous among warriors;
we cut them open
with the edge of our swords,
blood from their wounds
made our weapons red.

16.
"Now we are here
in the hall of the king,
shown no mercy
we're made to be slaves;

---

[109] «*...the grey-clad people. ...*»: Possibly the 'Ulfhednir', the warriors who took on the shape of wolves during battle.

our heels are chafed,
and we're chilled from above,
we're at the old grind,
it's gruesome at Frodi's.

17.
"Let the mill halt
and the hands rest,
I've done my share
of dour grinding!"
Menia, said:
"We shan't stop grinding
to get some rest,
till Frodi tells us
our task is through!"

The first sister, Fenia, said:
18.
"Our hands shall hold
hard weapons
all wet with blood.
Wake up, Frodi!
Wake up, Frodi,
if you want to hear
the sound of our songs
and sagas of old!

19.
"I see flames
East of the hall,
tidings of war,
a warning call;
like an avalanche
an army is coming,

it will burn to ashes
the Budling's farm.   *Frodi belongs to the clan of Budlings*

20.
"The throne at Leire   *the ancient seat of the Danish kings*
will be lost to you,
and the red gold
and the gods' mill;
take a firm hold
of the handle, sister!
The blood of the warriors
hasn't warmed us yet!

21.
"My father's girl   *She talks of herself in the third person*
ground powerfully,
she saw men who fell,
many were slain;
chunks were broken
from the base of the mill,
the iron hoops gave –
let's go on working!"

Menia said:
22.
"Let's keep at it,
so that Yrsa's son
may bring Frodi down
for the death of Halfdan;
he is, they'll say,
her son and brother –
it's bound to happen
as both of us know."

23.
The girls worked on
using their strength,
the young ones were
in the iotun mood;
the shafts were rattling,
rending the beam,
the splendid stone
was split in two.

24.
Then they spoke,
and this they uttered:
"We were made to grind
at the mill, Frodi,
and we have borne it
till the bitter end!"

The Spells of Groa
– GRÓGALDR –

Svipdag wakes his deceased mother Groa to seek her advice in his difficulties. His stepmother has ordered him to go and see the goddess Freyia, but for the meeting to take place he needs to make a journey into unknown worlds and dimensions. This seems now to be his unavoidable fate, which is why he goes to the grave of his mother, the shamaness Groa, in order to procure her help.

This poem is taken from a paper manuscript from the latter part of the 17th century. For this reason it is not included in most translations of the Eddic poems. We have chosen to include it, because we find its content valuable. The metre is liodahatt.

Svipdag said:
1.
"Wake up, Groa,
wake up, good woman!
I wake you at the doors of the dead!
Do you recall,
I could come if I needed
to your burial mound to meet you."

Groa said:
2.
"My only son,
what ails you now,
how is it that you have been harmed,
since you appeal to your mother
who's been put to rest
and has left the realm of the living?"

Svipdag said:
3.
"A foul hand she dealt,
the fiendish woman,   *Svipdag's stepmother*
the bride who embraces my father;
she told me to leave
for a land unknown,
and there to meet with Menglod."   *Freyia,*

Groa said:
4.
"Far is the journey
and further the trails
– far roam the minds of men –
if so it be
that you obey your wish,
you'll fulfill your debt to destiny."

Svipdag:
5.
"Sing chants for me
that will make my passage!
Mother, save your son!
I fear these roads
may render me dead,
I'm just too young for this journey."

Groa:
6.
"The first one I chant
– which is foremost of help –
that Rani[110] sang to Rind,   *Rind, an asynia*
so you may shake from your shoulders
the shackles that bind you,
yourself shall govern yourself.

---

[110] *Rani:*   ON: Hrani, an Odin-alias.

7.
"The next one I sing
if you're in need of help
and aimless on endless roads,
may the charms of Urd[111]
always guard you,
if you're stranded in dire straits.

8.
"I sing you the third,
if threatening rivers
swell to swallow you,
let them hurry toward Hel
– Horn and Rudr – *mythological rivers*
may they always shrink from you.

9.
"I sing you the fourth
if foes approach you
ready with a rope for your neck,
their minds will turn
attuned to you,
their souls will be set at peace.

10.
"I sing you the fifth,
if they swaddle you in chains
and fetter you hand and foot,
I'll chant for your legs
a loosening-spell,
so the lock springs from the latch
and your feet become unfettered.

---

[111] *Urd:*   Goddess of fate, one of the three norns.

11.
"I sing you the sixth,
if the sea rises
higher than men can imagine,
the wind will join
with the waves to let you
always pass in peace.

12.
"I sing you the seventh,
if you're sought by frost
in the high and hoary mountains,
the deadly cold
won't claim your body,
you will stay safe and sound.

13.
"I sing you the eighth
if sundown gets you
on far and foggy roads,
you'll still be safe
should you see the corpse
of a Christian woman walking.

14.
"I sing you the ninth
if you need to argue
with a war-seasoned iotun,
you'll find that you have
in your heart and mind
wit and words to beat him.

15.
"Never dally
where danger lurks,
may peril be kept from your path!
On a sturdy rock[112]
I stood, indoors,
chanting these charms for you.

16.
"What your mother says,
son, you must heed,
bury it in your bosom!
Health and riches
you shall have, always,
if you remember these words of mine."

---

[112] *On sturdy rock...:* It was a custom to stand on a stone or rock solidly embedded in the ground, for a person when performing magic.

The Tale of Fiolsvinn
– *FJǪLSVINNSMÁL* –

The Tale of Fiolsvinn *is a continuation of* The Song of Groa. *The poem tells of the battle of wits between Svipdag, Groa's son, and Freyia's guardsman, Fiolsvinn. Like* The Song of Groa, *this poem is taken from a paper manuscript from the latter part of the 17th century, and for this reason it is not included in most translations of the Eddic poems. Its metre is liodahatt.*

1.
Out on the road,
while riding, he saw
the realm of the giants arise.
Svipdag said:
"What sort of rogue
do I see in the yard,
flittering around the flames?"

Fiolsvinn said:
2.
"Where are you going,
what are you searching,
loser, what is it you want?
Get lost, loner,
leave and vanish,
there is no home for you here!"

Svipdag said:
3.
"What sort of vermin
do I see in the yard,
who doesn't welcome wayfarers?

All your life
you've lived without manners,
get yourself gone from here!"

Fiolsvinn said:
4.
"They call me Fiolsvinn,
I'm clever and mindful,
I don't freely share my food!
You shall never enter
within this courtyard,
be off with you, stray like a wolf!"

Svipdag said:
5.
"What I long for
are lovely visions,
that easily catch the eye;
these halls are a-glow
with golden roof-tops;
here is my heart's delight."

Fiolsvinn said:
6.
"Tell me, young man,
who your mother is,
and where your father is from?"
Svipdag said:
"Wind-Cold I'm called,
Spring-Cold was my father,
whose father, again, was Full-Cold.

7.
"I ask you, Fiolsvinn,
for I wish to know,
if only you will tell:
Who owns this realm
and rules these lands,
its territories and treasures?"

Fiolsvinn said:
8.
"Menglod she's called, = *Freyia, "she who loves jewelry"*
her mother got her
by the son of Svavrthorin;
she owns this realm
and rules these lands,
its territories and treasures."

Svipdag said:
9.
"I ask you, Fiolsvinn,
for I wish to know,
if only you will tell:
What's the name of this gate?
Never a man saw
a more awesome gate in Asgard!"

Fiolsvinn said:
10.
"It is called Thrymgioll,
three men built it,
the sons of Solblindi;
way-farers are fettered
and fastened tightly,
if they begin to open this gate."

Svipdag said:
11.
"I ask you, Fiolsvinn,
for I wish to know,
if only you will tell:
The name of the wall
that worries one more
than any you'll see with the aesir?"

Fiolsvinn said:
12. "It's called Gastropnir,   *"the one which strangles guests"*
I crafted it
from the limbs of Leirbrimi;   *a giant*
I've made it so strong
it will stand erect
as long as the world shall last."

Svipdag said:
13.
"I ask you, Fiolsvinn,
for I wish to know,
if only you will tell:
What's the name of these dogs?
Nowhere have I seen
hounds so fierce and fiendish!"

Fiolsvinn said:
14.
"One is called Givr
and Gevir the other,
since you need to know;
they guard the eleven
great women   *perhaps all the asynior*
until the aesir go under."

Svipdag said:
15.
"I ask you, Fiolsvinn,
for I wish to know,
if only you will tell:
Can any man
enter the hall
while the watch-dogs sleep?"

Fiolsvinn said:
16.
"An uneasy rest
is all they know,
they're born and bred to be watch-dogs;
one sleeps by night
and the other by day,
not one is allowed to enter."

Svipdag said:
17.
"I ask you, Fiolsvinn,
for I wish to know,
if only you will tell:
What kind of grub
can I give these dogs
so I may enter while they eat?"

Fiolsvinn said:
18.
"Two wings lie
in the lap of Vidovnir,   *see st. 24*
if you want to know;
it's the only grub
a guy should bring
so he may enter while they eat."

279

Svipdag said:
19.
"I ask you, Fiolsvinn,
for I wish to know,
if you only will tell:
What's the name of the tree
that neatly covers
all the lands with its limbs?"

Fiolsvinn said:
20.
"Mimameid's the name,   *'Mim's tree'*
it's known by few
from where its roots arise;
not many know
what can knock it down,
neither fire nor iron can fell it."

Svipdag said:
21.
"I ask you, Fiolsvinn,
for I wish to know,
if only you will tell:
What happens to the fruit
of this forceful tree,
as neither fire nor iron can fell it?"

Fiolsvinn said:
22.
"You must place the fruit
on the fire if you wish
to aid a woman in labour,
to bring that out
which is within;
this is what's meant for man."   *mankind*

Svipdag said:
23.
"I ask you, Fiolsvinn,
for I wish to know,
if only you will tell:
What's the name of the cock
which crows in that tree
and is all a-glow and golden?"

Fiolsvinn said:
24.
"Vidovnir he's called,
he crouches weatherbeaten
on Mimameid's branches;
he brings on worry
endlessly
to Surt and Sinmara."   *fire-demon and his consort*

Svipdag said:
25.
"I ask you, Fiolsvinn,
for I wish to know,
if only you will tell:
Is there a weapon given
that can get Vidovnir
to sink to the seat of Hel?"

Fiolsvinn said:
26.
"Lopt has made
a Limb-of-Harm   *a spear, arrow or club*
behind the gates of Hel;
Sinmara keeps it
in a casket of iron,
laden with nine locks."

Svipdag said:
27.
"I ask you, Fiolsvinn,
for I wish to know,
if only you will tell:
What does it take
to return safely,
after you've fetched the weapon?"

Fiolsvinn said:
28.
"A guy may return
who has gone out
to steal the harmful stick
– which few men own –
if when he fetches it
he gives it to the golden goddess." *Freyia*

Svipdag said:
29.
"I ask you, Fiolsvinn,
for I wish to know,
if only you will tell:
What would be fitting
for a fellow to bring
that could please the pale iotun?" *Sinmara*

Fiolsvinn said:
30.
"Take the shining scythe
in its sheath of wood,
which is kept in Vidovnir's casket,
give this to Sinmara,
and she will grant you readily
the stick of harm instead."

Svipdag said:
31.
"I ask you, Fiolsvinn,
for I wish to know,
if only you will tell:
What's the hall called
which is covered all over
in magical flickering flames?"

Fiolsvinn said:
32.
"Hyrr is its name,
it will hover a long time,
trembling on the tips of spears;
throughout the ages
only rumors
were heard of this treasure-trove."

Svipdag said:
33.
"I ask you, Fiolsvinn,
for I wish to know,
if only you will tell:
Who[113] has made
those marvelous things
within your yard, guardsman?"

---

[113] «*Who has created...*»: The ON text gives «Which sons of the gods have created...». In stanza 34 are listed the names of several dwarfs as an answer. The originator of this poem apparently presupposes that the listener/ reader knows that the gods created the dwarfs. Cfr. Voluspa, stanza 9.

Fiolsvinn said:
34.
"Uni and Iri,
Ori and Bari,
Varr and Vegdrasill;
Dori and Uri,
Delling, Atvard,
[Lidskialf, Loki.][114]"

Svipdag said:
35.
"I ask you, Fiolsvinn,
for I wish to know,
if only you will tell:
Which is that mountain *Freyia*
where the much-cherished woman
keeps her hearth and home?"

Fiolsvinn said:
36.
"It is called Lyviaberg, *a place of healing, a mountain*
and has long been
the solace of the sick and wounded;
each woman is cured
who climbs that hill
when burdened with barrenness."

Svipdag said:
37.
"I ask you, Fiolsvinn,
for I wish to know,
if only you will tell:

---

[114] *[Lidskialf, Loki]:*   this line is evidently an erroneous insertion.

What do you call the maidens
at Menglod's knees,
who sit in glad agreement?"

Fiolsvinn said:
38.
"One is Hliv,
another Hlivthursa,
the third is Thiodvarta,
Biort and Blid,
Blidr, Frid,
Eir and Aurboda."

female mythological beings:
'Protection',
'Protection-giantess'
'Lady-in-waiting'
'Light' and 'Merry'
'Merry-maker', 'Delight'
'Mercy'; 'Loam-bringer'

Svipdag said:
39.
"I ask you, Fiolsvinn,
for I wish to know,
if only you will tell:
Will they save the ones
who bring offerings to them
if real need should ever arise?"

Fiolsvinn said:
40.
"They save the ones
who serve them with
offerings at the altar;
no danger is so mighty
that they may not sweep away
all woes from their worshippers."

Svipdag said:
41.
"I ask you, Fiolsvinn,
for I wish to know,
if only you will tell:
Has any fellow
found a way
into Menglod's arms?"

Fiolsvinn said:
42.
"Not one fellow
has found a way
into Menglod's arms,
except for Svipdag
whom the sunbright maiden
was spoken for as his spouse."

Svipdag said:
43.
"Rap on the door
give room at the gate,
here you see him: Svipdag!
Few know yet
whether Menglod
will join me in blissful joy."

Fiolsvinn said:
44.
"Listen, Menglod,
a man has come,
go and greet your guest;
the hounds hail him,
the house opens up,
I'm certain it is Svipdag."

Menglod said:
45.
"Clever ravens
shall rip your eyes out
high up in the great gallows,
if it's a lie you tell me,
that at long last
a man has come to my mansion!"

Svipdag enters and Freyia speaks to him:
46.
"Where do you come from,
why did you leave
and what do you call your clan?
Your name and kin
will clearly show me
if I'm spoken for as your spouse."

Svipdag said:
47.
"Svipdag's my name,
Solbiart was my father,
icy winds sent me away;
you never gainsay
a gift from Urd,
whatever fate befalls you."

Menglod said:
48.
"I bid you welcome,
my will is fulfilled
and I seal what I've said with a kiss;
most people are glad
to glimpse a future
where they live with their beloved.

49.
"A long time I sat
on Lyviaberg,
waiting for *you* night and day;
now it has happened
just like I hoped for:
youth, you've returned to my yard!

50.
"Great was my longing
for your love and for you,
you wanted my eager consent;
it has truly been stated
we shall stay together
for time and eternity."

The Song of the Spear
– *DARRADARLJÓÐ* –

This poem, The Song of the Spear *is taken from* Njal's Saga. *A man called Darrad witnesses twelve norns or valkyries weaving the Battle of Clontarf, 1014 AD, while it was in progress. Here the woven cloth with its warp and weft is a metaphor for human fate.*

We have chosen to include the poem in our Eddic anthology because of its mythological content. It is also worth noting that the main characters are twelve women. The poem is composed in fornyrdislag.

On Good Friday it happened in Caithness that a man whose name was Darrad went outside. Then he saw a flock of twelve riding towards the women's workroom there, and all of them vanished inside. He approached the house and peeped through a small window and noticed that women were there. They had set up a loom, and the weights were men's heads, warp and weft were men's guts. The shuttle was a sword, and the reel was an arrow.

1.
Thrown wide open
for warriors to fall,
the warp-cloud is ready,
it is raining blood;
the loom is steadied
with steel-grey spears,
we are making a matrix
for men-folk now,   *we, norns/valkyries, here called* friends
for the end of Randve.   *Odin*

2.
This warp is made
from men's guts,
and tightened hard
with the heads of warriors;
the rods are spears
splashed with blood,
the heddle frame is of iron
and arrows for shuttles.
With swords we shall weave
the web of victory!

3.
Hild starts weaving   *'Battle'*
and Hiorthrimul,   *'Sword-fighter'*
Sanngrid, Svipul   *'Truly eager', 'The swift one'*
with swords drawn;
spears shall shake
and shields shall break,
helm-harrowers
shall hash the armour.

4.
Wind it up, wind it up,
the weft of Darrad,
which the young king
had owned before;
we shall go forward
and wade through the ranks,
where our friends swing
their swords in battle.

5.
Wind it up, wind it up,
the weft of Darrad,
then we'll rally round
the royal heir;
there Gunn and Gondul   *'Battle'; 'The one with the wand'*
shall get to see
men covered in blood,
who battled for the prince.

6.
Wind it up, wind it up,
the weft of Darrad,
where banners fly
over brave warriors;
let us not cause
his life to be taken –
choosing the dead
is down to us valkyries.

7.
Those people shall rule
the realm and the land,
who used to live
out on the skerries;
I say that the king
meets with certain death,
by the spears' edges
the earl sank dying.

8.
The Irish shall suffer
and certainly grieve,
it shall stick in the minds
of men forever.

Now the weft is ready,
and red is the battle-field,
this evil news
shall be known through the lands.

9.
It is terrifying
to try to look round,
as the blood-red clouds
cross the heavens,
and people's blood
shall blemish the air,
as we sisters know how
to sing our battle-song.

10.
Well did we chant
for the young king
our songs of triumph,
let us singers be saluted!
And may he learn
– he who listens now
to the tune of the spear-women –
and may he tell it to all!

11.
Let us mount our horses
and hurry on bareback,
with our weapons drawn,
away from here!

With this they tore down the cloth and ripped it to pieces, each keeping what she held in her hands. Darrad stepped away from the window and went home; but they mounted their horses and rode off, six to the South and six to the North.

APPENDIX I
On the sequence and age of the poems in Codex Regius

Many theories about the sequence and age of the Eddic poems have been presented. None have so far proved to be conclusive, and the various theories differ quite distinctly, one from the other, showing that even those who are most versed in the topic of eddic poetry are not in agreement here.

However, we find that one theory has particularly captured our interest, the one launched by Leiv Olsen. He bases the sequencing of the poems on a careful examination of grammatical characteristics, in short, on how Old Norse has changed over the centuries, changes which Olsen shows are reflected in the poems themselves.

According to Leiv Olsen the concepts presented in these poems must have existed in the North in pagan times.

The sequence of all the poems in CR, with Leiv Olsen's ranking of their age,[115] here represented by **a (the oldest)**, b (middle) and c (the youngest), is as follows:

    a The Sibyl's Prophecy
    a The Tale of the High One
    a The Tale of Vavthrudnir
    a The Tale of Grimnir

    b The Tale of Skirnir
    b The Song of Harbard
    b The Poem of Hymir

    a Loki's Quarrel
    a The Poem of Thrym
    a The Poem of Volund

    b The Tale of Alviss

---

[115] «...*ranking of their age, ...*»: See p. 19.

c The Poem of Helgi Hiorvardsson
c The Poem of Helgi Hundingsbane I
c The Poem of Helgi Hundingsbane II
c Gripir's Prophecy

b The Tale of Reginn
b The Tale of Favnir

a **The Tale of Sigrdriva**
a **Fragment of a Poem of Sigurd**
a **The First Poem of Gudrun**

b The Short Poem of Sigurd
b Brynhild's Ride to Hel
b The Second Poem of Gudrun
b The Third Poem of Gudrun

a **Oddrun's Lament**

b The Poem of Atli

c The Tale of Atli
a **Gudrun's Egging On**
a **The Tale of Hamdi and Sorli**

The anonymous editor behind CR placed the Poem of Volund among the poems of the gods. The majority of these belong to the oldest group of Eddic poems. The heroic poems in the anthology begin with four young poems, and following the criteria suggested by Leiv Olsen no more than six heroic poems should be counted with the oldest group.

The characters in the story of Volund, moreover, have no connection to those in the rest of the CR anthology. Volund is addressed as 'Prince of Elves' in three stanzas. He flies in the air and proves to be able to make his cut sinews heal. All things considered, the choice of place for the Poem of Volund by the editor behind CR seems not entirely unreasonable.

APPENDIX II
A brief note on The Song of Hyndla

It is well known that The Song of Hyndla contains a sequence (stanzas 29-44) which is reminiscent in certain ways of The Sibyl's Prophecy. Within this sequence, there is a smaller one (the nine stanzas 35-43) concerning Heimdall and his chief adversary Loki. Here Heimdall is, so to say, *alpha and omega*, and G. Dumézil compared him to Ianus – yet there seems to be two endings (stanzas 43 and 44), which are puzzling at first sight.
Thorough treatment of the symbolism and general coherency of The Song of Hyndla has been undertaken by Gro Steinsland, to quote from the English Summary of her doctoral thesis on Holy Marriage and the Norse ideology of kingship:

> "In *Hyndluljóð* the idea of the marriage between gods and giantesses as the genetic source of the prototypic ruler is transferred and ultimately transcended by a new, mythical idea. The revelation of Hyndla culminates in a vision of the ruler of the future world, a mythical, nameless sovereign who is to be revealed after Ragnarok. Through analysis of the structure and conception of the poem, it is revealed that this mythical figure is not Christ, as earlier contributors state, but rather a transformed or revived Heimdall."
> Page 350, *Det hellige bryllup og norrøn kongeideologi*, Oslo 1991.

Later, Steinsland has modified certain of her points of view, cfr the article "*Vǫluspá* and the Sibylline Oracles, with a focus on 'the Myth of the Future'" from *The Nordic Apocalypse*, Acta Scandinavica 2, Brepols 2013 – suffice it to say that the jury is out on the question of the identity of the Future Lord in *The Song of Hyndla*.

APPENDIX III
The Sibyl's Prophecy, a table of comparison

We find it important to demonstrate how The Sibyl's Prophecy has been altered as time has passed. Therefore we have made this table of comparison which shows some major differences between Codex Regius (***CR***), the older manuscript, and Hauksbók (***H***), the younger one.

The left column refers to Sophus Bugge's unified text (***SB***) from his edition Norrœn Fornkvæði 1867. Bugge included verses from Hauksbók with the stanzas and the order from Codex Regius. In the younger version, H, the sibyl seems compelled to prophesize and she ends by foretelling a future lord. These traits are reminiscent of the *Sibylline Oracles* and of an apologetic paradigm from the Middle Ages: 'a pagan prophetess foretelling the coming of the Messiah'.

Our table of comparison suggests a change of values, in that the younger version seems more influenced by Christian ideas than the older one. Stanzas quoted in mss of Snorri's 'Younger Edda' are marked – regardless of extent or deviation – by the letter q added to their SB number, and stanzas whose content is referred to in prose there, are designated by an asterix (*).

SB	*CR*	*H*	*A few guidelines*
1	1	1	H says 'holy' audience, and that the sibyl must tell of Odin's works
2	2	2	She remembers the giants, and 9 women-in-the-tree
3q	3	3	Ymir lived before our world was created
4	4	4	The sons of Bur heave up the lands
5q	5	5	Sun and Moon face the boundless
6	6	6	The gods assemble and give names
7*	7	7	The aesir make tools, in CR they also establish temples
8*	8	8	Golden tablets; three giant women arrive
9q	9	9	The gods assemble, creation of the dwarfs
10q	10	10	The dwarfs make man-copies *in* (H) or *of* (CR) earth

11q	11	11	Keeping up the sky
12q	12	12	Veigr/Veggr and Gandalf
13q	13	13	Fili, Kili
14*	14	14	Dwarfs have to move
15q	15	15	Draupnir as a dwarf
16q	16	16	The tale (*þula*) of the dwarfs (10-16) comes to an end
17*	17	17/18	The number 'three' is feminine, yet the three gods are male
18*	18	19	Three gifts to vivify us
19q	19	20	The World Tree conceived as vital circulation
20*	20	21	The goddesses of fate assume their work
21	21/22	26	First war between armies
22	23	27	Heid
23	24	28	The gods assemble and assess damages
24	25	29	Odin flings his spear; **the middle of the poem in H**
25q	26	22	The gods assemble to overrule a marriage
26q	27	23	Oaths are dishonoured
27	28	24	Heimdall's hearing etc; **1st 'Do you know it all now'**
28q	29	-	She sat outside at night; **CR 2nd 'Do you know it all now'**
29	30	-	Presents and Prophecy; **the middle of the poem in CR**
30	31	-	The valkyries ride
31	32	-	Baldr is fated to die
32	33	-	Loki coaches Hod
33	34	-	Revenge on Hod; **CR 3rd 'Do you know it all now'**
34	-	30	Revenge on Loki, details by H; **H 3rd "Do you know it all now"**
35	35	(30)	In the likeness of sadism; **CR 4th 'Do you know it all now'**
36	36	-	Sheath
37*	(36)	-	Twin halls

38q	37	34	A (third) hall to the North
39q	38	35	Nidhogg; **"Do you know it all now" H 4th, CR 5th**
40q	39	25	The Old One at Ironwoods; **H 2nd "Do you know it all now"**
41q	40	(25)	Another creature sucking life-force; **CR 6th 'Do you know it all now'**
-	-	31	**Garm is barking, refrain recurring 5 times in H**
42	41	32	Merry shepard
43	42	33	Goldencomb
44	43	36	**Garm is barking, refrain recurring 3 times in CR**
45q	44	37/38	Brothers fall out
46q	45	39	Mim's sons play, the horn is sounded
47	(45)	40	First semistanza: Yggdrasil shivering
(47)	-	(40)	Second semistanza: Scary road to Hel
48q	-	41	What is it with the aesir; **H 5th "Do you know it all now"**
49	46	42	**Garm is barking**
50q	47	43	Hrym
51q	48	44	Keel
-	49	-	What is it with the aesir; **CR 7th 'Do you know it all now'**
52q	50	45	Surtr
53q	51	46	Hlin's second sorrow
54	-	47	**Garm is barking**
55q	52	48	Vidar kills the wolf
56q	53	49	Thor dies, no complaints uttered
57q	54	50	Sun turns black
58	55	51	**Garm is barking**
59*	56	52	Second Coming of the goddess Earth
60*	57	53	Male Gods Only
61*	58	54	Tablets of gold, runes of power
62*	59	55	Return of Hod and Baldr; **CR 8th 'Do you know it all now'**
63	60	56	Hoenir chooses another Tree; **CR 9th 'Do you know it all now'**

64q	61	57	Glorious Gimle
65	-	58	A Future Lord descends
66	62	59	Now she may let herself go

When reading the two salvaged versions of The Sibyl's Prophecy as two separate poems, one may easily discover that the introductory stories are quite different.

Hauksbók, the younger manuscript, seems to be strongly influenced by the Christian religion. Here the sibyl is compelled to speak about Odin's exploits, and is lowered into her grave by a demon of death, Nidhogg, when she has served her purpose. Everything goes to pot, they all kill each other, but One shall descend from above – to be exact in Hauksbók st 58 – and will set things right. The meaning is clear: the heathen soothsayer is passive, Christianity is bound to conquer.

In Codex Regius, the older manuscript, we meet a self-confident sibyl who – just like the sibyl in Baldr's Dreams – even employs the pronouns *I* and *me* to rhyme with other words in the text. She challenges Odin: 'Is this right, Corpse-Father, that you truly want me to tell...?' And when she 'sinks down' in the last stanza, it is not difficult for anyone to visualize a soothsayer letting go of her focus and returning to the more common state of an ordinary human being. In short, it is the behaviour, role and rank of the sibyl, and consequently also Odin's, which has been changed from CR to Hauksbók.

The same becomes evident when you reach the key stanzas CR 29-30 (in our translation, st 28-29), which also indicates the centre and turning point of the poem. These stanzas, as well as almost the entire Baldr-mystery, are missing in Hauksbók.

It seems that only a few have understood that the third line in CR st 29 actually is an apposition describing Odin's gifts to the sibyl. An exception here is Vigfusson/Cleasby.

A quaint detail in both mss is that they never mention any of the goddesses dying at Ragnarok. In terms of the spirit of The Sibyl's Prophecy in Hauksbók, it is no wonder that the goddesses are not mentioned, while the CR version seems to suggest that the goddesses all survive Ragnarok.

The refrain 'Do you know it all now...' – a bold and challenging statement on the part of the sibyl – occurs as many as 9 times in CR but only 5 times in H. At the same time the hound of Hel – 'Garm is barking' – ocurs only 3 times in CR and as many as 5 times in H.

APPENDIX IV

JOHANN ERNST HARTMANN
A MELODY FOR THE SIBYL'S PROPHECY

[Musical notation with lyrics:]
Ár var ald - a par er Y - mir byggði, var-a san-dr né saer né sval-ar unn - ir; jörð fannskaev - a né upp - him - inn; gap var Ginn - un - ga, en gras hver - gi.

Text here shown is a reconstructed text from the French edition

In 1780 Jean-Benjamin de la Borde published 'Essai sur la musique ancienne et moderne,' thanking both monsieur Jacobi, the secretary of the Danish Royal Society of Science and Research, and monsieur Hartmann, musician at the Royal Court of Denmark, for their contributions, some of which were considered rather exotic. Johann Ernst Hartmann, who had been living in Copenhagen since 1762, had sent him the above musical material, which he had noted after having heard Icelanders sing it in Copenhagen.
However, at the time that Codex Regius was rediscovered in Iceland in the 1640s, bishop Brynjulf and his collaborators had no knowledge of the Edda-collection existing as a living tradition. After almost 800 years of Christianity it seems rather unlikely that people in Iceland would still be singing the 'heathen' poem *The Sibyl's Prophecy*. If this had this had been a reality, it would have meant that the oral tradition had been an unbroken one, lasting even to the end of the 18th century.

Nevertheless, Icelanders had apparently kept up a living song tradition, being especially partial to poems in the metre of fornyrdislag. As mentioned, this metre has been renamed *ljúflingslag* in modern times. To sing different poems using the same melody was common. (The Swedish trubadour Bellman is famous for his wonderful songs where the text was new, his own in fact, but the melodies were familiar to everybody, since they were already popular melodies.)

After having conducted an in-depth research on the topic, Jón Helgason pointed to the learned Icelander John Olafsen as the probable source for Hartmann and Jacobi. (Gardar, 3, 1972, p. 15-49)

We find this melody quite interesting, and recommend it for further experimentation.

INDEX of MYTHOLOGICAL NAMES

Name	ON	Meaning
Aegir,	Ægir	'Water' cfr aqua; one of the ancient giants, representing one of the four elements. His brothers were Logi, *Fire,* and Kari, *Wind/Gale.* The fourth element was personified by Thor's mother *Earth.* A. was married to Ran (see R.); Hler (*Hlér*), meaning 'Shelter', is an alias for Aegir. *Grím 45; Hym 1-3, 39; Lok*
Aesir,	sg: áss; pl: æsir	The war gods, goddesses and their progeny; probably the last family of gods to enter into the heathen pantheon prior to the advent of Christianity. All the male aesir die at Ragnarok, except two of Thor's sons, Modi and Magni, and two of Odin's, Vidar and Vali. Baldr and Hod also return after Ragnarok.
Agnar (1),	*Agnar*	Brother of king Geirrad. *Grím prose*
Agnar (2),	*Agnar*	Son of king Geirrad. *Grím 2, 3*
Agitator	*Þióðreyrir*	He who agitates people; a dwarf who taught Odin runes. *Háv 160*
Aï,	*Aï*	'Great-grandpa'; ancestor of the thralls. *Ríg 2*
Aldafather,	*Aldafǫðr*	'Father of All', alias Odin. *Vaf 4, 53*
Ali,	*Ali*	Ancestor of the Skioldungs; one of Ottar's ancestors. *Hynd 1*
Allgreen,	*Algrœn*	A mythological island *Hár 16*
Almveig,	*Almveig*	'Yielding + fluid '; wife of Ali. *Hynd 15*
Alsvinn	*Alsviðr*	'Fully wise'; Sun's horse. *Grím 37*
Althief	*Alþjófr*	A dwarf. *Vsp 11*
Alvaldi,	*Ǫlvaldi/Allvaldi*	A giant; the name means either 'he who takes care of the brewing of ale' (ON: *Ǫlvaldi*); or 'the all-powerful one' (ON: *Allvaldi*); father of Thiatzi. *Hár 19*

Alviss, *Alvíss*	All Wise; omniscient; a dwarf who contends with Thor in the poem 'Alviss' Speech'.	
		Alvíssmál
Alvrodul, *Alfrǫðull*	'Elf-blush'; Another name for 'Sun'.	
		Vaf 47; Skírn 4
Am, *Ámr*	'Rusty'; one of Ottar's ancestors.	*Hynd 18*
Amma, *Amma*	Grandma, ancestor of farmers; with Avi mother of 'Carl'.	*Ríg 16*
Andhrimnir, *Andhrímnir*	'Sooty-face'; A giant; the cook in Valhall; He boils the pig Saehrimnir in the kettle Eldhrimnir.	
		Grím 18
Angantyr, *Angantýr*	'Smelly warrior' (?); Ottar's competitor.	
		Hynd 9
Angeyia, *Angeyja*	'Narrow island'; a giantess; one of Heimdall's nine mothers.	*Hynd 37*
Angrboda, *Angrboða*	'The one who brings of sorrows'; a giantess; with Loki she is mother of Fenrir, the World Serpent and Hel.	*Hynd 40*
Asgard, *Ásgarðr*	The realm of the war gods; the dwelling place of the aesir and ásynior.	*Grím 8; Hym 7; Thrym 5, 9, 18*
Ask, *Askr*	The Ash tree, a tree; the name of the first man; the World Tree. Yggdrasil is also implied to be an oak.	*Vsp 17, 19*
Asvinn, *Ásviðr*	'Quick-to-act'; a giant; renowned for his knowledge of the runes.	*Háv 143*
Asynia (sg), *ásynja,* asynior (pl), *ásynjor*	'Beloved by the aesir'; goddesses in Asgard; some of the asynior were originally giantesses: Skadi, Ran and Gerd.	
		Lok 11, 31; Bdr 1; Hynd 10
Atla, *Atla*	'She who intends'; a giantess; one of Heimdall's nine mothers.	*Hynd 37*
Atrid, *Atríðr*	'Attacker on horseback', alias Odin.	*Grím 48*
Aurboda (1), *Aurboða*	'The one who brings loam'; a giantess married to Gymir; mother of Gerd and Beli.	*Hynd 30*
Aurboda (2), *Aurboða*	A maiden associated with Menglod/Freyia.	*Fiolsv 38-40*
Aurgelmir, *Aurgelmir*	'Loam-roarer'; a giant; according to Snorri Ymir was called Aurgelmir among the giants.	*Vaf 29, 30*
Aurnir, *Aurnir*	'He who makes loam'; a giant.	*Gróttt 9*
Avi, *Afi*	Grandpa; ancestor of farmers; with Amma father of Carl.	*Ríg 16*

Baldr, *Baldr*	'Lord'; one of the aesir; the whitest of gods; son of Frigg and Odin; married to Nanna ('the competent one'), and they had the son Forseti; during Baldr's funeral Nanna died of grief, so they laid her on the funeral pyre together with him. *Vsp 31-33; (Vaf 54-55); Grím 12; Lok 27, 28; Bdr 1, 7-11; Hynd 29, 30-31*	
Baleyg, *Báleygr*	'The one with a flaming eye', alias Odin. *Grím 47*	
Barri, *Barri*	A grove where Gerd will meet Freyr. *Skírn 39, 41*	
Beli, *Beli*	'The one who hollers'; a giant; son of Gymir and Aurboda; Gerd's brother'. *Vsp 53; Skir 16*	
Bergelmir, *Bergelmir*	'He who roars like a bear'; one of the ancient giants; son of Thrudgelmir and grandson of Ymir; with his wife B. was ancestor to all the giants; he and his wife were the only giants to survive the flood when Odin and his brothers killed Ymir. *Vaf 29, 35*	
Bestla, *Bestla*	'She who binds'; a giantess, daughter of Bolthorn; with the god Burr she had Odin, Vili and Ve. *Háv 140*	
Beyla, *Beyla*	'Swelling'; a maid of Freyr; Byggvir's wife. *Lok 55-56*	
Bileyg, *Bileygr*	'The cross-eyed one', alias Odin. *Grím 47*	
Billing, *Billingr*	'Twin'; an androgynous giant; perhaps Rind's father, with whom Odin had the son Vali. *Háv 96-101*	
Bilskirnir, *Bilskírnir*	'Crack-of-Lightning'; Thor's hall in Asgard. *Grím 24*	
Bivlindi, *Biflindi*	'Shield-shaker', alias Odin. *Grím 49*	
Blaïn, *Bláinn* from	'The Black one', alias Ymir; cfr Y.'s bones which rocks and mountains were made. *Vsp 9*	
Bolthorn, *Bǫlþorn*	'Harmful thorn'; a giant; Bestla's father and Odin's grandfather. *Háv 140*	
Bolverk, *Bǫlverkr*	'Damager', alias Odin. *Háv 109; Grím 48*	
Bragi, *Bragi*	'Outstanding'; one of the aesir; the god of skaldic (bardic) poetry. *Grím 44; Lok 8-19*	
Brainy, *Vitr*	A dwarf. *Vsp 12*	

Brave, *Þorinn*	A dwarf.	*Vsp 12*
Breidablikk, *Breiðablik*	'Shining far and wide'; Baldr's home in Asgard.	*Grím 12*
Brimir, *Brimir*	'He who foams'; a giant alias Ymir; a metaphor for the foam-crested wave.	*Vsp 9, 37*
Brisingamen, *Brísingamen*	'Glittering jewel'; cfr Beowulf *Brosenga;* Freyia's most precious jewel, made by the four dwarfs Alvrigg, Dvalinn, Burling and Grer who each got to spend a night with her for their troubles; a breast-plate, perhaps associated with her role as a military leader.	*Þrym 13,15,19*
Bumbling, *Bǫmburr*	A dwarf.	*Vsp 11*
Bur, *Burr*	'The one who is carried forth/borne'; the first god; with the giantess Bestla he had Odin, Vili and Ve.	
Byggvir, *Byggvir*	'Barley'; a servant of Freyr; married to Beyla.	*Lok 43-46, 56*
Byleist, *Byleistr*	'The cock-eyed one'; alias Odin.	*Vsp 51; Hynd 40*
Carl, *Karl*	'Man'; married to 'Snor'; their 22 children are listed in 'The Tale of Rig', st. 24 and 25.	*Ríg 21*
Concealer, *Fialarr*	A dwarf.	*Vsp 16*
Courage-Muncher, *Móðsognir*	A dwarf.	*Vsp 10*
Crooked-elf, *Vindálfr*	A dwarf.	*Vsp 12*
Day, *Dagr*	Son of the god 'Delling', and goddess 'Night'	*Vaf 25*
Dainn (1), *Dáinn*	'Ghost'; an elf knowledgable in runes.	*Háv 143*
Dainn (2), *Dáinn*	One of the four harts grazing on the World Tree.	*Grím 33*
Dainn (3), *Dáinn* 'Pale'; a dwarf.		*Hynd 7*
Damager, *Dólgþrasir*	A dwarf.	*Vsp 15*
Dan and Danp, *Danr* and *Danpr*	Dane. These were legendary Danish kings.	*Ríg 48*
Darrad, *Darrað*	'Spear'; A person in the prose introduction to 'The Song of the Spear' in *Njal's Saga*	
Dashing, *Þekkr*	A dwarf.	*Vsp 12*
Deceiver, *Ginnarr*	A dwarf.	*Vsp 16*
Delling (1), *Dellingr*	'The proud one'; a god married to Night; they had the son Day.	*Háv 161; Vaf 25*
Delling (2), *Dellingr*	Maybe the same as Delling 1.	*Fiolsv 34*
Dis (sg),	Goddesses; common term for asynior, nornir,	

Disir (pl), *dís, dísir*	valkyries and other feminine spirits.	*Grim 53*
Dithering, *Báfurr*	A dwarf.	*Vsp 11*
Draupnir, *Draupnir*	'The one that causes dripping'; Odin's arm ring, created by the dwarfs Sindre and Brokk (Snorri's Prose Edda).	*Skír 21*
Drop-maker, *Draupnir*	A dwarf.	*Vsp 15*
Duneyr, *Duneyrr*	'Downy-eared'; one of the four harts grazing on the World Tree.	*Grím 33*
Durathror, *Duraþrór*	'Thriving'; one of the four harts grazing on the World Tree.	*Grím 33*
Dvalinn (1), *Dvalinn*	'Sleepy'; one of the four harts grazing on the World Tree.	*Grím 33*
Dvalinn (2), *Dvalinn*	Mythological being who carves runes for the dwarfs; maybe the dwarf who helped create Brisingamen.	*Vsp 11, Háv 143; Alviss 16*
Eager-hothead, *Eikinskialdi*	A dwarf.	*Vsp 13*
Earl, *Jarl*	Son of' Mother'; married to Erna; their sons are listed in 'The Tale of Rig', st. 41 and 42.	*Ríg 34*
Earth, *Jǫrð*	One of the ancient goddesses; Thor's mother; her alias, Fiorgyn (*Fiǫrgyn*), means 'Thunder-clap'; her alias Hlodyn means perhaps 'Friendly support' (*Hlóðyn*) or 'She of the starry band' (*Hlǫðyn*).	*Vsp 56; Hár 56; Lok 26, 58; Thrym 1*
East, *Austri*	A dwarf.	*Vsp 11*
Edda, *Edda*	Great-grandma; ancestor of thralls.	*Ríg 2*
Edge, *Jari*	A dwarf.	*Vsp 13, 14*
Eggther, *Eggþér*	'Armed guard'; herdsman with the giants.	*Vsp 42*
Egil, *Egill*	'Awe-inspiring'; a farmer who lives on the border of Iotunheim, the realm of the giants, and takes care of the goats.	*Hym 7, 37-38*
Eikin, *Eikin*	'Hot'; a mythological river in Asgard.	*Grím 27*
Eikthyrnir, *Eikþyrnir*	'Oak-pesterer'?; a hart, gnawing on the tree Laerad in Valhall.	*Grím 26*
Eir, *Eir*	'Gentle'; an asynia who gives help and shelter.	*Fjolsv 38-40*
Eistla, *Eistla*	'The stormy one'; a giantess; one of Heimdall's nine mothers.	*Hynd 37*
Eldir, *Eldir*	'The igniter'; a servant at Aegir's place.	*Lok 1-5*
Eldhrimnir, *Eldhrímnir*	'Sooted by fire'; the kettle in Asgard, in which the pig Saehrimnir was boiled.	*Grím 18*

Elivagar, *Élivágar*	'Icy showers'; border rivers between Asgard and the realm of the giants.	*Vaf 31; Hym 5*
Elf, *Álfr*	A dwarf.	*Vsp 16*
Elves	A class of mythological beings often associated with the dead; elves were regarded as powerful and at times hostile spirits; in the poems they are consistently mentioned together with the aesir.	
Embla, *Embla*	'Young elm tree'; the name of the first woman.	*Vsp 17*
Erna, *Erna*	'Eagle'; wife of Earl; their sons are listed in 'The Tale of Rig', st. 41 and 42.	*Ríg 39*
Eyrgiava, *Eyrgjafa*	'She who gives golden water'; a giantess; one of Heimdall's mothers.	*Hynd 37*
Fair, *Litr*	A dwarf.	*Vsp 12*
Falhovni, *Falhófnir*	'The one who moves his hooves speedily'; one of the aesir's horses.	*Grím 30*
Famed, *Frægr*	A dwarf.	*Vsp 13*
Farmatyr, *Farmatýr*	'God of trade', alias Odin.	*Grím 48*
Fast, *Frár*	A dwarf.	*Vsp 13*
Father, *Faðir*	Ancestor of the class of earls; married to 'Mother'.	*Ríg 27*
Favnir, *Fáfnir/Fáðmir*	'He who guards the gold'; a dragon.	*Hynd 25*
Fenia, *Fenia*	'The one of the marshes'; a giantess; with her sister, Menia, she works the mill 'Grotti'.	*Song of Grotti*
Fenrir, *Fenrir*	'He of the marshes'; The cosmic wolf; son of Loki and Angrboda; brother of Hel and the World Serpent.	*Vsp 40, 44, 49-55, 58; Váf 46-47, 53; Grím 39; Lok 38-41; Hynd 40*
Fertile, *Þrór*		
Fensalir, *Fensalir*	'The halls of the marshes'; Frigg's homestead.	*Vsp 33*
Fialar (1), *Fjalarr*	'He who conceals'; a giant, alias Skrymir, alias Utgarda-Loki.	*Hárb 26*
Fialar (2), *Fjalarr*	A dwarf in the story of the bardic mead.	*Vsp 16; Háv 14*
Fialar (3), *Fjalarr*	A cock in the Iron Wood;.	*Vsp 42*
Filer, *Fili*	A dwarf.	*Vsp 13*
Fimafeng, *Fimafengr*	'He who delivers quickly'; a servant at Aegir's place.	*Lok prose*
Fimbulthul (1), *Fimbulþulr*	'The mighty singer of religious texts'; alias Odin.	*Háv 80, 142*

Fimbulthul (2), *Fimbulþulr*	'The mighty roarer'; a mythological river flowing from Hvergelmir.	*Grím* 27
Fimbultyr, *Fimbultýr*	'The mighty god', alias Odin.	*Vsp* 6
Fiolnir (1), *Fjǫlnir*	'He who knows much', alias Odin.	*Grím* 47
Fiolnir (2), *Fjǫlnir*	A Swedish legendary king.	*Grotti prose*
Fiolsvinn, *Fjǫlsviðr*	'The very wise one', alias Odin.	*Grím* 47; *Fjǫlsvinnsmál*
Fiolvar, *Fjǫlvarr*	'Tremendously careful'; a giant; a travelling companion of Odin.	*Hár* 16
Fiorgyn, *Fjǫrgyn* Fiorgynn.	See: *Earth*. F. has a male counterpart,	
Fiorgynn, *Fjǫrgynn*	'Thunderer'; a giant; Frigg's father.	*Lok* 26
Fiorm, *Fjǫrm*	'The busy one'; a river that runs through Asgard, having its origin in the well Hvergelmir.	*Grím* 27
Fitiung, *Fitjung*	'Adopted heir', A giant living in the bogs; possibly an ancestor of farmers.	*Háv* 78
Folkvang, *Fólkvangr*	'Drill ground'; Freyia's homestead; F. is the place where the hall 'Sessrumnir' stands, the place of many seats; a realm of the dead where half of those who die in battle go.	*Grím* 14
Forseti, *Forseti*	'He who presides and settles law suits'; one of the aesir; son of Nanna and Baldr.	*Grím* 15
Foundling, *Fundinn*	A dwarf.	*Vsp* 13
Freki, *Freki*	See: Geri.	
Freyia, *Freyia*	'Lady'; reckoned as one of the asynior, originally one of the vanir; sister of Freyr, daughter of Niord; goddess of love, beauty, life and death; wife of Odr (Odin), and they have two daughters, Hnoss and Gersemi, both meaning 'Valuable Possession'/'Gem'; half of those who die in battle belong to Freyia, while Odin gets the rest; she owns the legendary jewel, the large breast-plate Brisingamen; she rides the golden boar *Hildisvín*, Battle-swine; she is the object of men's intense desire. Freyia has many aliases: Gevn/Gevion (*Gefn/Gefjon*), 'The giving one'; Hledis (*Hlédís*), 'She who protects'; Horn (*Hǫrn*), 'Goddess of flaxen', 'Goddess of the harvest'; Mardoll (*Mardǫll*),'She who makes the sea blossom'; Menglod (*Menglǫð*),	

	'She who is fond of jewels'; Syr (*Sýr*), a sow, the symbol of fertility; her place in Asgard is Folkvang (see F.) *Grím 14; Lok 29-32; Thrym; Hynd*
Freyr, *Freyr*	'Lord'; reckoned as one of the aesir, originally one of the vanir; a fertility god; god of the good harvest; son of Niord and Niord's sister; brother of Freyia; his wife is the giantess Gerd (see: Gerd), they had the son Fiolnir; an alias is Yngvi (*Yngvi*) meaning 'the fecund one', who was the progenitor of the Ynglings, a family of princes. *(Vsp 53); Grím 5, 43; Skírnismál; Lok 35-37, 41-44; Hynd*
Frid, *Fríð*	'Beautiful'/'Undamaged'; one of the maidens who accompany Menglod; she could cure diseases. *Fiǫls 38-40*
Friend, *Ánn*	A dwarf. *Vsp 11*
Frigg, *Frigg*	'Beloved'/'Lady'; one of the asynior; wife of Odin; mother of Baldr and Hod; she knows the fate of everyone; she was also called Hlin (*Hlín*), 'Protectoress'; she may also appear as Saga (*Ság a*), 'She who sees'. *Vsp 33, 53, Váf 1-4; Grím pr; Lok 25-29*
Frodi Fridleifsson, *Fróði Fríðleifssonr*	Legendary mighty king of Denmark; Snorri compared 'Frodi's Peace' with 'Pax Romana'. *Gróttasǫngr*
Frosty, *Frostri*	A dwarf. *Vsp 16*
Fulla, *Fulla*	'Full larder'; a maid at Frigg's; she is unmarried and wears a head band with her hair hanging loose. *Grím prose*
Fylgia, *fylgia* pl fylgior, *fylgior*	'Follower'; guardian spirit.
Gagnrad, *Gagnráðr*	'The one who gives useful advice'; a disguise for Odin. *Vafþrúðnismál*
Gangleri, *Gangleri*	'Tired of walking', alias of Odin. *Grím 46*
Garm, *Garmr*	'Growler'; the dog guarding the path to Hel, the underworld or the realm of the dead. *Vsp 44, 49, 54, 58; Grím 44; Bdr 2, 3*
Gastropnir, *Gastropnir*	'The one who strangles the guests'; The gate to Menglod's/Freyia's place. *Fiolsv 12*
Gatherer, *Finnr*	A dwarf. *Vsp 16*
Gaut, *Gautr*	Ancestor of the Goths, alias Odin. *Grím 54*
Geironul, *Geirǫnul*	'Spear-fencer'; a valkyrie in Valhall. *Grím 36*

Geirrod, *Geirröðr*	A king who was Odin's favourite.	*Grímnesmál*
Geirskogul, *Geirskǫgul*	'Spear-fight'; a valkyrie.	*Vsp 30*
Geirvimul, *Geirvimul* river	'She who shakes the spear'; a mythological in Asgard.	*Grím 27*
Gerd, *Gerðr*	'Fence'/'Yard'; a giantess; daughter of Aurboda and Gymir; sister of Beli; wife of Freyr.	*Skírnismál*
Geri and Freki, *Geri* and *Freki*	Odin's wolves 'Greedy' and 'Brazen'	*Grím 19*
Geri and Gifr, *Geri* and *Gifr*	Menglod's/Freyia's dogs.	*Fiolsv 1*
Gevion, *Gefjon*	'She who gives'; an asynia, alias of Freyia.	*Lok 19-21*
Giallarhorn, *Giallarhorn*	'The sounding horn»; Heimdall's horn.	*Vsp 27, 46*
Giants/iotuns	The first beings to live in the world; the giants are generally huge, ill-tempered and dangerous; they are often connected to natural phenomena such as frost, wind, fire, rivers, the sea, mountains, etc.; it is known that giants were worshipped; e.g. Skadi was seen as a protectoress of hunters in the wild; due to their being very ancient the giants were often considered to possess great knowledge. By the names giants/iotuns we translate a whole group of ON names: *jǫtnar, þursar, risar, hrímþursar, bergrisar* and *troll.*	
Gimle, *Gimlé*	'Gleaming shelter'; a place where virtuous people dwell; this concept, Gimle, is probably added in Christian times.	*Vsp 64*
Ginnunga-gap, *Ginnungagap*	'Magical Chasm'; The magically vibrating universal void; between Nivelheim to the north and Muspelheim to the south huge streams of ether appeared, gradually asuming the shape of the celestial cow Audhumbla and the primeval giant Ymir. *Vsp 3;* See also Snorri Sturluson's *'Gylfaginning'*	
Gioll, *Giǫll*	'She who makes noise'; a mythological river originating in Hvergelmir.	*Grím 28*

Giolp, *Gjǫlp*	'She who cries out'; a giantess; one of Heimdall's nine mothers; probl. daughter of the giant Geirrad.	*Hynd 37*
Gipul, *Gípul*	'She who snatches'; a mythological river in Asgard.	*Grím 27*
Gisl, *Gísl*	'Bolting'; one of the aesir's horses.	*Grím 30*
Gladr, *Glaðr*	'Happy'; one of the aesir's horses.	*Grím 30*
Gladsheim, *Glaðsheimr*	'Home of joy'; the site in Asgard where Valhall was erected.	*Grím 8*
Glapsvinn, *Glapsviðr*	'The impish one'; alias Odin	*Grím 47*
Glowing, *Glói*	A dwarf.	*Vsp 15*
Gnipahellir, *Gnípahellir*	'Protruding rock'; the cave that leads to Hel.	*Vsp 44, 49, 58*
Goinn, *Góinn*	'Of earth'/'Crawler'; a serpent gnawing at one of Yggdrasil's roots; son of Gravvitnir; Moinn's brother.	*Grím 34*
Golden-Comb, *Gullinkambi*	A rooster in Valhall.	*Vsp 43*
Golden top, *Gulltoppr*	'Golden Mane'; a horse belonging to Heimdall.	*Grím 30*
Goll, *Gǫll*	'Wham!' a valkyrie in Valhall.	*Grím 36*
Gomul, *Gǫmul*	'The old one'; a mythological river in Asgard.	*Grím 27*
Gondlir, *Gǫndlir*	'He who handles the wand', alias Odin.	*Grím 49*
Gondul, *Gǫndul*	'The One with the wand'; a valkyrie.	*Vsp 30*
Goodly, *Ánarr*	A dwarf.	*Vsp 11*
Gopul, *Gǫpul*	'She who gapes'; a mythological river in Asgard.	*Grím 27*
Grabak, *Grábakr*	'Grey-back'; a serpent gnawing at one of Yggdrasil's roots.	*Grím 34*
Grad, *Gráð*	'She who troubles the waters'; a mythological river in Asgard.	*Grím 27*
Grandpa, *Afi*	A dwarf.	*Vsp 15*
Gravvitnir, *Grafvitnir*	'Grave-dweller'(?); a serpent gnawing at Yggdrasil's roots.	*Grím 34*
Gravvolud, *Grafvǫluðr*	'Grave-ruler'; a serpent gnawing at one of Yggdrasil's roots.	*Grím 34*
Great-grandpa, *Aï*	A dwarf.	*Vsp 11*
Greip, *Greip*	'She who grasps'; a giantess; one of Heimdall's nine mothers.	*Hynd 37*

Greybeard, *Hárbarðr*	'Grey-bearded', alias Odin.	*Grím 49; Hárbarðsljóð*
Greyhair, *Hár*	A dwarf.	*Vsp 15*
Grim, *Grímr*	'The masked one', alias Odin.	*Grím 46, 47*
Grimnir, *Grímnir*	'The masker', alias Odin.	*Grím prose, 47*
Groa, *Gróa*	'Growth'; a sibyl: wife of Aurvandil.	*Grógaldr*
Grotti, *Grótti*	The great magical mill pulled by Fenia and Menia, which was owned by king Frodi.	*Gróttasǫng*
Gulltopp, *Gulltoppr*	'Golden mane'; one of the aesir's horses.	*Grím 30*
Gullveig, *Gullveig*	'She who is consecrated to gold'(?); possibly a name for Freyia. It seems she may have been a leader of the vanir in their battle with the aesir.	*Vsp 21*
Gunnlod, *Gunnlǫð*	'She who invites battle'; a giantess, daughter of Suttung; she guarded the bardic mead for her father.	*Háv 13, 105, 108, 110*
Gunnthorin, *Gunnþórin*	'She who is eager for battle'; a mythological river in Asgard.	*Grím 27*
Gunnthra, *Gunnþrá*	'She who longs for battle'; a mythological river in Asgard.	*Grím 27*
Gyllir, *Gyllir*	'Golden'; one of the aesir's horses.	*Grím 30*
Gymir, *Gymir*	'The sea'; a giant; married to Aurboda; they have the daughter, Gerd, and the son, Beli.	*Lok 42; Hynd 30*
Habrok, *Hábrók*	'Short-pants'; a hawk.	*Grím 44*
Handle, *Hepti*	A dwarf.	*Vsp 13*
Har, *Hár*	'The grey one', alias Odin.	*Vsp 21; Háv 109; Grím 46*
Hati, *Hati*	'He who hates/pursues'; a giant in the shape of a wolf; he pursues Moon and will eventually swallow him.	*Grím 39*
Heid (1), *Heiðr*	'Clarity'/'Honour'; a sibyl; in our interpretation she is identical with the speaker in 'The Sibyl's Prophecy'.	*Vsp 22*
Heid (2), *Heiðr*	A giantess.	*Hynd 32*
Heidrun, *Heiðrún*	'From whom clarity flows'; a goat on the roof of Valhall, who munches off the branches of Laerad; from her teats flow the beer that the warriors drink each night.	*Grím 25; Hynd 46-47*

Heimdall, *Heimdallr* — 'He who makes the world blossom'; one of the aesir; one of Rig's aspects, see: Rig; he is the personification of sensual perceptions; he has nine mothers (giantesses) who all are sisters: Gialp, *Gjalp* (= she who cries out), Greip, *Greip* (= she who grasps), Eistla, *Eistla* (= she who swells); Eyrgiava, *Eyrgjafa* (= she who gives golden water), Ulfrun, *Ulfrún* (= wolf-woman), Angeya, *Angeyja* (= she who confines), Imd, *Imðr* (= she who tosses and turns), Atla, *Atla* (= she who intends), Iarnsaxa, *Jarnsaxa* (= she who cuts like a dagger); H. guards the rainbow Bivrost; Heimdall and Loki fight in the shape of seals for Freya's jewel, Brisingamen; as Rig (*Rígr*) he is progenitor of the three basic social classes: workers, peasants and princes. Two aliases for Heimdall are: Hallinskidi (*Hallinskíði*) meaning probably 'The World Axis', and 'Wind-shelter' (*Vindhlér*), closely associated with 'the World Tree'.
Vsp 1, 27, 46; Grím 13; Lok 47-48; Thrym 15-16; Rígsþula; Hynd 35

Heimdall's nine mothers: Giolp, Greip, Eistla, Eyrgiava, Ulvrun, Angeyia, Imd, Atla, Iarnsaxa, see Heimdall. These names may allude to the stages in the process of giving birth. *Hynd 37*

Hel, *Hel* — 'She who conceals'; a giantess, daughter of Loki and Angrboda; she rules the realm of the dead under the ground. *Vsp 43, 47, 52; Grím 28, 31; Skír 27; Alv 26; Bdr 3*

Helblindi, *Helblindi* — 'The one who blinds', alias Odin. *Grím 46*

Herfiotur, *Herfjǫtur* — 'She who spellbinds the army' a Valkyrie in Valhall. *Grím 36*

Heriafather, *Heriafǫðr* — 'Father of armies', alias Odin. *Vsp 43; Vaf 2; Grím 19, 25, 26; Hynd 2*

Herian, *Herian* — 'Head of the army', alias Odin. *Vsp 30; Grím 46*

Hermod, *Hermóðr* — 'He who rages in the army'; son of Odin. *Hynd 2*

Herteit, *Herteitr* — 'He who is happy to be in the army', alias Odin. *Grím 47*

Hialmberi, *Hialmberi* — 'Helmet-bearer', alias Odin. *Grím 46*

High One, *Hávi* — 'The High One', alias Odin. *Háv 164*

Hild, *Hildr* — 'Battle'; a valkyrie. *Vsp 30; Grím 36*

Hildi-swine, *Hildsvíni*	'Battle-boar'; a boar made by the dwarfs Dainn and Nabbi for Freyia.	*Hyndluljóð*
Hildolf, *Hildolfr* 'Battle-wolf',alias Odin.		*Hár 8*
Himinbiorg, *Himinbjǫrg*	'Heavenly mountains'; Heimdall's place at the end of the rainbow.	*Grím 33*
Hlebard, *Hlébarðr*	'Big-beard'; a giant.	*Hár 20*
Hledis, *Hlédís*	'She who gives shelter'; Ottar's grandmother.	*Hynd 13*
Hlidskialv, *Hliðskiálfr*	'Seat on top of the gatehouse'; Odin's high seat in Valhall from where he can look into all worlds. *Prose intro to Grímnismál and Skírnismál*	
Hlin, *Hlín*	'She who protects'; alias Frigg.	*Vsp 53*
Hliv, *Hlíf*	'Protection'; one of Menglod's maids,	*Fiolsv 38-40*
Hlivthursa, *Hlífþursa*	'She who protects'; one of Menglod's maids.	*Fiolsv 38-40*
Hlodyn, *Hlóðyn*	See: *Earth*.	
Hlorridi, *Hlórriði*	'He who rides noisily forth', alias Thor. *Hymiskviða; Lok 54-55; Þrym 7, 8, 14, 31*	
Hlokk, *Hlǫkk*	'Racket'; valkyrie who serves the warriors in Valhall.	*Grím 36*
Hnikar, *Hnikarr*	'The one who eggs on', alias Odin.	*Grím 47*
Hod, *Hǫðr*	'Battle'; one of the aesir; the blind god, tricked by Loki to kill his own brother Baldr.	*Vsp 32, 62; Bdr 9, 10*
Hoenir, *Hænir*	'He who up-lifts'; one of the three gods who create man and woman, giving them emotional life; H. was given as hostage to the vanir.	*Vsp 4, 18, 63*
Holl, *Hǫll*	'Slanting'; a mythological river in Asgard.	*Grím 27*
Horn, *Hǫrn*	'Flaxen'; an alias for Freyia; in the poem she appears as a river.	*Grotti 8*
Horned, *Hornbori*	A dwarf.	*Vsp 13*
Horses:	Glad and Gyllir (*'Happy' and 'Golden'*), Gler and Skeidbrimir (*'Shiny' and 'Foamer'*), Gisl and Falhovnir (*'Bolt' and 'Speedy-hoof'*) ; Gulltopp and Lettfeti (*'Golden-top' and 'Lightfoot'*).	*Grím 30*
Hraesvelg, *Hræsvelgr*	'He who swallows corpses'; a giant; in the shape of an eagle he creates all wind that exists in the world.	*Vaf 37*

Hrid, *Hríð*	'Strife'; a mythological river in Asgard.	
		Grím 28
Hrimfaxi, *Hrímfaxi*	'Icy mane'; a horse driven by Night (*Nótt*).	
		Vaf 14
Hrimgrimnir, *Hrímgrimnir*	'Frosty-mask'; a giant.	*Skír 35*
Hrimnir, *Hrímnir*	'He who causes frost'; a giant, father of the valkyrie, Liod.	*Skír 28; Hynd 30*
Hrist, *Hrist*	'She who shakes'; a valkyrie in Valhall.	
		Grím 36
Hronn, *Hrǫnn*	'She who grunts'; a giantess; a mythological river in Asgard.	*Grím 28*
Hropt, *Hróptr*	'The chanter', alias Odin.	*Vsp 62; Háv 142; Grím 8; Lok 45*
Hroptatyr, *Hroptatýr*	'The screaming god'; alias Odin.	*Vsp 160*
Hrym, *Hrymr*	'The Roarer'; a giant who sails the ship Naglfari at Ragnarok.	*Vsp 50, Grím 54*
Huginn and Muninn,	*Huginn* and *Muninn*, Odin's two ravens 'Mind' and 'Capability'.	*Grím 20*
Hymir, *Hymir*	'Sluggard'; a giant and father of Tyr; owner of the large cauldron that is used to make beer at Aegir's; H.'s mother has nine hundred heads.	*Hymiskviða; Lok 34*
Hyndla, *Hyndla*	'Bitch'; a giantess, Freyia seeks her out to achieve wisdom.	*Hyndluljóð*
Ialang Heath, *Jalangrsheiði*	Jelling Heath at Vejle in Denmark, at one time a royal estate.	*Grott prose*
Ialk, *Jálkr*	'Gelding'; alias Odin.	*Grím 49, 54*
Iarnsaxa, *Jarnsaxa*	'She who cuts like an iron dagger'; a giantess, one of Heimdall's nine mothers.	*Hynd 37*
Iavnhar, *Jafnhár*	'Equal-in-height', alias Odin.	*Grím 49*
Idavoll, *Iðavǫllr*	'Field of intense activity'; the place where the gods gathered and played in the earliest days; the gods who survive will return there after Ragnarok.	*Vsp 7, 60*
Idi, *Iði*	'The industrious'; a giant, brother of Thiatzi.	*Grótt 9*
Idunn, *Iðunn*	'She who activates'; one of the asynior, wife of Bragi; owner of 'the apples of life', which keep the gods young until Ragnarok.	*Lok 16-18*
Im, *Ímr*	'Dust-covered'; a giant, son of Vavthrudnir.	*Vaf 5*

Imd, *Imðr*	'She who tosses and turns'; a giantess; one of Heimdall's nine mothers.	*Hynd 37*
Iord, *Jǫrð*	See: Earth.	
Iormungand, *Jǫrmungandr*	'Big staff'. See: The World Serpent.	
Iotuns/giants	See: Giants.	
Iotunheim, *Jǫtunheimr*	'The Realm of the giants'; a mountainous, inhospitable region outside the world of human beings.	*Vsp 8, 48; Skír prose*
Iron Woods, *Járnviðr*	Mythological place where giants are born.	*Vsp 40, 42*
Ivaldi, *Ívaldi*	A dwarf; his sons made magical objects.	*Grím 43*
Iving, *Ífing*	'The turbulent one'; a border river between Asgard and the realm of the giants.	*Vaf 16*
Kerlaugar, *Kerlaugar*	'Bathing pools'; twin mythological rivers in Asgard.	*Grím 29*
Kialar, *Kjalarr*	'Sleigh-driver', alias Odin.	*Grím 49*
Kioll, *Kiǫll*	'Keel'; the ship that carries the sons of Muspel to Ragnarok.	*Vsp 48*
Kormt, *Kǫrmt*	'Framed'; a mythological river in Asgard.	*Grím 29*
Laerad, *Læráð*	'Harmful advice'; a tree in Valhall off which the goat Heidrun and the hart Eikthyrnir feed in Valhall; possibly an aspect of the World Tree.	*Grím 25, 26*
Lauvey, *Laufey*	'The Leafy island'; a giantess, maybe an elf; mother of Loki with Farbauti; an alias is Nal (*Nál*, meaning 'needle').	*Lok 52; Thrym 18, 20*
Leift, *Leiftr*	'Glittering'; a mythological river in Asgard.	*Grím 28*
Leire,	Lejre; ancient seat of the Danish kings.	
Lettfeti, *Léttfeti*	'Light-foot'; one of the aesir's horses.	*Grím 30*
Lingerer, *Lóni*	A dwarf.	*Vsp 13*
Liv, *Líf*	'Life'; together with Livthrasir they are the only humans to survive Ragnarok.	*Vaf 45*
Livthrasir, *Lífþrasir*	'Life-striver'; see: Liv.	
Loam-heath, *Aurvangr*	A dwarf.	*Vsp 13, 14*
Loddfavnir, *Loddfáfnir*	A mythological character who is given advice by Odin in 'Odin's Speech'.	*Háv 112-163*
Lodur, *Lóðurr/ Loðurr*	'The allurer' (?); one of the three gods who create man and woman, giving them motion, Maybe an alias for Loki.	*Vsp 18*

Loki, *Loki*		One of the aesir, originally of the family of giants; The name may imply: fire, shutting, bog or destruction; or it may be an abbr. of Lodur. Loki is probably the child of an elf mother, Laufey, and a giant father, Farbauti; he became blood brothers with Odin; he was married to the asynia Sigyn and had a son by her, Narvi; he had another son, Vali; with the giantess Angrboda he bred the World Serpent, Fenrir and Hel; with the stallion Svadilfari, he became the *mother* of Odin's horse, Sleipnir; through all his mischief he is the one who always instigates creative action; his alias, Lopt (*Loptr*) is associated with 'air'. *Vsp 35, 51, 55; Lokasenna; Þrymskviða; Bdr 14; Hynd 40-41*
Lopt, *Loptr*		'The airy one'(?); alias Loki. *Lok 6, 19; Hynd 12, 41; Fjolsv 26*
Lyviaberg, *Lyfjaberg*		'The life-giving mountain'; Menglod sits there with her maidens, curing illnesses. *Fjolsv 36, 49*
Magni, *Magni*		'The strong one'; one of the aesir, son of Thor and the giantess Iarnsaxa; brother of Modi. *Vaf 51; Hár 9, 53*
Maid, *Þir*		Wife of 'Thrall'; ancestor of the class of servants. Their children are listed in 'The Tale of Rig' st. 12 and 13. *Ríg 10*
Meadwolf, *Mioðvitnir*		A dwarf. *Vsp 11*
Meili, *Meili*		'The mild one'; Thor's brother. *Hár 9*
Menia, *Menia*		'Maid'; a giantess; with her sister, Fenia, she works the mill 'Grotti'. *Gróttasǫngr*
Menglod, *Menglǫd*		See: Freyia.
Midgard, *Miðgarðr*		'Middle earth'; the realm of mankind; M. lies between the Realm of the Giants and Asgard. *Vsp 4, 7, 38; Háv 107; Grím 8, 41; Hár 23; Hynd 11, 16*
Midgardsorm, *Miðgarðsormr*		See: World Serpent.
Midvitnir, *Miðvitnir*		'He who drinks up the mead' (?); a giant. *Grím 50*
Mimameid, *Mímameiðr*		'Mim's tree'; a tree in Menglod's yard; possibly the same as the World Tree. *Fiolsv 20, 24*

Mimir/Mimr/Mimi *Mímir/Mímr/Mími*		'Memory'/'The function of memory'; a wise giant; he had been beheaded, but Odin kept his head alive in order to gain wisdom from him. *Vsp 28, 46*
Miodvitnir, *Mjǫðvitnir*		'Mead-wolf'; a dwarf. *Vsp 11*
Miollnir, *Mjǫllnir*		'He who crushes something into powder'; Thor's hammer. *Vaf 51; Hym 36; Lok 57; 59, 61, 63; Þrym 30*
Miskorblindi, *Miskorblindi*		Possibly 'He who mixes the mash'; a giant; perhaps Aegir's father. *Hym 2*
Mist, *Mist*		'Fog'; a valkyrie in Valhall. *Grím 36*
Modi, *Móði*		'The raging one'; one of the aesir; son of Thor, half-brother of Magni. *Vaf 51; Hym 34*
Moinn, *Móinn*		'Moor-creeper'; a serpent gnawing at one of Yggdrasil's roots, Goinn's brother; son of Gravvitnir. *Grím 34*
Moon, *Máni*		The moon is masculine in Norse mythology; he is son of Mundilfari and brother of Sun, who is feminine in Norse mythology. *Vsp 5; Vaf 23*
Mother, *Móðir*		Ancestor to the class of earls; wife of 'Father'. *Ríg 27, 31, 34*
Mound-stepper, *Haugspori*		A dwarf. *Vsp 15*
Mundilfari, *Mundilfari*		'He who travels in intervals'; father of Sun and Moon. *Vaf 23*
Muninn		See: 'Huginn and Muninn'.
Murky Woods, *Myrkviðr*		A mythological forrest. *Lok 42*
Muspelheim, *Muspellheimr*		*Muspell* may mean 'Destruction of the world'. M. is the hot side of Ginnunge-gape. *Vsp 51; Lok 42*
Muspell, *Muspell*		See: Muspelheim; a giant; a forceful destroyer; owner of the ship Naglfari. *Vsp 51; Lok 42*
Mysing, *Mýsingr*		A sea king. *Grott prose*
Nabbi, *Nabbi*		'Stout'; a dwarf. *Hynd 7*
Naglfari, *Naglfari*		A ship made of nail-clippings, carrying dead people. *Vsp 5*
Nanna, *Nanna*		'The competent one'; an asynia; wife of Baldr, see: Baldr.
Nari, *Nari*		Son of Loki and Sigyn, brother of Narvi. *Lok prose end*
Narvi, *Narfi*		Son of Loki and Sigyn, brother of Nari. *Lok prose*
Nastrand, *Nástrǫnd*		'Beach of the dead'; murderers, oath-breakers and fornicators go there when they die. *Vsp 38*

Naut, *Naut*	'Sacrifice'; a mythological river in Asgard.	
		Grím 28
New, *Nýr*		
(CR gives Nár = Dead)	A dwarf.	*Vsp 12*
New-Counsel, *Nýráðr*	A dwarf.	*Vsp 12*
New Moon, *Nýi*	A dwarf.	*Vsp 11*
Nidafell, *Niðafjǫll*	'The shadowy mountains';	*Vsp 66*
Nidavellir, *Niðavellir*	'Murky meadows'; the home of Sindri's clan;.	
		Vsp 37
Nidhogg, *Níðhoggr*	'Spiteful Biter'; a serpent feeding on the dead and tormenting them.	*Vsp 39, 66; Grím 35*
Night, *Nótt*	A giantess married to Delling, one of the aesir; they had the son Day; she drives Hrímfaxi across the sky every night.	*Vsp 6; Vaf 25; Alv 30*
Niord, *Niǫrðr*	'The forceful one'; one of the vanir; associated with the element water; father of Freyia and Freyr; given as hostage to the aesir; married to the giantess Skadi.	*Vaf 38, 39; Grím 16, 43; Skír 38, 39, 31; Lok 33-36; Þrym 22*
Nivlhel, *Niflhel*	'Misty realm of the dead'.	*Vaf 43; Bdr 2*
Noatun, *Nóatún*	'The shipyard'; Niord's home.	
		Grím 16; Thrym 22
Nonn, *Nonn*	'She who masters'; a mythological river in Asgard.	*Grím 28*
Norn, *Norn*	Goddess of fate; the chief norns were Urd, Verdandi and Skuld (past, present and future); it was believed that norns decided the fate of each new-born child.	
Norr, *Nǫrr*	'Father of Night'; a giant.	*Vaf 25; Alv 29*
North, *Norðri*	A dwarf.	*Vsp 11*
Nyt, *Nyt*	'Useful'; a mythological river in Asgard.	
		Grím 28
Odin, *Óðinn*	'He who agitates'; the one-eyed god of war of the clan of the aesir; master of runes; he also practised the art of seid (magic) which otherwise was a prerogative of the goddesses; he is son of the first god Bur and the giantess Bestla; allegedly he was the father of nearly all the other male gods; Odin and his brothers killed the primeval giant Ymir and used his body parts to create our world; he is married to Frigg with	

	whom he has Baldr and Hod; with the giantess Grid he had a son, Vidar, who later killed Hod in revenge for Baldr; he owns the ravens Huginn (mind) and Muninn (capability); he also consults with the head of a giant, Mim/Mimir (memory); he steals the skaldic (bardic) mead from Suttung. *Vsp 18, 24, 28, 31, 32, 46, 53, 56; Háv 98, 110, 138, 143; Vaf 5, 52, 54, 55; Grím 3, 7, 9, 10, 14, 19, 44, 51, 53, 54; Skír 21, 22, 33; Hár 9, 24, 56; Hym 21, 35; Lok 9, 22; Þrym 21; Bdr 2, 3, 4, 8, 9, 11, 13, 14; Hynd 44; Grott prose*
Odr, *Óðr*	'Agitation'; in all likelihood a short form of the name Odin; a myth tells that he was married to Freyia, he disappeared, and Freyia searched for him all over the world, crying tears of gold in her grief. *Vsp 13, Hynd 47*
Odrerir, *Óðrerir*	'The one that stirs up frenzy'; one of the kettles containing the bardic mead. *Háv 107, 140*
Okolni, *Ókolni*	Brimir's beer hall; 'Never-freezing'. *Vsp 37*
Omi, *Ómi*	'The roarer', alias Odin. *Grím 49*
Ormt, *Ǫrmt*	'Heated'; a mythological river in Asgard. *Grím 29*
Oski, *Óski*	'The one who wishes', alias Odin. *Grím 49*
Ottar,	'Fearsome'; Freyia's lover; see: 'Song of Hyndla' *Hyndluljóð*
Ovnir (1), *Ófnir*	'The one who eggs on', alias Odin. *Grím 54*
Ovnir (2), *Ófnir*	'The one who eggs on'; a serpent gnawing at one of Yggdrasil's roots. *Grím 34*
Passionate, *Þráinn*	A dwarf. *Vsp 12*
Potion, *Veigr*	A dwarf. *Vsp 12*
Quick-wit, *Ráðsviðr*	A dwarf. *Vsp 12*
Radgrid, *Ráðgríðr*	'Ready-to-rule'; a valkyrie in Valhall. *Grím 36*
Ragnarok, *Ragnarǫk*	'The end of the powers'; the fate of the war gods/the male aesir. *Vsp 44, 49, 58; Bdr 14; Vaf 38, 42*
Ran, *Rán*	'Theft', a giantess; married to Aegir; goddess of the sea; mother of nine daughters (ocean waves); she rules a realm of the dead in the sea.
Rani, *Hrani*	'Burly'; prob. an alias for Odin. *Gró 6*
Randgrid, *Randgríðr*	'Shield-ready'; a valkyrie in Valhall. *Grím 36*
Ratatosk, *Ratatoskr*	'Gnawing tooth'; the squirrel that runs up and down the World Tree delivering messages between Nidhogg at the bottom of the tree and the eagle at the top. *Grím 32*

Rati, *Rati*	Odin's drill or drill-bit.	*Háv 106*
Realm of the Giants/ the giants' realm, *Jǫtunheimr*	The mountainous, uninhabited area where the giants/iotuns live, regarded as a dangerous place.	*Háv 108; 40; Þrymskvíða*
Reginleiv, *Reginleif*	'Daughter of the powers'; a valkyrie in Valhall.	*Grím 36*
Rennandi, *Rennandi*	'Running'; a mythological river in Asgard.	*Grím 27*
Rig, *Rígr*	'He who governs'; one of the aesir; Heimdall is one of Rig's aspects; see 'Heimdall'.	*Rígsþula*
Rin, *Rín*	'Flow'; a mythological river in Asgard.	*Grím 27*
Rind, *Rindr*	'Rambler'; regarded as one of the asynior; may be the daughter of the giant Billing, as alluded to in 'Odin's Speech'; with Odin she had the son Vali.	*Bdr 11; Gró 6*
Roskva, *Roskva*	'Fertile'; Thor's maid; daughter of the farmer/shepherd Egil; Thialvi's sister.	*Hym 7, 37-38*
Ruler, *Reginn*	A dwarf.	*Vsp 12*
Ruling Powers, *Regin, Rǫgn, Bǫnd, Hǫpt*	The gods regarded as a collective entity.	
Saehrimnir, *Sæhrímnir*	The pig that Andhrimnir boils in the kettle Eldhrimnir for the aesir in Asgard; perhaps meaning 'Sea' + 'Soot'.	*Grím 18*
Saga, *Sága*	'She who sees'; one of the asynior; wife of Odin.	*Grím 7*
Samsey, *Samsey*	'Samsø'; a Danish island.	*Lok 24*
Sann, *Saðr*	'The true one', alias Odin.	*Grím 47*
Sanngetall, *Sanngetall*	'He who guesses the truth'; alias Odin.	*Grím 47*
Seid, *Seiðr*	'Magical bond'; a technique of magic and divination; mainly a woman's prerogative.	*Vsp 22; Lok 24; Hynd 32*
Sekin, *Sekin*	'The convict'; a mythological river in Asgard.	*Grím 27*
Shearer, *Skirfir*	A dwarf.	*Vsp 15*
Shelter-yard, *Hlévangr*	A dwarf	*Vsp 15*
Shingle, *Skafiðr*	A dwarf	*Vsp 15*
Shivering, *Bifurr*	A dwarf	*Vsp 11*
Shorn, *Nori*	A dwarf	*Vsp 11*

Sid, *Síð*	'The deep one'; a mythological river in Asgard.	*Grím 27*
Sidgrani, *Síðgrani*	'Long moustache', alias Odin.	*Alv 6*
Sidhott, *Síðhǫtr*	'A brimmed hat', alias Odin.	*Grím 48*
Sidskegg, *Síðskeggr*	'Longbeard', alias Odin.	*Grím 48*
Sigfather, *Sigfǫðr*	'Father of Victory', alias Odin.	*Vsp 55; Grím 48; Lok 58*
Sigmund, *Sigmundr*	'Power to win'; one of the clan of the Volsungs.	*Hynd 2*
Sigyn, *Sigyn*	'Victory + Friend'; one of the asynior; married to Loki, and they have a son, Narvi.	*Vsp 35; Lok prose*
Silvrintopp, *Silfrintoppr*	'Silver-mane'; one of the aesir's horses.	*Grím 30*
Sinir, *Sinir*	'Sinewy'; a horse belonging to the aesir.	*Grím 30*
Siv, *Sif*	'She who relates'; one of the asynior; personification of kin and family; she is married to Thor and they have a daughter, Thrud; she is also thought to be the mother of Ull.	*Hár 48; hym 3, 15; Lok 53-54*
Skadi, *Skaði*	'Shade' or 'Harm'; counted among the asynior, a giantess, daughter of Thiatzi; wife of Niord; she is termed 'ski-goddess' (ǫndurdís), implying that she used skis like Ull; in very old sources Scandinavia is sometimes called 'Scadinavia', implying that Skadi may be a goddess much older than the aesir.	*Grím 11; Skír 1; Lok 49-52; Hynd 30*
Skeggiold, *Skeggjǫld*	'Axe-age'; a valkyrie in Valhall.	*Grím 36*
Skeidbrimir, *Skeiðbrimir*	'Foaming during the race'; one of the aesir's horses.	*Grím 30*
Skidbladnir, *Skíðblaðnir*	'The one that spreads the boards'; Freyr's ship that could sail both on land and sea, and which he could fold up and carry in his pocket.	*Grím 43, 44*
Skilful, *Hannarr*	A dwarf.	*Vsp 13*
Skilving, *Skilfingr*	Ancestor of the Skilvings, alias Odin.	*Grím 54*
Skilvings, *Skilfingar*	A clan of people descending from Skilving.	*Hynd 11, 16*
Skinfaxi, *Skinfaxi*	'Shining Mane'; the horse driven by Day; its mane lights up the sky and the earth.	*Vaf 12*

Skinny, *Náli*	A dwarf.	*Vsp 15*
Skiold, *Skjǫldr*	'Shield'; legendary ancestor of the Skioldungs.	*Grott Prose*
Skioldungs, *Skioldungar*	A Danish dynasti descending from Skiold.	*Grott prose*
Skirnir, *Skirnir*	'The shining one'; Freyr's servant.	*Skírnismál*
Skogul, *Skǫgul*	'She who causes battle'; a valkyrie.	*Vsp 30; Grím 36*
Skoll, *Skǫll*	'Deceiver'; a wolf who chaces Sun across the sky.	*Vaf 47; Grím 39*
Skrymir, *Skrýmir*	'He who boasts'; a giant.	*Hár 26; Lok 60-62*
Skuld (1), *Skuld*	'She who shall be'; a norn, one of the three goddesses of fate: Urd, Verdandi and Skuld.	*Vsp 20*
Skuld (2), *Skuld*	'She who brings the future'; a valkyrie.	*Vsp 30*
Sleipnir, *Sleipnir*	'The One who glides'; Odin's eight-legged horse; S. was mothered by Loki, its father was the stallion Svadilfari; it takes Odin everywhere on land, sea and air.	*Grím 44; Bdr 2; Hynd 40*
Slid, *Slíð*	'Sheath'; a mythological river in Asgard.	*Grím 28*
Slumber, *Dvalinn*	A dwarf.	*Vsp 12*
Snor, *Snǫr*	'Daughter-in-law'; wife of Carl; their 22 children are listed in 'The Tale of Rig', st. 24 and 25.	*Ríg 23*
Sokkmimir, *Sǫkkmímir*	The meaning is obscure; a giant, fooled by Odin.	*Grím 50*
Sokkvabekk, *Sǫkkvabekkr*	'A treasure chest'/'a sunken bench'; a mythological place beneath the ocean's surface where Odin and Sága are seated.	*Grím 7*
Solblindi, *Solblindi*	Meaning obscure; a giant; his sons made the gate at Menglod's place.	*Fjǫlsv 10*
South, *Suðri*	A dwarf.	*Vsp 11*
Spawny, *Yngvi*	A dwarf.	*Vsp 16*
Staff-elf, *Gandalfr*	A dwarf.	*Vsp 12*
Strond, *Strǫnd*	'Shore'; a mythological river in Asgard.	*Grím 28*
Summer, *Sumar*	A giantess, daughter of Sweet One.	*Vaf 27*
Sun, *Sól*	One of the asynior; daughter of Mundilfari; Moon's sister; her daughter takes her place after Ragnarok.	*Vsp 5; Vaf 23, 47; Grím 37; Alv 16, 35*

Surt, *Surtr*	'The black one'; a fire demon from Muspelheim.	
	Vsp 47, 52-53; Vaf 17-18, 50-51	
Suttung, *Suttungr*	'He who sucks'; the keeper of the bardic mead; a giant; his daughter, Gunnlod, let Odin have the bardic mead in exchange for three nights of love-making.	
	Háv. 104, 109, 110, 140; Skír 34; Alv 34	
Svadilfari, *Svaðilfari*	'He who travels in slippery places'; a horse; Sleipnir's father with Loki as mother.	*Hynd 40*
Svarang, *Svárangr*	'The Difficult one'; a giant.	*Hár 29*
Svarthovdi, *Svarthǫfði*	'He with the black head'; ancestor of sorceresses.	*Hynd 33*
Svavnir (1), *Sváfnir*	'The one who calms', alias Odin.	*Grím 54*
Svavnir (2), *Sváfnir*	'The one who calms'; a serpent gnawing at one of Yggdrasil's roots.	*Grím 34*
Svidrir, *Sviðrir*	'The one who whirls', alias Odin.	*Grím 50*
Svidur, *Sviðurr*	'The whirling one', alias Odin.	*Grím 50*
Svipall, *Svipall*	'The quick one', alias Odin.	*Grím 47*
Svol, *Svǫl,*	'The cool one'; a mythological river in Asgard.	*Grím 27*
Sweet One, *Svásuðr*	A giant, father of Summer.	*Vaf 27*
Sylgr, *Sylgr*	'She who swallows'; a mythological river in Asgard.	*Grím 28*
Thekk, *Þekkr*	'Dashing', alias Odin.	*Grím 46*
Thialvi, *Þjálfi*	'He who strives ardently'; son of the farmer/shepherd Egil; Thor's servant; Roskva's brother.	*Hár 39; Hym 7, 37-38*
Thiatzi, *Þjazi*	'Fatso'; a giant; son of Alvaldi; father of Skadi; he stole Idunn and her apples and was killed in the skirmishes that ensued.	
	Grim 11; Hár 19; Lok 50-51; Hynd 30; Grott	
Thiodnuma, *Þjóðnuma*	'She who grabs people'; a mythological river in Asgard.	*Grím 28*
Tholl, *Þǫll*	'Toil'; a mythological river in Asgard.	*Grím 27*
Thor, *Þórr*	'He who thunders'; the great protector ; one of the aesir, originally one of the vanir; he was son of the goddess Earth; god of lightning and thunder; as god of the weather he was guardian of farmers and their homesteads, and as such they simply called him 'Karl' (the man); his	

	hammer, Miollnir, was used in connection with weddings to consecrate the bride; he is Siv's husband and they have two children, Modi and Thrud; he also has a son Magni with a powerful giantess; he kills the World Serpent at Ragnarok but dies himself from its venom; his regular occupation is to keep the giants at bay. *Vsp 26; Grím 4, 29; Skír 33; Hár 9, 18, 22, 24, 26, 28, 32, 36, 38, 50, 56; Hym 23, 28; Lok 58, 60; Þrym 9, 15, 17, 19; Hynd 4*
Thrall, *Þræl*	Son of Edda and Aï; married to 'Maid'; their children are listed in 'The Tale of Rig' st. 12 and 13. *Ríg 7, 11*
Thresher, *Lofarr*	A dwarf. *Vsp 14, 16*
Thridi, *Þriði*	'The third one', alias Odin. *Grím 46*
Thror, *Þrór*	'The thriving one', alias Odin. *Grím 49*
Thrudr (1), *Þrúðr*	'The powerful one'; daughter of Siv and Thor. *Alv 1-8*
Thrudr (2), *Þrúðr*	'The powerful one'; a valkyrie in Valhall. *Grím 36*
Thrudgelmir, *Þrúðgelmir*	'He who hollers loudly'; an ancient giant; so of Ymir; father of Bergelmir. *Vaf 29*
Thrudheim, *Þrúðheimr*	'Home of strength'; Thor's homestead; here lies Thrudvangar, the fields where Thor's hall, Bilskirnir, stands. *Grím 4*
Thrym, *Þrymr*	'He who makes noise'; a king among the giants; he stole Thor's hammer and demanded Freyia, Sun and Moon. *The Tale of Thrym*
Thund (1), *Þundr*	'The one who expands', alias Odin. *Háv 145; Grím 46, 54*
Thund (2), *Þundr*	A river at Valhall. *Grím 21*
Thyn, *Þyn*	'Torment'; a mythological river in Asgard. *Grím 27*
Turner, *Virfir*	A dwarf. *Vsp 15*
Tyr, *Týr*	'God'; an ancient god; son of the giant Hymir, whose mother had nine hundred heads; he sacrificed his right hand in order to put the wolf Fenrir in chains. *Hym 5-9; Lok 37-40*
Ull, *Ullr*	'He who brings bounty'; one of the aesir; a partially forgotten god; temples would have a ring, which was named after Ull, and whoever touched that ring saved his life; this custom of asylum has lived on up to the present day; Ull was called 'ski-god' (ǫndurgoð); he was also

	described using bow and arrow; he was called upon when duelling. *Grím 5, 42*
Ullinn, *Ullinn*	In all likelihood the same as Ull, see: Ull.
Ulvrun, *Ulfrún*	'Wolf-woman'; a giantess; one of Heimdall's nine mothers. *Hynd 37*
Unn, *Unnr*	'He who wins', alias for Odin. *Grím 46*
Urd, *Urðr*	'She who was'; a norn, one of the three goddesses of fate: Urd, Verdandi and Skuld. In 'Beowolf' the word 'Urd' appearing as Wyrd (hence weird) has acquired the general meaning 'Providence'. *Vsp 20; Háv 111*
Utgarda-Loki, *Útgarða-Loki*	Alias Skrymir, perhaps alias Loki; Utgard was in a way synonymous with Iotunheim, the realm of giants; once Thor was fooled by U. *Lok 60-62*
Vak, *Vakr*	'He who is awake', alias Odin. *Grím 54*
Valaskialv, *Valaskjálfr*	'The seat of Vali'; Vali's dwelling in Asgard. *Grím 6*
Valfather, *Valfǫðr*	Corpse-Father', 'Father of the fallen warriors', alias Odin. *Vsp 1, 27, 28; Grím 48*
Valhall, *Valhǫll*	'The hall of the fallen warriors', Odin's hall located in Asgard; here they feed on the pig Saehrimnir and drink beer from the goat Heidrun; during the day the warriors fight, and in the evening they all enjoy their meal, those who died having revived. *Vsp 33; Grím 8-10, 23, 25-26; Hyn 1, 6, 7*
Vali (1), *Váli*	Meaning obscure; one of the aesir, son of Odin and Rind; Vali killed Hod, thus wreaking vengance for Hod having killed Baldr. *Vsp 34; Vaf 51; Bdr 11; Hynd 29*
Vali (2), *Váli*	Son of Loki. *Lok prose*
Valkyrie, *Valkyrja*	'Corpse-Choser', 'She who choses who is to die'; female deities who pick out the warriors that Odin has decided shall die in battle. *Vsp 30; Grím 36*
Valland,	Norse name for celtic areas, esp. Northern France. *Hár 24; Hynd 9*
Van, *Vón*	'Wish'; a mythological river in Asgard. *Grím 28*
Vanaheim, *Vanaheimr*	Home of the vanir. *Vaf 39*
Vanr (sg), vanir (pl),	'Friend'; the fertility gods. This clan of gods

Vanr, Vanir	were specific to Scandinavia. The main gods of this clan were Niord, Freyia and Freyr, but quite a few other female deities were worshipped for their capacity to promote fecundity and secure health.
Var, *Vár*	'Oath; one of the asynior; goddess of oaths, betrothals, promises, etc.; she punishes those who break their oaths. *Þrym 30*
Vavthrudnir, *Vafþrúðnir*	'He who tightens the web'; a wise giant; outwitted by Odin. *Vavthrudnir's Speech*
Vegsvinn, *Vegsvinn*	'Quick passage'; a mythological river in Asgard. *Grím 28*
Vegtam, *Vegtamr*	'Weary-of-Travel', alias Odin. *Bdr 6, 13*
Verdandi, *Verðandi*	'She who becomes'; a norn, one of the three goddesses of fate: Urd, Verdandi and Skuld. *Vsp 20*
Verland, *Verland*	'The world of mankind'; a mythological place; Odin says that Thor will meet his mother there. *Hár 56*
Veurr, *Véurr*	'He who guards the temple', alias Thor. *Vsp 56; Hym 11, 17, 21*
Vid, *Við*	'The wide one'; a mythological river in Asgard. *Grím 28*
Vidar, *Víðarr*	'He who rules far and wide'; one of the aesir; son of Odin and the giantess Grid; he kills the Fenris wolf and revenges his father Odin; V. shall survive Ragnarok. *Vsp 55; Vaf 51, 53; Grím 17; Lok 10*
Vidolf, *Viðólfr*	'Wood-wolf'; a magician who was the teacher of the sibyls. *Hynd 33*
Vidovnir, *Viðófnir*	A rooster in Mimameid at Menglod's (Freyia's). *Fjolsv 18, 24, 25, 30*
Vidur, *Viðurr*	'Weather-beaten', alias Odin. *Grím 49*
Vidrir, *Viðrir*	'He who makes weather', alias Odin. *Lok 26*
Vilmeid, *Vilmeiðr*	'Wand of magical power'; ancestor of sorcerers. *Hynd 33*
Vin, *Vin*	'Desire'; a mythological river in Asgard. *Grím 28*
Vina, *Vina*	Perhaps the river Dvina; a mythological river in Asgard. *Grím 28*
Vond, *Vǫnd*	'Troublesome'; a mythological river in Asgard. *Grím 28*

Waning, *Niði*	A dwarf.	*Vsp 11*
Warfather, *Heriafǫðr; Herfǫðr*	'Father of armies', alias Odin.	*Vsp 29*
Wastrel, *Svíurr*	A dwarf.	*Vsp 13*
Wedge, *Kili*	A dwarf.	*Vsp 13*
West, *Vestri*	A dwarf.	*Vsp 11*
Will, *Vili*	A dwarf.	*Vsp 13*
Wind-cool, *Vindsvalr*	A giant; father of Winter.	*Vaf 27*
Wingthor, *Vingþórr*	'Thor Victorious', alias Thor.	*Þrym 1; Alv*
Winter, *Vetr*	A giant; son of Wind-cool.	*Vaf 27*
World Serpent	A cosmic monster; son of Loki and Angrboda; brother of Hel and Fenrir; the serpent is sometimes called 'Iormungand', 'the mighty staff'; and 'Midgardsorm', the serpent who surrounds all lands.	*Vsp 50, 56; Hym 22-24*
World Tree	See: Yggdrasil.	
Ydalir, *Ýdalir*	'The valleys of the ewe tree'; the home of Ull.	*Grím 5*
Ygg, *Yggr*	'The terrifying', alias Odin.	*Vsp 28; Vaf 5; Grím 53, 54; Hym 2*
Yggdrasil, *Yggdrasill*	'He who carries the Awesome One (Ygg/Odin)'; the World Tree seen as Odin's gallows.	*Vsp 19,47,50,55,56; Grím 29-35, 44; Hym 22-24*
Yggiung, *Yggiungr*	'The terrifying one',	*Vsp 28*
Ylgr, *Ylgr*	'She-wolf'; a mythological river in Asgard.	*Grím 28*
Ymir, *Ymir*	'The Twin'; the primeval giant(ess) who is androgynous; the natural world was created from her/his body parts; ancestor of all the giants.	*Vsp 3; Vaf 21, 28; Grím 40; Hynd 33*
Ynglings, *Ynglingar*	One of the royal families claiming to descend from the gods. See: Freyr.	
Yrsa, *Yrsa*	She was wife of Adils; mother of Rolf Kraki (a legendary Danish king from the 6th C AD) by her father Helgi Halfdansson. For a fuller story, see Snorri Sturluson's 'Skaldskaparmál'.	*Grott 22*

Made in the USA
Columbia, SC
09 April 2023